FOWLERI:
ANTIBODIES AMASSED

T.R. ANTHKO

Copyright 2024 by Andrew Kosakowski Production
copyright by Andrew Kosakowski
Published by Anthko's Ideas

Triggers Page

Ambiguous Consent: There is a scene where a person is forced into a hotel room and coaxed into sex. A scene where a character believes sex is the best way to accomplish a mission then changes the opinions during sex. There are multiple scenes where a character is overpowered for sexual purposes and forced to continue while experiencing deep emotions, as that is the way that the character enjoys sex.

Assumed Sexual Assault: There is a scene where the characters assume they are hearing a sexual assault.

Bondage: There are scenes where characters are bound for sexual gratification.

Consensual Torture: There is a scene where a character willingly submits to torture.

Execution Arousal: A character stops mid-execution in this book to achieve sexual gratification with the victim.

Eroticism: There are multiple scenes of graphic adult erotic acts contained within the book that include heterosexual, male-with-male, female-with-female, multiple males with a single female, and multiple females with a single male encounters.

Forced Abortion: A character chemically aborts a pregnancy without consent from the mother.

Gore: There are places where wounds that are inflicted are described in a level of specificity that exceeds generalities.

Gun Violence and Military Combat: There are scenes where gun violence occurs as part of military-type encounters.

Murder: There are several scenes where characters are directly murdered or where their murder is suggested.

Nonconsensual Torture: There is a scene where a character is ordered to torture a person to death. The character follows orders.

Table of contents

Prologue

Lift Them to Benghazi

Prepparing the Target
Unusual Gameplay
How to Win

General Vilonka

Facing Danger
Compromising Emotions
Woken President

Unwanted Attention

Receiving the Boot
The Rendezvous
Climatic Events
Avoiding Capture

Pulaxo's Final Act

Planning Ahead
Staging the Players
Treachery

Opportunistic Exits

Time to Break Away
Pompous Return
A Drink to Remember
Heartbreak Railways

Retirement

Uninvited Guests
Private Party
Ceremonial Displays

Breaking In

Nasir
Sword Dancing
Sisterhood
Distress Undressed

The Layover

Speedy Relocation
Taking Inventory
Embracing Family

Returning Home

Stuck in the Past
No Escape
Arboretum Delights
Taking the Reigns

Full Circle

Embarassing Ignorance
The Dance Continues
Unsettling Arrivals

Final Twists

Bathroom Issues
One Happy Ending

Epilogue

I thank the United States Under Secretary of Defense and the U.S. Office of Special Counsel. It is my opinion that if they had taken my whistleblower reports seriously, conducted full, transparent, independent investigations, and protected my legally required whistleblowing activity, I would not have had the time and opportunity to write this book.

Disclaimer: All characters and events in this book are fictional. Any technologies, events, places, or persons in this novel that appear to be related to technologies, events, places, or persons that have or will materialize in the real world have been entered into this work by coincidence and, thus, should not be construed as related to one another. This book is a work of fiction. The technologies are a work of fiction, the places are a work of fiction, the characters are a work of fiction, and the events are a work of fiction.

Prologue

"Thank you everyone for attending. You should be able to see each of your selected representatives standing behind me. As I unseal your ballot boxes, you will receive an encrypted message asking you to verify your vote. Please verify your selections to ensure the agenda is not delayed. I will announce the council's confirmed results once all the ballot entries have been entered into the ledger. We should be finished within eight minutes," the attenuated, solemn woman spoke to the laptop camera.

"Green, step forward. Place your box in the camera frame, then return to your spot," the woman instructed.

The man at the end of the line behind her obeyed. She broke the wax seal of the leather-clad oak box. It contained three tea biscuits, each with a different design baked into the top.

"I have read the vote. Council member of the Northern and Western European expanse, please verify your votes as they appear on your screen."

The woman navigated several screens on the laptop and tapped on the keyboard to forward her confirmation request. Seconds later, a green box appeared on her screen.

"Your ballot has been verified. I will record and consume the vote," the woman stooped to mark a page in a linen-bound book with a quill.

The pages had dried and yellowed since it had felt its first entry, causing the ink from the quill to puddle at the beginning and ending of each cursive word. Once the pages had finished drying in the breeze from her oscillating face and pursed lips, the woman stood and ate the encoded cookies.

"Your vote has been recorded and consumed. Red, please step forward with your box."

The voting continued until all boxes were opened, and all votes were recorded and consumed. It appeared the woman struggled when it was time to consume the fish-eyed tart ballot, but she maintained her composure.

"I have verified, recorded, and tallied the votes. I am setting aside vote two because we must contact the adjudicator for final clarifications. The results for vote one are as follows: the U.K. Prime Minister has become problematic and will be replaced. The votes indicate we should disgrace the Prime Minister with the 'Party Gate' plan. Additionally, we will punish the U.K. by increasing inflation and flooding the country with migrants. Are there any entries of dissent or objection?"

The woman looked at the computer screen for several minutes.

"I see no communications from the council, so I will read vote three. After the Chinese twenty-two went dark, the council was asked how to proceed. The votes indicate a new twenty-two will be inserted into position. We trust the current operatives located in China and see no reason for more substantial changes. We will cause a flood and sandstorm as a consequence for the loss of our Ghost. Any dissent or objections?" She waited.

"If everyone would like to take a five-minute break, I will get the adjudicator on the line to resolve the second vote. I thank everyone for your cooperation and patience."

The woman opened a new window on the laptop. A telephone keypad appeared, and she dialed a number.

"Hey, long time no see," said a voice. "How have you been?"

"The council needs adjudication for vote two," the woman replied.

"Are they on the line?" The voice sounded inquisitive.

"One moment," the woman said as she changed screens on the computer. "Can all council members please inform me when they have returned?" Colorful pop-ups flashed on the screen.

"Adjudicator, can you still hear me?"

"It is so beautiful today. Would you believe it is 75 degrees in May?" The voice responded.

"Can all council members hear the adjudicator?" The screen flashed with colorful boxes.

"Adjudicator, please provide the decision. I will record it in the ledger."

"Whoa. . . Calm down. There is no need to drop the 'F' bomb in polite company. Are you in polite company? No, then drop the 'F' bomb, but don't do anything I wouldn't do. Did I mention I love your voice? What else is going on?"

"Thank you. I am recording the decision. Do any council members have any dissent or comments about implementing the 'Fowleri protocol' while the adjudicator is on the line?" The woman paused to ensure there were no responses.

"Thank you, adjudicator. The council has accepted your decision, and we have nothing further."

"No worries, I will see you later tonight. I must return to work before the boss gets after me. Love you, bye." The call disconnected.

"I want to thank the council for their continued commitment to evolving this world. It is an honor to serve. I will ensure the secrecy of this vote as required. Anyone who wants to disconnect can. Anyone who would like to watch me secure this vote may."

The woman withdrew a gas mask from beneath her clothing and pressed a button on the computer. The room filled with a thick yellow gas. Some of the council's ballot-holding representatives ran for the door, but the gas overpowered them, molesting their eyes, mouths, esophagus, and lungs.

The council watched as their representatives fell to the floor, vomiting and clutching their faces. The gas melted through their eyes as molten serum drooled from the sockets. Their skin was slower to react as the bodies convulsed.

"I am going to be quick about this because I am getting overheated," the woman said from beneath the mask as she lifted the laptop.

She carried it around the room to show that each representative had succumbed to the gas. Their faces melted, eyes liquified, and all struggling stopped. She thanked the council and closed the lid. The woman placed the device in a large metal trash can and filled it using a large container of liquid. She sprinted from the room and plunged into the waiting pool.

Lift Them to Benghazi

Preparing the Target

"Long time, stranger," Sam spun towards the voice which tickled his ears, Sarah was a few yards behind him in the long, narrow hallway.

The fluorescent lights were accentuating her curves marvelously. "What are you doing in the nest? I thought perch boys never departed their roost."

"I thought you were still on assignment. It's good to see you," his dopey smile was uncontrollable despite his best efforts. "I am getting a new phone."

"Why do you need a new phone, got a stalker?" Sarah made a face as she neared. "I arrived last night. We should catch up over drinks after work," she bit her lower lip.

Sam's mind flashed to their night together, the profound love and safety he experienced. He remembered her words and hoped she did as well. She knew his mark, and he had seen hers. Sam wanted her offer to be real but knew in his life, all such offers were no more than fantasies.

"I do not believe we are allowed to fraternize," he frowned. "I wish I could, but you know how things are with the rules and stuff."

"I know. Meet me at eight. Same place as before." Sarah's perfume penetrated and delighted his senses. Sam closed his eyes and appreciated the moment. "I play for keeps. I wish I could stay longer, but I have a briefing. If I'm a minute or two late, order my favorite. I'll need it."

"Bye, Sarah," his sloppy smile recurring.

Sam continued walking towards the Information Technology service desk. As he walked, he fantasized about lying naked with Sarah, the embrace they shared, and how much he enjoyed listening to her heart as she stroked his hair.

"Sam," Valerie whispered from her office. "We need to talk. Also, what's with the goofy smile?"

Sam had not seen Valerie since the day they made it home from the Middle East. Somehow, her breasts looked fuller, and her face was glowing. Had the fertility drugs he slipped into her drinks worked?

"Valerie, I thought you ghosted me. I assumed you were distancing yourself from me and the perch," Sam's smile disappeared.

"Not here," she led him into a stairwell by the arm. "I have taken three pregnancy tests. I am pregnant. I do not know how this happened. I am on birth control."

"Your tits look amazing," Sam pressed her against the wall as he stared into her eyes. "You are glowing, it's a huge turn-on."

"I am serious, Sam, what am I going to do?" Valerie was unable to control her volume due to the hormones. "You know this baby is wrong. I can't have it."

"Val, I told you before, you're mine. Plus, I was being serious," Sam rubbed his fingers across the top of Valerie's breast. "I want more than you have been offering."

"I am scared," her eyes grew large and misted. "What can I do?"

"Relax," Sam held her nape and kissed her deeply.

He ensured her breasts were pressed against his chest while he crouched to her level. Sam slid his hand into her pants and pulled Valerie against his growing member as he pushed his tongue between her lips. Sam felt Valerie's fingers tighten in his hair as she pulled his head.

"You better not be fucking with me. I am super emotional, and my hormones are making me super needy," Valerie's free hand rubbed Sam's swollen staff.

"Over here," Sam kept his tone low, pulling Valerie to the stairwell. He pressed her toward the four-bar railing. "Turn," he unbuttoned her pants and pressed her belly against it.

"We will get caught," she rebuffed with hushed tones and a slap to his hand.

"I do not care. I want you. You have driven me crazy since I first saw you and those sexy calves," Sam lowered all clothing away from her sex with one swift motion. "Are you ready?"

"Be gentle," Valerie turned her head and pulled Sam in for another kiss. She leaned over the top rail as she continued stroking him through his pants.

"I have you," Sam lifted her onto the railing as he lowered his pants and underwear. "Are you okay? Is the railing hurting you?"

"I need this," Valerie clutched the middle two bars of the railing, trying to steady her body and keep her balance as her feet dangled.

Valerie's lips were somehow firmer than he had imagined as he kissed and licked. Valerie was not lying about needing this; she dripped with desire.

"Stop teasing me," she groaned. "I have earned this."

Sam rose and pressed his head into her but stopped before the shaft made entry.

He held her hips, "Hold on."

"I am so ready," she whimpered.

Sam pressed forward with a clap. Valerie lifted her legs to grab Sam, but her pants prevented it. Sam pressed forward with another clap. Valerie grunted loudly.

"Quiet," she held an index finger to her face.

Sam clapped harder as he moved his hands from her hips. He placed one hand on the small of her back and pulled her hair with the other to force her to arch.

"Yes," Valerie purred, "Fuck me the way I know you fuck other women. Fuck me like you fucked Sarah the night she stole you from me."

Sarah flashed in Sam's mind, and he felt ashamed but had to focus on the task at hand. He pushed into Valerie harder and faster. Sam continued to increase his momentum until the clacking of his scrotum against her pubis mirrored a metronome. Valerie was grunting with every advance and purring with every retreat through one hand as she kept steady with the other.

"God, Val," Sam leaned forward and praised. "This is better than I ever fantasized. I love..." Sam paused to let Valerie's imagination finish the thought before he continued, "How perfect this feels."

"Stop talking," Valerie panted as she clawed his thigh.

Sam could feel her nails squeeze his flesh as she wrapped her legs around him. Accepting her pants were still in the way, Valerie grabbed Sam's knees with her feet and pulled, almost collapsing him to the ground. Sam grabbed the railing and drew closer, making shorter, quieter penetrations. He could feel her sex grasping at his rod with each ram. Her legs and arms trembled.

Sam pinned Valerie still as he pushed in. This time, Sam held himself inside as he, too, felt his sex quiver. As he exploded inside Valerie, she released an ungovernable exhalation of passion before squirming to lay sideways on the top rail.

Valerie rested with the rail along the shirt buttons between her breasts while she maintained her balance by holding the railing between her bent knees. She tucked an arm under her head as a pillow as she looked into Sam's eyes with a lover's smile. He wondered if that was the way he had been looking at Sarah.

As Sam took a step backward, he used his fingers to explore Valerie's suckling sex. They heard a loud thud several floors above. Sam yanked his pants up and tucked his undershirt and button-up into the waistband. Valerie rolled off the railing and landed on her hands and knees. As she sprang to her feet, she pulled up her underwear and pants while tucking in her shirt. Her agility impressed and surprised him.

"And that is why I need a new phone. Do I need to see you and the acquisitions department, or should I head to I.T.?" Sam asked as a suit rounded the stairwell and produced a peculiar expression at the pair.

"That is I.T. I have no idea why so many new employees are so helpless or why they insist on bothering me in the hallways. I can't even take a piss in peace. I do have an office," Valerie berated.

"I apologize. I am still learning who everyone is and how things work," Sam sounded nervous.

The suit opened the stairwell door and paused. It glanced back at the two, shook its head, then continued into the hall without a word.

As the door shut, Sam quipped, "Should I kill him? Does he know all our secrets? That was a pretty serious head nod."

"It doesn't matter who knows, and I don't care," Valerie seemed to have missed the silliness as she pulled Sam to her lips. "I like you, and I am yours. We still need to talk more about things." Valerie rubbed her abdomen.

"Do you believe there are cameras in the stairwell?" Sam examined the ceiling.

"No, there aren't any. They don't monitor the stairs. It's a fire hazard or something like that." Valerie grabbed the sides of Sam's head. "What should we do about being pregnant? I don't know what to do. I have no idea what I am going to do. Talk to me."

Sam kissed Valerie's forehead. It seemed like he did not need the recording of her biracial gang bang after all, but it was always good to have a backup plan.

"If you can't have the baby because you have a problem with its daddy, you can have an abortion," he was sure to scowl as he spoke.

"I am catholic. You know what my religion means to me," Valerie grimaced as her eyes floated to the floor.

"You are also racist, and your family is racist. What will your mom say when she finds out you got pregnant by someone who isn't white or Filipino? You are carrying the child of an African warlord, what will she say about that?"

Sam lifted her chin so their eyes met.

"Whatever you choose, I support you no matter what. You are mine, and I take care of my things," He pecked their lips together.

"What happens if I have my baby? What happens with us and my job? If it's a boy, I want to name him Larry after my father. If it is a girl, she will be named Lily after my grandmother," Valerie wrapped her arms around Sam and pulled their bodies together.

"You know you will be taken care of at work," Sam smiled. "You are a stickler for the rules. You know more than the human capital department."

"What about you, Sam? What benefits and rights have I earned with you?" Valerie was becoming misty.

"You are mine. In this situation, you can't make a wrong decision. How I feel about you will not change," he stroked her hair.

"One more for the road," Valerie pulled Sam down, holding their lips together longer as she pressed her tongue across the threshold. "Go get your new phone and return to work, babe."

"We need to do this more often, *babe*," Sam accentuated the word as he winked. Opening the door for Valerie, he added, "After this, I am headed back to the White House. We should plan to get together later this week."

"I am all yours, just not in this minute. If I don't get back soon, my coworkers will assume I am goofing off," Valerie hurried down the hall. "Message me," she called before disappearing into her doorway.

As she disappeared, Sam wondered if she was acting. This all seemed too simple. How could a woman as intelligent as Valerie fall for such a simple ruse? He pushed it aside, but it continued to plague his mind throughout the rest of the morning.

Unusual Gameplay

Not long after entering, Sam realized someone had set the stage to manipulate the president. The television was broadcasting the Iranian delegate's speech. A stack of classified files lay on the broad mahogany desk for the president to review. The file on top was open to a page documenting Iran's criticisms of the president. The words "weak," "pathetic," and "insignificant" were in bold font.

"If they continue to hit us in Syria, we'll hit them harder, we'll make it count. What are our options?" the president questioned an advisor as he strode across the elegant, natural-fiber carpeting.

"I will get the Pentagon on the phone to discuss options," the advisor replied.

"Ahh, Sam," the president took his position in the deep maroon leather chair. "Did you get the phone situation worked out?"

"I'm good," Sam replied, holding up a phone. "I hope the team has been taking care of you," Sam motioned toward Todd, Paul, and Ben. "Ben, you can go home. Please apologize to your wife and let her know I won't be keeping you late anymore."

"Thanks," Ben replied as he rushed toward the door. "Last time I was late, she chopped my balls off. She thought I was cheating. I may have her call you."

"Gentlemen," the president raised his voice as Ben closed the door behind him. "Ben's balls may be important, but can we focus on the current situation?"

The president read the open file, and Sam could see the president's fingers find the highlighted words. The president closed the file.

"Is the Pentagon on the line yet?" The president asked.

"They are being patched through the system," the advisor responded.

The president turned his attention to the television. The Iranian representative described the evils of the West and how the Iranian Supreme Leader was the last bastion of righteousness. Sam watched the president let his ego take over. The president's brows furled, his lips tightened, his nostrils flared, and a deep crimson blanketed his face.

"I have them, they are holding on the line," the advisor activated the phone's speaker. "I have the president. Has everyone been briefed on the situation with Iran?"

"You've got General Avery. We have been briefed. I'll be the liaison and will provide the response options. We believe the sensitivity warrants providing options orally."

"Avery," the president interrupted. "I suggest a limited strike against the proxies and economic sanctions."

"Yes, sir, that is part of two different options compiled as a holistic proportional response, but we have limited confidence it will act as a reasonable deterrent against future aggressions toward our assets."

"Cut the shit, Avery," the president barked, "if that will not work, say it. What options do you folks believe demonstrate the desired message?"

"We have three options from passive to near-war level: a targeted bombing of known proxy ammunition depots designed to degrade their near-term capabilities; the removal of their finance minister using our special operators to impact their ability to maintain the economy; finally, attack their supply routes out of Iran. The last option may be interpreted as an act of war."

"An assassination is not an act of war?" The president was incredulous.

"No, sir," Avery responded. "The special operators have unique skills and abilities to prevent the Iranians, or anyone else, from proving we killed the bastard."

"Can we bomb the ammo depots and kill the finance minister?" The president asked.

"Excellent Idea, Mr. President. That's why you get paid the big bucks. We believe your recommendation is the best option. We will host a presser to say the ammo depot hits were our response while celebrating the benefit of the disrupted Iranian economy," a smile was heard in Avery's voice. "We have intelligence which indicates the Russians have started borrowing money from the Iranians, so the hit is a two birds response."

"When was I going to be briefed about the Russians?" The president leaned toward the speaker.

"In tomorrow's national security meeting. It is a minor change, and we did not believe interrupting your schedule was merited," the response cool and confident.

"I want the Russians and Iranians to suffer for challenging me. How long until we can have the operators take action?" The president tightened his fists, pushing them on the desktop toward the information.

"We have assets in the region. We can have them in play within the hour," Avery informed.

"It's a go," the president's mouth frothed. "I am moving to the war room."

"Good to go. I will reconnect in five minutes with the generals on the line. Avery out."

The president turned to the advisor, "Get the crew. Have them join me in the War Room. We have an assassination to watch." The president turned to Sam, "Tell Deloris to order cold cuts for everyone. This is going to be a long night."

"I'm on it," Sam said as he opened the door and motioned for everyone to exit.

The president watched the speech being delivered by the Iranian representative for an extended moment before following the group exiting toward the War Room.

"I wish we could assassinate him," the president confided to Sam.

As they entered the hall, Sam concurred, "Me too. I will meet everyone in the War Room after I let Deloris know she has been selected to provide us with a feast."

As the entourage closed the War Room door, Sam pulled a black cellular from his pocket and reentered the Oval Office. He flicked off the television and dialed.

"We have a problem," his voice was stern. "US1 ordered the assassination of your finance minister. They will be landing within an hour. I am sending you the details, let me know when you see them. Do not let this attack happen. Capture the Americans without killing any. Offer to sell them back. They will pay the ransom. I wish you and yours a life of transparency, honesty, and good consequences." Sam paused, waiting for the correct response before disconnecting.

Finding Deloris was easy; she was the most jovial person in the building. She was always laughing. She claimed it was a nervous reaction, but Sam suspected there were deeper psychological issues she was hiding. He didn't believe anyone could be that happy and wondered what dark secrets she hid.

Naturally, she accepted the assignment to order sandwiches from the bulk food store, even going so far as to offer to drive and purchase them. Sam assured her the standard delivery options and procedures were adequate. She should not trouble herself.

Sam strolled to the War Room, stopping at the bathroom to splash cold water on his face and investigating his suit in the mirror to ensure the creases were crisp and all fuzz, real and imagined, was removed.

Every seat at the table in the War Room was filled. The Secretary of State was the most prominent figure. Her entire life had revolved around silencing all stories about her deeds and promoting her political ambitions, so it seemed fitting to Sam that she would be included in assassination attempts and coverups.

"The seals have landed," a man at the end of the table stated as two helicopters appeared on the large screens that covered the wall at the far end of the table.

Dots descended from the helicopters and remained motionless until their hovering helpers departed.

Sam took mental notes while the players discussed the progress of the dots on the screens as radio communications sounded over the conference line. Occasionally, radio communication required an authorization, but for an assassination attempt, this seemed boring.

"How long until they reach the target?" The president asked.

"We are anticipating two more hours until arrival. We inserted them thirty miles off target to avoid detection. They take 30 minutes to rest around this time so they are not fatigued as they make the assault," the man sitting below the edge of the screens informed.

"Sam," the president turned, "Have the sandwiches arrived?"

"I'm headed to Deloris," Sam answered as he exited the room.

He pulled the cell from his pocket and dialed.

"The American team is at the coordinates I am forwarding. We need our asset to make her way there and ensure they are delayed. I am giving the Iranian twenty-two the same coordinates. I know we have an operation against him, but we need to ensure the Americans do not spoil ours first. Our operative has two hours before the Iranians can reach the Americans. Make sure she delays them and gets out before the Iranians arrive. I wish you and yours a life of transparency, honesty, and good consequences,"

Sam ended the conversation as he forwarded the coordinates. He dialed the Iranian.

"It's me. I am sending the coordinates where the Americans will stop. Wait at least two hours before deploying any troops into the area, or you may spook them. We must ensure they do not evade capture." Sam hung up and texted the information before walking in the direction of Deloris's area.

"Deloris, you are a lifesaver. The president was asking about that platter," he smiled.

"Perfect timing," she chuckled. "It arrived minutes ago. I have procured the finest cheap deli meats on stale bread from a wholesaler. Bring the wealthy, powerful, starving politicians the best money can buy; On the double, their bellies deserve the best." She handed Sam the platter with a cackle.

"I like you," Sam took the platter as he fantasized about Deloris's secret life.

He imagined her holding a whip and ordering some middle-aged lobbyist to kiss her black leather thigh-highs. Sam could see her yanking on the chain attached to the poor man's collar as he returned to the War Room.

"What's happening, why did the screens shut off?" Asked the president.

Everyone was leaning across the table in the direction of the man at the end. The feed on the wall had stopped. Sam was invisible as he opened the platter and placed the sandwiches in the center of the table. The man was talking into the conference line, asking why they had lost visuals and how they would be restored.

"We have lost visuals. We are working to restore them. It appears to be a satellite disruption. Patching comms through," the voice in the speaker was frantic. "Let me know if you can hear them."

"She is sexy for a towel head," the line crackled with static from the unfiltered radio transmission.

"Who's on the line?" The president demanded and received no acknowledgment. "This is the president, who is on the radio?"

"Fuck you, I get to go first. I am squad leader. Bring her."

"This is the resident of the United States. Who is on comms? The entire War Room can hear you. Identify yourself," the veins in the president's neck bulged as his eye twitched.

"What are you doing? Hold her arms. Bend her over the front seat. You two spread her ankles."

"Oh my god!" screamed the Secretary of State in disgust. "They are raping a local." She shot up. "This is the Secretary of State. Stop what you are doing before you embarrass me and this administration. You are on an official, sanctioned mission."

"Sorry, Ma'am," apologized the man at the end of the table. "We are trying to reestablish comms. It is not clear why we can hear them, and they cannot hear us."

"God damn it!" She exploded. "We have the best technology in the world, and we cannot figure out how to work a fucking radio? They are done. All twenty-two of them are out. As soon as they get back, their records are being scrubbed. I am going to make sure the V.A. wipes their memories, I mean *vaccinates* them, with opioids." She used air quotes to accentuate the word. "Their brains will be so scrambled they will die as homeless dip-shits with mush for brains. Nobody creates a scandal that can be traced to me."

"Ma'am," the man at the end of the table growled. "They are property of the Department of Defense, not the Department of State. They will be handled per the U.C.M.J., plus, it's not opioids, the V.A. uses other drugs to wipe the brains of veterans with P.T.S.D., Do your research."

The Secretary was about to lose her shit but was interrupted by the radio. There was a scream, the sound of a woman crying, and multiple sounds of slapping.

"Fuck, Sandoval. Stop fucking her ass so hard. I can feel your dick rubbing mine through her pussy wall."

"Mute it," the Secretary of State cried out.

"No," overruled the president. "We must listen and hear everything. It is our job to monitor the situation. Especially when our people lose sight of the mission and could get ambushed or detected," he didn't bother hiding the fact he was adjusting his crotch.

"They are already detected," she protested. "They aren't raping one of their team members! That isn't a man crying!"

"Sit down and shut up," the president pointed to her chair with a hand still in his lap. "We are going to wait until the mission is over before turning the feed off." He turned his attention to the man at the end of the table, "Restore our visuals. We need to see what is happening."

It took over ninety minutes for the radio to indicate everyone had taken their turn with the woman. The entire room listened in silence as the operators agreed to take a twenty-minute nap before proceeding to the target.

"Jones," a voice spoke. "Make sure to get everyone up in twenty. Do not let her get away. We will release her after we snipe."

"Got it," another voice responded.

Eight minutes into the impromptu nap time, there was more chatter. It was moaning, followed by the sound of several gunshots and a thunderous bang. One of the voices screamed in pain. Several voices were shouting over each other and were incomprehensible.

"We have restored visuals," the man at the end of the table announced.

"Where is it?" The president hollered over the radio.

"Bringing it online... Ah, here it is," the man pointed. "We have switched to thermal video to track our people better."

There was a figure lying on the ground with a growing spot beside its face. Several others surrounded him as they worked. A few yards away, another group was working on the leg of someone else. The satellite view zoomed out, and nobody could spot any other life forms in the area. The woman had vanished.

"Report," the man at the end of the table commanded.

"A hostile sniper hit Jones and our high-value asset," someone squawked. "We are patching Jone's face, but it's bad. The asset was hit in his leg. It was a clean shot through the calf. He will be fine. The sniper is down four hundred yards to the northwest."

"Can you complete the mission?" The man inquired.

"We're good, but we are sending Jones, Sandoval, and Brooks to the extraction point so we can finish strong."

The satellite feed lit up with countless dots and rectangles entering the screen from all directions as the transmission ended.

"Dear god," the Secretary of State whispered as she put a hand over her mouth. "It's going to be a blood bath. They have to surrender."

The man at the end of the table turned to the president.

"Kill the mission. There is no way to keep this quiet," the president confirmed.

"No-go, team leader, stand down," the man at the end of the table repeated into the conference line. "Swarms of hostiles in every direction. Surrender for diplomatic extraction. Do not engage. I repeat, do not engage. Surrender for diplomatic extraction."

The room was commandeered by scenes of the American operators being beaten and loaded onto trucks. Everyone watched while the vehicles drove to a remote prison.

When the trucks were arriving, the man at the end of the table stood, "I have Turkey on the line. They are patching Tehran through to us. Are we prepared to take the call?"

"Put it through," the president waived a hand.

"Is this the Americans?" A boorish voice demanded.

"This is the Secretary of State," she entered the conversation.

"We discovered a handful of Americans lost in our desert. We were worried they might die in such an environment. Please do not worry; we have rescued them. We used manpower and fuel to reach them, and one of our people was injured. We request your help paying for the assistance we have rendered as a 'thank you' for saving so many Americans," his voice sounded mechanical like he was reading a speech. The Secretary motioned for the phone to be muted.

"They could have killed everyone. The best option is to pay the ransom and extract our people. We can still cover this up," she rationalized.

"Can we rescue them?" The president stared into the face of the man at the end of the table.

"We do not have additional special operators in the area, and we have no intel on the prison where they are being held. We can try to rescue them, but it would take several days and is almost guaranteed to result in many lost operators."

"Unmute the phone," the president puffed out his chest. "Who is on the line? This is the President of the United States."

"Hello, Mr. President," the voice responded. "I am the representative of the Iranian leadership. My president sits beside me but will not speak. He is a pious loyalist and is forbidden by his convictions from conversing with Western leaders. I am his voice."

"Release our people, or you will feel the full weight of the United States," the president snarled.

"Do your citizens know you are sending these people to their deaths? We are not even at war, how would your congress act if they knew you were doing such things? Is the value of secrets worth less or more than the lives of your people? You have created so many secrets in one day. How much are you willing to pay to keep your secrets?"

"We keep no secrets from our citizens. You have one hour to release our people, or we will be forced to retaliate," the president kept his voice strong as he grimaced and wiped his brow.

"Mr. President, we will release your people. We do not want them. Reimburse us seventeen million dollars for our rescue efforts, and we will guarantee they leave Iran."

"If it is discovered you took a bribe from us, you will be destroyed by your people," the Secretary blurted.

Sam held back a snicker at the comment. She was far closer to the truth than anyone in the conversation knew. He looked at his watch. It was less than 23 hours before the Iranian negotiator would be tortured and killed.

"Women are not meant to interrupt the conversations of negotiating men," the voice replied to the Secretary. "It seems there was a rounding error when we calculated the cost of rescuing your people. We are requesting a reimbursement amount of twenty-six million dollars."

"We will send drop-off coordinates. You will be paid after we verify our people are safe. Their radios must be derived with them," the president responded, motioning for the phone to be muted. "Find me a place near one of our diplomatic sites. We don't want them to be returned to where it sounded like they raped a woman. That would be begging for trouble. Unmute the phone."

"They did rape a woman," the Secretary mumbled.

"I haven't heard you speak," the president called out. "Are you still on the line?"

"We are waiting for the coordinates," the voice announced to the silent room.

"Forwarding the coordinates," the president turned to the Secretary of State. "Choose a place where you are sure we control the situation."

Her expression brightened, "By Rasht. We will lift them to Benghazi. I control everything that happens there."

How to Win

The air was thick with stale beer in the bright, stuffy bar when Sam arrived. Sarah's nude-tan pencil dress matched her heels, and Sam was not her only fan that evening. She was chatting with a man at the far end of the honey-colored counter.

"Just in time for last call. If you slam it, I can get you something," the bartender offered. "You missed the rush, but there are a few groups scattered around. See anyone you know?"

"I was the D.D., but it looks like she has another ride planned," Sam lied to protect his ego as he tilted his head and pointed his chin at Sarah.

"Yeah, she's been getting free drinks all night. Better luck next time," the bartender lifted two half-filled pint glasses and dumped them into the sink.

Wishing he had been able to make it earlier and hating himself for not interrupting Sarah's conversation, Sam walked outside. The cool air felt good on Sam's face and helped wash the stench of the bar from his nostrils. A few seconds into the walk to where he parked, Sam heard the tapping of running heels on cement behind him.

Sam spun and prepared himself for the attack but was surprised by an unexpected ambush. His lips were met with the sweet taste of Sarah. She grabbed his head with one hand and hugged him with the other. He wrapped his arms around her, pulling their chests together until he could feel their warmth combine and her nipples stiffen. Sam let Sarah use her tongue to spread his lips and explore the inside of his mouth.

"I missed you," Sarah admitted when she pulled herself away from Sam's face. "You weren't going to try to leave without me, were you? I play for keeps, remember?"

"God, you're fucking amazing," Sam's eyes sparkled as he kissed her. "I had to work late; there was a situation."

"No explanations required," Sarah pressed a finger against his lips. "I know who and what you are, you owe me nothing. But, we should agree to some ground rules, considering we are fraternizing with the enemy."

Sam released her at the word 'enemy' and thought about the word. He had never considered any five-point, especially Sarah, to be enemies. The treaty was still enforceable, and even if it wasn't, they didn't have different goals: a better future for humanity. Although, the word did make sense as he contemplated Sarah's meaning. The five-points always settled things with war. It was reasonable to believe that anyone who did not align with their ventures would be considered an enemy.

Sarah, seeming to notice Sam had got lost in thought, linked their arms at the elbow. Appearing to have been discontent with his reaction, she interlaced her fingers with his and pulled him in for another smooch.

"Sam," she interrupted his thoughts. "No matter what our people do, I want to be with you. I know what and who you are, and I know you will not be around long. While you are here, you are mine, ok?"

"Sarah," he sighed. "I wish I could keep you; you are so gorgeous and amazing."

"Thank you for not calling me a beauty. I know there are women you target to complete your assignments; I'm fine with that. We all do things to get the job done. But while you are here, you are mine, ok?"

"Sarah, you can claim me as yours as long as you are mine."

Sam paused and wondered if the infatuation and excitement he felt was how normal people loved. Sarah was not part of the plan, and talking to her could get them both killed, it was exhilarating.

"Do normal people take risks to be with the ones who make them feel loved and safe?" Sam wondered.

"Naturally! Don't give me anything I can't wash off in the shower. Always wear a condom," she squeezed Sam's hand.

"Do you have something I cannot wash off in the shower?" Sam pulled their bodies together and gazed into her eyes.

"No," She looked puzzled as she walked, pulling Sam by the hand. "Also, you are not allowed to use me for info on the five-points. I know you are searching for the Pentagon twenty-two we took hostage, but I cannot reveal the dark site. We have to leave our organizations out of our relationship."

"What the fuck?" Sam thought. *"When did they take a hostage? What else does she know?"*

"You know the capture is a violation of the treaty, and the death would be an act of war, right?" Sam asked.

Sarah stopped, it was her turn to pull their bodies together. They stared at the reflections of themselves in each other's eyes under the street light's orange glow.

"Stop!" She almost begged. "There are those among us who want to return to the old ways: the time before the treaty. Those are not my people, the ones I know and respect. That faction has lost their values and way. There are still good people in the five-points. We are battling to maintain control. Promise me," a tear formed at the inner edge of Sarah's eye as she raised both of Sam's hands to her heart, "Promise me that your people will not start a war before we have retaken our organization."

"Sarah, you don't know what you are asking me to do," Sam was blindsided by the entire conversation. "This is beyond my authority."

"Don't report it. The council doesn't need to know. Give us time to fix this," she pleaded.

"Are you here as a bribe?" Sam felt used, humiliated, and disgusted.

"Never, you know rainbows do not use sex as a mechanism. You are here for me. I don't care what they do to me. I want to keep you; you're mine. We are Herolma and Cheoliba reincarnate."

"God, I love you," Sam's boyish pleasure reshaped his face. "I mean, I love how your brain works. The capture of our twenty-two cannot be ignored. We will be coming, and it will be brutal, but we will not interfere with the five-point's power struggles. To make sure we are on the same page about everything and have no more secrets, I can tell you are half-frozen. Look at those nips. They are about to slice through your dress. That's my car," he pointed across the street. "Let's hop in and get you warmed, up or naked, lady's choice."

"Warm me here first," Sarah lowered their hands to their sides.

Sam could feel his pants begin to tighten as she pressed herself against his chest. She let Sam taste her lips before twirling on her toes as she crossed the street. They agreed to drive to Sarah's home; it was closer. Sarah scoured the radio until she found the perfect song,

"*You Belong to Me,*" Sarah sang as Sam wondered if she knew about his work with Valerie.

"Park behind the red car up there. I don't know why I said that you know where I live," Sarah ran her hand up his leg.

"Of course," Sam put a hand on Sarah's knee and squeezed.

An odd feeling swept over him. He wasn't trying to manipulate her; he wasn't sure why he was touching her. It happened, and it felt good. It wasn't part of some job it was a weird thing that happened without planning or reason. For the first time in his life, Sam believed doing things without a reason was a reasonable thing to do.

"I haven't let myself be with anyone else since you," Sarah rose from the seat. "Even when I was on a mission, I couldn't. I am yours, and you are mine. You belong with me."

"No, you belong with me," he replied as he locked the car, grabbed her by the waist, and pulled her close to look into her face.

He examined it, trying to see if he could find any tells, anything that would expose her. Was she manipulating him, or could this dream be real?

"Come with me," Sarah pulled Sam to her door. "We need to consummate our agreement," she said in a high-pitched, bad English accent. The bolt on the door slid open. "In we go," Sarah yanked Sam inside.

It was dark except for a warmer in the corner that filled the room with a light pumpkin spice aroma. The sound of unzipping grabbed his attention. Sarah shimmied her dress to the floor. To Sam's surprise and delight, a garter with stockings remained on the otherwise naked goddess.

"Do they look ok?" She asked, turning a knee sideways to cover her sex with her thigh.

"Have I mentioned how perfect you are?" Sam couldn't stop staring.

In his mind, there were a number of discoverable absolute truths, Sarah's perfection was an absolute truth that forced mania.

"Come on," she whispered, leading him up the stairs. In her bedroom, she produced another deep kiss. Sam was powerless to resist. He enjoyed the sweet taste that somehow persisted. "I will be back. Make yourself comfortable," Sarah blew a kiss as she walked into the bathroom.

"Wait," Sam called as she reached for the door.

"Yes?" Sarah raised an eyebrow as they locked eyes in the mirror.

"Leave the garter and stockings on," his face glowed with excitement.

Sarah winked as she closed her leg in the door. She slipped her leg into the bathroom before it was pinched, letting the door close with a click. Sam scrambled to remove his clothes.

"Why did this shirt have so many buttons? Who needs this many buttons?"

He thought as he yanked it open and let the last three fly. He crumpled his pants to the floor but couldn't remove his briefs, Sarah made her way to the bed.

"Come," she beckoned from the comforter, her knees bent over the edge, her stockinged feet flat on the carpet.

Sam had fine-tuned his routine and moved into the first position. The tactile sensation of Sarah's calf muscles clad by stretched nylon excited his pleasure. Sam tucked his forearms beneath Sarah's knees, grabbed her lower thighs, and lifted as he pulled her to the edge. He stroked Sarah's thighs through her stockings as he knelt. He removed his underwear then raised his arms to glide her knees to his shoulders.

He could smell the cake frosting cream she applied and kissed the inside of her left knee, then her right. He approached her sex as he crisscrossed his kisses, biting through the stockings as he moved. When he reached the top of the nylon, he stopped kissing and opened his mouth wide.

As Sam glided his hands across Sarah's cool white skin, he exhaled on her sex, warming it. He felt Sarah's legs tighten around his head as his hands passed her belly button. He exhaled. The tip of Sam's fingers found Sarah's nipples and pinched as he exhaled. He felt Sarah's back arch as she moaned.

"No," Sarah whispered as she sat up and placed her feet on the floor. "You are not at work. Come,"

She bit Sam's lip as she pulled their faces together.

"Come on, we are going to cuddle." She interlocked her fingers with his before scooting backward on the bed and lying on the pillow.

"Cuddling sounds amazing. I call big spoon," Sam laughed as Sarah pulled him onto the bed.

He couldn't wait to cuddle because that was when he felt the closest to her. Although, her quirky adamance about wrestling the comforter over their bodies before spooning perplexed him.

"Roll on your side," Sarah bit her lip. "I am the big spoon tonight."

Sam wondered how Sarah always made him feel safe, loved, and at peace despite being a life-threatening risk. Being with her was a thrill, but not like the killings, the mind games, or the torture. He had always felt pity for the sheep who believed in innocent romance and love, but here he lay, being held by sublimity.

Sarah's body was warm between the cool sheets. She pushed her hand under his arm and held his heart. Sam noticed Sarah working her foot between his feet, and her leg followed upward until his thighs hugged the intruder. Her nylon tickled his scrotum as it took position.

Sarah's exhalations excited Sam's nape as their breathing synchronized. The fuzz on his abdomen prickled as Sarah crept her hand south with every breath she drew. It was ten minutes before her hand rested between the head of his erect excitement and his belly button.

Sarah bit Sam's neck as she whispered, "I hope you're ready." Nipping his flesh, she wrapped her fingers around the base and stroked upward.

As it made its way back to the head, it tightened before lowering to the starting position. She pulled her hand away and returned it covered in a slick moisture.

Sam licked his lips as he noticed how dry they had become, closed his eyes, and enjoyed the divine attention. He rolled onto his back. His leg fell between Sarah's and found itself trapped. The feeling of her nylon against his thigh intensified the stimulation. He tucked his bicep under her head as they kissed. Sarah continued her slow, firm strokes as their mouths made tender love.

She rocked her mound against Sam's leg as her hand continued its work. The moisture on his member dried and chafed. He freed his leg and pleasure as he rolled to face her.

"Come to me, perfection," Sam requested as he merged their mouths.

Sam pressed the head of his love between the sides of her tender opening. He knew as long as they played face-to-face, the best he could do was tantalize her clitoris, and it was working.

Sarah rolled to face away from him and scooted her ass against his abdomen. He pressed between her shoulders as he glided inside. Sarah bent forward as he pulled her sex down his member until she pressed against his scrotum. Sarah lifted her leg and spread her opening with a hand as Sam infiltrated and retreated from her fortress.

"Make sure you get yours," Sarah recommended as Sam wrapped his hands around her hips and pulled.

"I will," he smirked, transitioning from long, soft intrusions to short, hard thumping.

Sarah was dewy, but he thought she was much juicier last time. The added friction made it difficult to resist the nearing climax.

"mmmm, nobody compares to you, love," Sarah moaned as she turned her shoulders and scratched Sam's chest.

That was all he needed. His body shuddered as his finale filled her femininity. It was less than normal because of his morning work with Valerie, and he prayed Sarah would not notice. Sam decided she was oblivious when she rolled onto her back and continued to scratch his chest with a grin.

"My turn," Sarah seemed elated as she pushed Sam on his back and wormed beneath the comforter.

Her hands guided his knees apart as her tongue teased. It copied his earlier work, zig-zagging from leg to leg as it moved north.

When it arrived at the first pool of cooling juice, it stopped. Sam could feel Sarah's breath heating the wet flesh until she lapped it with a flattened tongue.

Sam was confounded and aroused at the same time. No woman had ever eaten the dried excitement from his skin. Sarah's hand had found the base of his desire, but this time, refused to advance as her tongue continued its journey.

When her heated exhalations found his manhood, they stopped traveling. Her eager oral passage engulfed his limp lance. The skillful maneuvering of her oral orchestra grew it into a formidable weapon that would intimidate the most experienced woman as it surrounded, pressed, and dampened.

Sarah's mouth was so magical that Sam rocked his hips. Sarah pulled back as Sam wove his fingers into her hair. She lifted away, but Sam pulled her down, forcing her to gag as he worked into her throat until her lips reached the bottom. When she pinched his thigh, he remembered where he was and who he was gagging. He released and pulled her up for a kiss to apologize.

"Time for me to get mine," Sarah exclaimed as she rose like a phoenix from the covers.

The comforter sailed off the bed as Sarah straddled Sam's body. Sarah lowered herself onto Sam's naked sex and let the shaft part her clamshell. Sam could feel his lance lubricate as she rocked her hips forward and found the tip. She wiggled from side to side as she placed both hands on his chest, forcing his weapon to enter her sheath.

He placed his hands behind his head, ogling Sarah's face as she rocked her hips, grinding her clitoris on his flesh. He was mesmerized, infatuated, and in love.

In awe of her continued perfection, he was unable to divert his gaze. Sam wondered if he would ever stop admiring her. Imagining what she would look like, overwhelmed and exhausted.

"*Even then, she would be flawless,*" he thought.

"Make sure you get yours," he grinned as he clamped her chest.

Sarah bent backward, placing her hands on his knees for support. Sam could feel his balls being drenched by Sarah's juices as she kept their eyes locked. The thorough lubrication had Sarah sliding with ease as she squinted. Sam could feel her fingers tighten around his knees as her sex clung to his manhood in spasming gratification. Sarah stopped sliding as her legs convulsed.

"Do you want to finish again?" She panted.

"I want you," Sam responded as he pulled her flat onto him. "Let's cuddle more," he insisted as he kissed her forehead. "Unless you need to clean up."

"Yes, but let me clean you first," Sarah rolled over and hopped off the bed. The cloth Sarah used to massage Sam's abdomen, sex, and her smeared passion was damp and warm. Sarah tossed the cloth into the bathroom with a light thud.

Sam pulled Sarah by the forearm as she squealed with glee. He wrapped his arms around her as she fell to her side in front of him. He could feel his sex stiffen as Sarah pressed her ass against it.

"I'm yours, and you are mine. We are joined," Sam promised as he drifted from his dream into a deep sleep.

General Vilonka

Facing Danger

"What are you saying?" Alya questioned. "Protect your finance minister. The council didn't order his death."

She knew the American's request was a bad sign.

"He's a twenty-two, like us. If he needs you to capture troops, then capture the troops."

Alya held back her rage. The incompetent and rebellious nature of the Iranian twenty-two had ground away all patience and understanding. She had started dreaming of being present when whoever had been selected tortured and murdered him. She could hear his screams, see the pain in his eyes.

"I am surprised you are not more accommodating. The council's warning seemed direct." Alya paused to listen for a response that never arrived.

"You are much braver than me. I would never be so bold as to question the strength of the Society. Work with the American; he represents the Council, like us." Alya grimaced as she swallowed at the thought of the Iranian being considered an equal.

"Now, I must work on my list of missions. I wish you and yours a life of transparency, honesty, and appropriate consequences."

She placed the phone in her pocket and opened the great doors. The Russian double was reading at the wooden desk under the high-arched window at the far end of the bright room. Two regal wingbacks were sitting across the desk from him. The walls were bare except for the cherry wood frames that rose high towards the arched ceilings on the three interior walls.

"We have a problem," Alya's words skipped across the floor.

"What?" The double held a finger where he stopped reading and looked up.

"I have one more call to make, and then I will provide an update. I apologize for the delay," she spun back toward the doorway.

"Important matters take precedence," he lowered his head and continued reading.

Alya closed the massive doors with a click and retrieved the phone from her pocket. She dialed the emergency line.

"We have a problem," Alya started. "The Americans are sending a hit team to kill the Iranian finance minister. Please verify the current mission."

Alya noticed the anticipation and nervousness swell in her head as she struggled to remain calm. It seemed like she had been waiting an eternity, her frustration was boiling when the emergency dispatcher responded. The council had already pushed the fog, and there was no turning back. Alya clenched her jaw to hold back jubilation. The ungrateful, disgraceful Iranian's fate was sealed.

"It is an honor to serve," she said through clenched teeth. "I wish you and yours a life of transparency, honesty, and good consequences."

Alya disconnected the call, removed the battery, placed them both in the metal trash can beside the door, and dumped the bottle of liquid from her pocket on top. Faint smoke billowed as the devices melted. Alya reopened the large doors.

"Dear president," she boomed. "Are you ready for an updated report from your most humble servant?"

Laughter burst from the double and danced in the room. "I hope the news is as good as your spirits."

"Nothing has changed," Alya's body floated to the desk above the tapping of her heels.

"Then why so happy?" The double closed his book.

"The five-points are attempting an assassination in Iran. The council said it will handle them. We still get to crash the helicopter." Alya used her hand to imitate a plane crashing into the desk.

"Let me rehearse before the generals and staff arrive," the double motioned for Alya to sit. "Our Iranian friends have betrayed us. They claim the Russians have become weak."

"Say, 'They claim the motherland is weak,' it will hurt their hearts more." Alya advised as she leaned forward in her chair.

"Our Iranian friends have betrayed us. They claim the motherland is weak," he paused to wait for a nod of approval from Alya. "They have sowed the seeds of a malevolent harvest across the globe."

Alya leaned forward, "Do not write poetry; these are Russian generals, not American coeds."

"I was planning to slam my fists every time I start a sentence. What are your thoughts?" He solicited Alya's advice.

"Let me see the speech," Alya took the paper. "When you say the words 'must' and 'today,' you should slam your fists. That was a good idea, well done. I will follow along. Start your speech."

"They have spread lies of Russian poverty. We must correct this injustice." He waited for a nod of approval after slamming his fists on the desk. "We must be strong with our reply. We must be true and brave with our aim. We must strike them with the Russian fist of power. We must knock the Iranians back. We must make the lips of their lies swell and bleed. Today, we make things right. Today, we lift the homeland and show the world our glory. Today, we make the world fear the sleeping bear that Iran has awoken. Tomorrow, we crash the helicopter of the Iranian president and snuff out those who lie about the motherland. We are the warriors who lift the Russian homeland. We make the homeland and all of Russia a gem to be worshiped by the world."

Alya analyzed the short speech for a moment while considering its delivery. She calculated all the possible interpretations and nuances before offering any more refinements. Overall, it was not bad, but it was not good either. It was adequate, and that was the cornerstone of Russian politics.

"Do not use the final line," Alya critiqued, "Russians do not seek the worship of their lands or government."

"Done," the double nodded. "Anything else?"

"No, it is adequate. We should move to the briefing place. Remember, you are the fearless leader. Every hint of an issue with your words, actions, appearance, or persona is an attack on the Russian president, yourself, and the council. They must be handled ruthlessly," Alya rose with the double.

"We can always replace generals," the double followed Alya's lead.

Alya paced the room as she and the double waited for the generals and staff to arrive. The double was sitting at the grand oak table that had marble inlay. The first to arrive was General Klopvor. He was followed by a new general, General Vilonka. General Vilonka had assumed the place of the general who had tripped and fell from his balcony. Alya wondered how his houseboy was doing.

General Vilonka's impressive dancer's body, from her time before the army when she was a ballerina, could not be concealed by her uniform. She was taller than Alya at five feet nine inches and used no makeup. She once stated it was because she did not want to hide her face's overwhelming beauty. As Alya watched the general, she understood why she made the claim.

Alya heard rumors about the new general. She had risen through the ranks due to her brutal betrayal and savagery against several Russian military leaders. She fantasized about joining General Vilonka as they murdered the corrupt men. Alya stepped behind a chair as she felt her panties moisten at the impromptu murderous fantasy. When the general looked at her and smiled, Alya's face pinked. She understood she had been gawking and missed the fact that the table had filled.

As the double greeted the final participants, Alya walked to the opposite end of the table. Painfully aware General Vilonka was still watching her with a smile, Alya took her spot. As the final staff members took their seats, the double rose, and the general returned her attention to the head of the table.

"Our Iranian friends have betrayed us," the double performed his speech and was rewarded with a standing ovation. General Klopvor remained standing as the ovation dissipated.

"Like you, your words are powerful. I am honored to serve a president who casts off all restraints when Russia is challenged." General Klopvor offered tribute.

The double raised both hands above the table and clapped until General Klopvor sat. General Vilonka rose.

"Mr. President, I have studied your career. I have modeled myself after you and thought I knew you, but still, you continue to teach me the meaning of Russian leadership. I am proud to serve such a wise and decisive mastermind," she honored the president.

The double looked past the standing general to Alya, who provided a subtle nod before he smiled and clapped. The remaining participants took turns praising and pledging tribute to the Russian presidency and the homeland.

"The strength of the motherland swells within us," the double shook a fist. "Go, let it flow from this room across the motherland, drown Iran, and flood the earth."

The double raised both arms towards the doors behind Alya as cheering swelled the room. Alya hid her disdain at the poetry as she opened the doors. Stepping to the side, she became a statue, part of the room's decorations, as everyone filed out.

General Vilonka remained in her chair until all others had passed. The general slowed as she approached Alya.

"I'm Talia. I will be at Central Station tonight. Find me," the general's hushed tone as she passed.

She kept her head unturned to ensure no others heard. Alya closed the doors and walked to the double.

"We may have a problem," she stated.

"I performed as you suggested," the double looked worried.

"Not you," Alya did not have time for his fear of consequences. "General Vilonka requested a secret meeting with me. I will meet with her to find out what she knows and if this is something we can contain or if this is something we need to pass on to the council. Do not contact me until I return, and do not have any meetings with any generals or politicians."

"I have plenty of reading to do," he replied. "Be safe, Alya, these are dangerous times." Alya ignored the sentimental old fool.

"All times are dangerous times," she thought as she departed.

Compromising Emotions

It had been a long time since Alya had been on a date and never with someone so attractive. She scrolled through her memories at the Harem while pulling clothes from the closet, holding them to her body, then tossing them onto a growing heap that covered the bed. The others from the Harem were beautiful, but they were lost to time and, most likely, the fire. Plus, that was different, those kinds of relationships had a single destiny: heartbreak.

The lingerie and underwear the council had furnished were the best in the world, but the clothes were modest and lacking in appeal. Alya wanted to look sexy for Talia. When her closet was empty, she dug through the mounds of rejects, mixing and matching. Deciding she looked good enough, Alya placed a bag of cocaine, a roll of cash, and a knife in her clutch beside her phone and condoms. Skipping out the door, she was aware she needed to prepare for the unexpected.

The bouncers had already taken their positions at the door. She knew none compared to her allure, but a single woman would not be able to get past face control. She scanned the approaching groups. One with well-dressed, laughing young men coming from the river side of the road was perfect. Their joy would get them inside.

"Serge, I cannot believe you are here tonight, my best love. We must dance, you are my absolute favorite," Alya walked toward the men with open arms, hoping one would reciprocate.

The two men in front descended into silence as they gave each other peculiar looks. The center man from the back three pushed through and ran to Alya.

He scooped her up in his arms, and her legs swung as he spun in a circle.

"I thought you went back to Romania," he exclaimed as she felt the earth beneath her. He had the heavy smell of Vodka mixed with cologne.

"No," Alya responded. "I leave tomorrow evening. We have one more night to dance."

"Who is she," the other men had caught up.

"This is Denisa. Remember, I met her two nights ago, and she brought the party," the man used his index finger to hold a nostril shut.

"Hello, Denisa," another man locked arms with Alya, "I am Petrov. We should be friends."

"You smell so yummy," Serge giggled to Alya as the group was inspected by the bouncer.

Alya feigned a laugh and made an immaculate smile in return. Impressed with their clothes, smiles, laughter, and male-to-female ratio, the bouncer let the group enter.

Alya turned and kissed the man, claiming to be Serge, "I do not know your friends, so I am going on my own." She took the cocaine from her purse and wrapped it in his hand, "Thank you for your friendship. Take this and have fun."

The man placed the bag in his pocket, kissed Alya's cheek, then yelled to the friends that surrounded the pair, "Come men, Denisa does not like the labyrinth, but we have a party to get started. She is on her own."

Petrov gave Alya a curious look before releasing her arm, "This is a shame, you look fun." He scampered after his group into the darkness.

The thumping music stifled Alya's senses as she circled the thick mass of bodies jostling each other under the rhythmic lighting. Faces flashed and disappeared in the crowd. Alya was on the hunt, and her prey was hidden. When she reached the edge of the stage, she spotted it across the room. It was looking towards the entrance, having missed her entrance.

Alya crouched as she made her way through the tall clumps of socialites. As she approached, she would raise her head enough to ensure her prey remained before she continued stalking. Alya slowed as she neared the target. She crept close to a dancing group and peered between its members. Talia was still oblivious, the perfect victim. Alya used a passing man to shield herself during the final approach. Alya sprang as the man passed the general's table, but Talia had vanished. Alya scanned the room to locate the target, wondering how the general had escaped.

"Good girl," yelled a voice as Alya felt a hand on the small of her back. "You know how to listen, but your hunting needs practice."

Alya whirled with an elbow bent, seeking a target. The elbow sailed over an evading face as a pair of hands grabbed her waist.

"Your reflexes almost match your beauty," Talia yelled over the music as she stood. "Only almost."

"We should drink!" Alya exclaimed.

"You're nervous?" Talia grinned as she pulled Alya to her. "You don't have to worry. I will play nice as long as you behave."

"You are..." Alya could not find of a word to describe how she was feeling.

"A woman?" Talia's face hardened.

"No, just, you are so strong and pretty, and you smell good, and..." Alya's mouth got dry, and she used her hands to cover her face as she hid how unimpressive she was compared to Talia.

"You're coming with me," Talia pulled Alya's arm. "This place is overstimulating you."

Alya let Talia lead her from the club. The tapping of her heels echoed in the quiet streets. She wanted to break the silence but was nervous she would say something embarrassing.

"Do you love him?" Talia's voice halted the tapping.

"What?" Talia's question was an unexpected and bizarre assault.

"The president. Everyone knows you are his mistress. Does he force you with threats, or do you love him?" Talia snapped as her face became scary.

"It's not like that," Alya rebutted as she freed herself from Talia's hold. She squatted with her thighs to her chest and hugged her legs, "You don't understand. I don't know why you invited me out."

"Do not pull away." Talia squatted beside Alya, wrapped her arm around her, and pulled her close. "Many men have threatened me and used me while I was in the ballet. It helped me learn how to use them when I became a soldier." She pulled Alya up as she stood, ensuring their bodies remained together.

"There is one man who threatens me and all of Russia. Also, I am not one of your men that can be used to advance your career," Alya pulled away.

"No," Talia turned and pulled their bodies together. "You are not important enough to help my career. You are here for fun. Tell me which man threatens you."

Alya wasn't sure if she liked the idea that Talia thought she was a plaything or if she was insulted. Ultimately, she decided the desire to have Talia was too strong to resist.

"General Klopvor is the most loyal general in all of Russia. It seems his ambitions are higher than his current position," she lied.

"We all have ambitions," Talia replied, texting someone. "Do not talk about work for the rest of the night."

The walk to Talia's home was short. The night was still, a single car passing as they walked. Talia lived in a quiet building not far from the club.

"Come," Talia pulled Alya as the apartment door shut. Talia slipped out of her shoes and led Alya to a large tan sofa on a dark brown shag rug that filled the side of the room. "Sit, you need vodka."

"Wine is easier for my belly," Alya liked the way Talia's hips swayed as she walked. Talia walked to the wall facing the couch. Beneath the television mounted on the white wall was a control panel. Talia played *Ты моя жизнь*.

"Red or white?" Talia asked over her shoulder as she crossed the bright-colored wood floor into the kitchen, stepping behind the white marble island.

"Red," Alya almost sang as she followed.

"I see we are still working on our listening skills," Talia pointed her chin at the couch as she made a bottle appear from below the counter and removed a corkscrew from a drawer. "You are new, so I will be nice. Sit on that stool," Talia's voice was stern as she pointed through the counter.

"Naturally," Alya responded as she sat. Talia popped the cork and returned the corkscrew to the drawer. "Your place is nice. I didn't know generals were paid so well."

Talia raised an eyebrow, "Do you always worry about the finances of others?"

"It is a nice place. You have so much. Why are you interested in someone like me?"

"Take this," Talia slid a half-filled glass across the counter. "Relax. I have benefactors who want me to be comfortable. I am sure a woman as beautiful as you also have some benefactors."

"Don't call me beautiful," Alya shrieked before adding, "I'm sorry, I didn't mean to have that reaction. That word hits my ear wrong. As for your question, I try to stay away from men. They are so terrible. I wish I could kill them all." Alya gulped the wine.

"Such an odd reason to get upset. It's a word. And, Yes, they are horrible, but also they are not horrible. You can either hate them for their desires, or you can use their desires to win. I have these things because I let my benefactors convince themselves they are getting what they want, and I win," Talia refilled the glasses.

"You are a prostitute," Alya had let the wine take over as she hunched and talked into her glass. She felt the pangs of her history as the words escaped.

"You are a disrespectful creature," Talia's face was stern but softened before Alya noticed. "What is wrong with giving men ten minutes with your body for them to give you all you desire? Plus, I do not have sex with them."

Alya straightened on her stool, "I didn't mean it in a bad way. We are all prostitutes in some ways."

She analyzed Talia's face for any new emotions. She knew she might have offended her host and feared rejection would soon follow.

"Have more wine; you are still in your head. The wine will help with what is coming," Talia refilled both glasses as she circled the island.

Talia turned Alya on the stool, placed the palms of her hands between Alya's knees, and pressed them open. Alya felt herself moisten as she returned the glass to the counter.

"Enough about men," Talia's fingernails scored Alya's skin as their fingers worked.

They started at the small of Alya's back, found untucked the camisole, worked their way around the waist of the black leather skirt as they freed it, finding Alya's belly button. The fingernails etched their way up Alya's stomach, revealing pale white skin.

"Off with your shirt," Talia lifted.

Alya raised her arms as Talia lifted it to freedom, tossed it on the floor, and took two steps backward. The air was cold on Alya's naked chest, but the way Talia was looking into her soul kept her from hiding or realizing how stiff her nipples had become.

"Stand."

"Now what?" Alya rose.

"Remove your boots and put them by the door," Talia's voice reminded Alya of the nuns from primary school.

The wood was icy beneath her naked feet as she scurried back.

"Good girl," Talia complimented without a smile, "Now your skirt."

Alya could feel embarrassment and shyness blossoming within as she struggled to unzip. She could only garner enough courage to look at Talia's manicured toes as her trembling fingers maneuvered. Alya folded the skirt and placed it on the stool.

"No!" Talia's rebuke was sharp. "Dirty girl, your skirt belongs on the floor."

Alya could feel a stinging in her eyes as she retracted the skirt, rotated, and let it fall on top of her shirt. Her embarrassment was overwhelming, and the frustration at her inability to anticipate something as simple as '*dirty clothes belong on the floor*' filled her with shame.

"Now your underwear," Talia's voice softened as Alya slid her lace thong to her knees, then crouched and removed them.

She pulled her thighs to her chest and hugged her legs as she stared at her clothes pile.

"You did a good job listening. Stand, you have earned a reward," Talia's voice seemed almost motherly.

Alya raised her eyes to watch Talia walk into another room. She reappeared with a cloth bag that she placed on the couch. Talia walked to Alya and waited. Alya took her time to straighten up. Her skin prickled with goosebumps from the cold. Talia took her hand and led her to the end of the sofa on the shag carpet.

"You did a good job listening, so you have earned a kiss," Talia pressed their lips together.

Alya could feel herself yearning for more compliments and affection and couldn't understand why. As their lips parted, Alya wanted to pull Talia, hoped to burn the taste into her memory, and needed to force more affection, but Talia was unwilling.

"Bend over the sofa," Talia commanded.

"What?" Alya scrunched her face and cocked her head.

Before Alya realized what had happened, her hips were mounted on the edge of the sofa, and her face was pressed against the cushion. She could still feel the shag beneath her feet, but she could not pull herself up. Talia was strong and pressing between her shoulders to keep her in place.

"You will learn to listen," Talia's voice was free from emotion as Alya felt something hard and flat strike her ass cheeks. "I will be nice. Two this time." Another sting warmed Alya's ass.

"Why?" Alya stated from the shock of the situation.

"You will learn to be my good girl," Talia's voice still emotionless. "You will listen to me and obey me, and you will always call me 'TaVi.' Do you understand?"

"But at work," thwap, Alya reminded the General about the dangers but was interrupted by another spank.

This one was harder, causing Alya's cheeks to feel numb as stinging tendrils wormed around the edges of her ass. She reached her hands back to protect her ass from any further assaults.

"You will always call me 'TaVi,' do you understand?" Talia repeated.

"Yes," Alya replied through clenched teeth, fighting back tears of embarrassment from her vulnerability.

Talia leaned on Alya's back with her forearm and pulled Alya's arms up her back, holding Alya's hands away from her ass as another wack interrupted the romantic Russian music. Alya squirmed and struggled to free herself from Talia, but the general was too strong. Alya could feel the general shift more weight onto her every time she struggled to get free.

"You will always call me 'TaVi,' do you understand?" Talia's voice still seemed calm and emotionless.

"Yes, TaVi," Alya sneered.

She could feel herself becoming angry at Talia. Angry that she had been promised a night of passion with a beautiful woman and instead was being abused for being human. She struggled more. As Talia wrenched Alya's arms to keep her in place, pain spiked in Alya's body.

Alya felt her face get hot with rage as all the pain seemed to disappear. She flailed her legs and thrashed her body, trying to break Talia's grip. She turned sideways. Used her thighs to pull her off the end of the sofa. She even stood, but Talia was too strong. Alya had one move remaining; she used all her might to crash to the floor. Even as she fell, Talia kept a grip on her arms and prevented her from hitting the carpet. Talia lifted Alya back to her perch.

"You are new. It is natural that you will try to fight against your fate, but you are my toy. Do you understand?"

Alya's rage boiled, and she felt defiant. Her way to fight back was silence. She refused to respond. Even after Talia repeated herself and gave her ass two more spanks, Alya could hear Talia digging through the bag for something. She turned her head to see what was coming, but the bag was behind her feet. Alya kicked the bag in protest, but it could not be emptied.

"You are a wild monster," Talia said. "You need to be taught. It seems like you have taken all the spankings you can manage tonight. We will progress to the next teaching method. I recommend that you start telling me how attractive I am."

"You know you are breathtaking, TaVi," Alya's rebelliousness still permeated her entire vessel, but she was scared about what might happen if she were rude.

"Good girl, open wide. You are going to want to bite down on this," Talia placed a round leather bar between Alya's teeth with her free hand.

It had two leather straps at each end. The shorter straps were wrapped around Alya's head and tightened to prevent Alya's tongue from pushing it out. Talia placed a cloth under Alya's chin as saliva warmed the corners of Alya's mouth and overflowed the bottom lip.

Alya could feel Talia lay the longer straps across her shoulders, down her back, and between her ass cheeks. Alya closed her eyes as they watered. Fur found its way to Alya's wrists with clicking. Talia released her arms. Alya pulled her hands apart, but they were cuffed. The same sensation wrapped Alya's ankles as they were cuffed to the feet of the sofa.

Alya opened her eyes and stood, but Talia pushed her down, "We are getting started."

Talia ran into the other room and returned with a stand of some sort. Alya shook her head to end the moment, but Talia wasn't interested in her protests. Talia placed the device behind Alya and spent several minutes adjusting the height and distance as Alya kept trying to stand.

"Almost ready," Talia half whispered as she lifted two phallic objects from the bag and attached them to the device.

"This is going to be cold," Talia smiled as she placed a towel between Alya's feet and lifted a bottle of liquid.

She drenched Alya's ass and sex, ensuring all parts were lubricated. Alya buried her face in the sofa cushion as her tears continued.

"Now," Talia stood with her hands on her hips, surveying the scene, "the machine is plugged in, the dicks are attached, you are lubed, you are secured, it looks like everything is set."

She knelt beside Alya and ran her hand through Alya's hair.

"You are so beautiful." Alya thrashed at the word. "Try to relax and enjoy the ride. It will help heal you. Maybe next time you will earn me," Talia kissed Alya on the forehead, stood, and walked to the machine.

Alya couldn't see Talia, but she could feel the two phallic objects press against her. One was pressing against the opening of her sex, and the other pressed her asshole open. A loud 'click' shattered Alya's struggle to see Talia. She could feel Talia's hands holding her ass open as the objects invaded. Talia was correct; her ass was on fire from the size and force of the intruder, and the leather in her mouth was vital as she screamed away the pain.

"Good girl," Talia purred as she released Alya's ass. "But you do not get to lay there and be lazy."

Alya could feel the reigns of her leather bit tighten.

"Up you go," the reigns pulled Alya's head back.

Alya could feel the cuffs on her hands being pulled rearward, too, lifting her chest from the fabric. This position forced the invasion deeper into her reaches. Talia walked beside Alya and crouched.

"You are going to be here a while. I am going to get into something more comfortable." Talia placed a hand towel below Alya's drooling mouth, then walked to the far wall and increased the music's volume before walking into the other room.

Alya almost stood, but the objects were inside her, and felt like they would cause serious damage if she changed position too much. She pushed the machine with her feet, but the ankle cuffs were too short. Like many past experiences, she decided she would have to take the abuse and survive.

Unfortunately, she couldn't make the attacker cum and then kill him. There was no way of knowing how long she would be abused. Her mind raced about all the potential outcomes. All of her worst experiences were relived as she was powerless: powerless to escape, powerless to hide, and powerless to forget.

She was trapped, and her brain forced her to compare her current predicament against every memory she had collected. When no more memories remained untouched, other ideas, ideas as far-fetched as Talia murdering her to Talia marrying her, raced in Alya's brain. For some reason, marrying Talia seemed to get stuck. She pushed the idea away to focus on her warming clitoris, but the image of Talia in a wedding dress kept returning. For some reason, it was a sad thought. Something that made Alya's eyes well.

Alya reminisced about her marriage, or at least the one she envisioned as a child. She had seen in magazines women in ornate gowns marrying men in fine black suits. Flowers everywhere, satin white cakes, doves, rolling green hills, and a burgh. She could even hear the sheep braying from a neighboring field.

Alya's mind struggled, *"Why am I thinking about these things? I am trapped between a leather bit and two fake dicks, humiliated by the first woman who asked me out in years, and unable to concentrate. What is wrong with me? And why the fuck are my shoulders and abs burning so badly? What is my next move? Come on, Alya. I know TaVi would be so sexy in a traditional wedding gown, fuck you brain! How can I get out of this?"*

Alya noticed Talia had returned as her brain continued to betray her, focusing on weddings and honeymoon lovemaking. Tears flowed freely, saliva streamed, and the cloth between Alya's legs was soaked.

"Good girl," Talia said as she sat.

She worked her foot and leg between Alya and the sofa. Alya could feel Talia petting her head and struggled to wipe her tears on the sofa so she could see. Talia was in a purple silk nightgown. Her vagina was inches from Alya's face, and it smelled delicious. The smell made Alya's mouth water even more.

"Do you mind if I play with myself while I watch?" Talia asked rhetorically.

Alya shook her head, and the restraints made her whole body sway. The sight of Talia was somehow comforting and helped Alya concentrate on the pleasure of the situation. As Alya watched Talia moisten her fingers and begin to pleasure herself, Alya could feel her pleasure begin to grow.

Now, Alya struggled not against the machine but towards Talia. The sweet scent of Talia's wet sex was intoxicating. Alya needed to have a taste, but as Alya pulled forward, the reigns prevented her advance.

"Good girl," Talia encouraged as she continued working her sex. "If you are good for TaVi, maybe you can earn a taste."

The words sent shivers through Alya. The machine was plugging her holes and forcing an odd kind of unexpected pleasure as she watched, yearned for, and needed Talia's climax.

As Talia grew closer to climax, her fingers dipped inside. Her hips rocked. With each rock, they swayed closer to Alya's face. Alya pressed against her bit and tried to touch Talia. She needed to feel Talia, even if it was a gaze on the tip of her nose, but the reigns were too strong.

The thumping in her ass and sex was beginning to overwhelm Alya, and struggling to touch Talia's sex was making her desire more desperate. The pounding was slow but potent. Talia huffed and trembled. The sound sent Alya's head into a spin. She started grunting at the sound of Talia unleashing some deep primordial satisfaction from the furthest reaches of her soul.

Alya felt rejected when she was denied Talia's sex and wanted to save face. If Talia didn't want her, she didn't want Talia. She rocked herself back against the machine, working both members with her holes as they pleasured her deepest need. She could feel herself grunting as she rode, and it was not long until she was trembling. Her orgasms started small and short but rolled into a second, then a third.

Her shoulders and abdomen were on fire, but she was too fatigued to do anything other than succumb to the machine's pounding. She felt a fourth orgasm claim her despite being too exhausted to participate.

"Good Girl," Talia whispered as she turned off the machine and moved it back to the other room.

Alya could hear a sink running as Talia washed the tools. As Talia removed Alya's cuffs and the bit, she continued to tell her how she was a 'good girl.'

Talia used a warm, damp cloth to massage the lubrication from Alya's still-raised ass and sex. Alya thought she felt Talia kiss her vagina but had no energy to check or find it exciting. Then Talia took the saliva cloth and the cloth from between Alya's feet and put everything in a basket hidden in a cabinet below the kitchen counter.

Talia took Alya's hand, "Come."

Alya was too exhausted to move, so Talia pulled her to her feet.

"Let's go; you have earned some cuddle time."

Talia half-carried Alya to a large bed with silk sheets. She helped Alya between the sheets and slid in behind her.

"Now, say good night," Talia whispered as she pressed against Alya's naked body.

Talia hung her arm around Alya's waist with her elbow bent and her hand cupping Alya's breast. She kissed Alya's neck and gave Alya a gentle but firm squeeze.

"Good night, TaVi, say you'll always remember me," Alya whispered in a delirium as she drifted to sleep.

Woken President

It had been three hours since Alya had arrived at the hospital. She knew the drugs would be wearing off, but the exact timing was fuzzy. The Russian resident's muscles had atrophied. Yet, he still appeared strong, discounting the tubes and medical equipment.

She rose from her chair and paced the dim room. Even the sky seemed to be melancholy, with its grey face peering through the windows. Alya knew she could no longer keep him under. It was time for his return. The president was opening his eyes. Alya knew she had seconds to act before the nurses returned.

"Welcome back, sir," she bent down beside his pillow. "You are using an alias. There was an assassination attempt on your life. You were poisoned after your surgery. I have not been able to find who poisoned you. I believe it was a close ally, someone who visited you in the hospital. Do you remember who came to see you?"

He removed the tube from his mouth before replying with a hoarse voice, "I remember my naked ass on a cold table, staring at a ceiling, waiting to be sliced: nothing more."

A curly-haired, brawny nurse with an infectious smile entered.

"Wow, we have a live one. Can I get a doctor? One of our patients is ready," she yelled into the hall.

The doctor was tall, pale, and cold. Alya imagined he took pleasure in torturing and releasing the souls of the unloved into the universe. The idea was furthered when she realized he enjoyed working with people who could not defend themselves.

"The morgue must be overflowing with his patients," she thought.

"This is unexpected," the doctor stated as he investigated the president's faculties. "I recommend you stick around for a while to recover. You must still feel ill."

"No," the president's tongue whipped. "I am leaving. Alya, my clothes," he pointed to a stack of clothing on the chair in the corner.

"How peculiar," the doctor rotated in the direction of Alya. "Do you bring clothes every visit?"

"Yes," Alya replied. "He is my husband. I knew he would wake up eventually, he needs his clothes."

"Very interesting," the doctor rubbed his chin. "You look so young, and he is advanced in age. Are you married?"

"I'm thirty-eight," she shook her head in disgust. "Why are you questioning our love?"

"Enough," shouted the president as he swung his legs over the side of the bed and removed the tubes from his arms. "My pants, Alya. Doctor, leave."

"Sir, I am making sure you will be safe," the doctor protested.

"I'm fine. If you need me to sign a paper, bring it. If not, leave. I want to finish dressing without an audience." The president stood, exposing his bare ass, as he pulled up his pants.

"Nurse," the doctor huffed on his way out of the room. "Apparently, these *patients* know more than us. Let's not interrupt their escape."

When the door finished creeping into its final resting position, Alya spoke, "A body double has been maintaining your position for you. There were two challenges to your leadership, but they have been removed. One was assassinated on a bridge by a criminal friend, and the other was sent to Siberia using the courts."

"Too much," the president raised a hand. "I cannot deny the things I know. Fewer details."

"Apologies," Alya continued. "The double was removed in anticipation of your return. Let me help with that," Alya held the free side of the president's dress shirt so he could find the armhole. "We suspect it was a general who poisoned you, but it may have been a staff member. It was not part of your security team, and it was not from the Society."

"Which general?" The president raised an eyebrow as he pulled a sock on.

"We are not sure, but a close one," Alya handed him his shoes. "The general had to get close enough to deceive you into trusting the food and drinks he or she offered."

"So, trust the new generals?" He asked with sincerity.

"No, that is not a good idea. The new generals may have questionable alliances. I recommend you test all food and drinks before consumption."

"By who?" He finished tying his shoes. "You, perhaps?"

"If you trust me, then yes. There must be someone you trust more. There is no need to endanger my life." Alya held the president's arm as he stood. His legs had grown weak. She ducked under his arm, wrapped it over her shoulder, and lifted.

"It seems my body has started to betray me," the president whispered.

"I can hear you whispering," Alya whispered in return. "I am here to help and protect you. Your strength will return, and until it does, I will be your might. I will test your food if you would like."

"You are too good to a weak old man, Alya. Come, we have a country to save. Call the generals and staff; I want a meeting today."

"We cannot have one today. There will be suspicion. I can schedule one for the day after tomorrow. All the generals and staff will anticipate it to be a normal brief."

"Schedule it," he groaned as they walked.

"I already have," her lips curled, creating deep dimples. "I have been preparing for your return."

Unwanted Attention

Receiving the Boot

"Take these," Muhammed sat on the front of his desk, holding a black chador and matching hijab. "It is time for you to rise up and prove you can become a defender of humanity."

"Wait, are you trying to be funny again?" Stacy asked, puzzled, but Muhammed was not smiling.

He offered the cloak and hijab with extended hand.

"Sorry," Stacy hunched her neck into her shoulders. "I am still figuring out our new dynamic," she half-whispered.

She removed her white hijab and pulled her leggings and underwear to her ankles.

"What are you doing?" Muhammed snickered. "This goes over your clothes."

Stacy's body shriveled further from embarrassment, "Um, yes, that's good information."

"I still remember the first time I saw you naked, look at you," Muhammed edged as her leggings modeled her vagina.

"You are the creepiest gay," Stacy laughed. "Are you sure you don't want a piece of this, Daddy?"

She teased as she leaned over the chair. She peeled her clothes down and opened herself with a mischievous wink.

"You couldn't handle me," Muhammed held the clothes beside her face. "Get dressed; we have a schedule to keep. I am heading to the runway, meet me when you are ready. Do not visit or speak with anyone before we leave."

"Yes, Daddy," Stacy teased as he exited.

When she finished dressing, she smelled smoke from the stack. Nancy was the eldest but had not reached the age of disownment, and no guests had been visiting. Her curiosity always forced her to be nosey, and this time was no exception. It propelled her through the garden to see who had been lost.

It was a lot easier for Stacy to sneak around and hide in her new black clothing, but she still had to be careful, especially if the French or Irish teams spotted her. The Irish still blamed her for Copper Brows, and the French were always disappearing and reappearing without explanation.

She thought she could hear singing as she crept between the hedges and the Arboretum. Peaking through the window of the kiln house, she heard singing. The window's edges were stained with dark soot, and the middle was blurry from years of dirt, but she could make out figures.

There were five naked women wearing moccasins who sat around a sixth. The women were covered in ash, and each dumped a pot of soil on the naked body in the center. One of the figures stopped singing and looked toward Stacy's window. She ducked, her heart pounding, hoping they had not seen.

Stacy crept away from the window and returned to Muhammed's office. After being satisfied that her new clothes would not reveal her adventure, she proceeded to the runway. A stealth jet was waiting with protectors guarding the entrance.

"Where is he?" Stacy yelled as she approached.

"He is inside," one of the women replied. Her voice carried the accent of Australia. "Better hurry, we need to be wheels up in five."

Stacy jogged to the door, smiling. "I have never been on a plane before. I hope all goes well."

"We will take care of you," the woman replied as Stacy passed. "Don't worry, we will get Nancy out," she whispered as she pushed Stacy inside and closed the door.

"I do not understand," Stacy could not comprehend the statement.

"Sir," the woman's voice rose. "Our final guest has joined us. We will begin our flight."

"Come," Muhammed motioned for Stacy to sit in an oversized leather chair that was installed on the opposite side of a glossy table. "I must congratulate you on finishing your training." One of the Australians placed a large, shallow wooden box between them. "Open it," Muhammed urged.

There were all varieties of luxury chocolates, botanical and fruit macaroons, sweet and traditional biscuits, and every kind of cheese available.

"I have a special treat for you," Muhammed continued as Stacy gobbled. "Bring the beverages."

The Australian protector wheeled a cart beside the table as the jet taxied to the end of the private runway. She bent down and locked the wheels into divots in the floor.

"I know your country is obsessed with eggnog and apple cider this time of year. I had it made for you," Muhammed tried to lift a bottle from the cart. "Show me how these come out," he recalled the Australian from her seat.

"Press the button beside the bottle you would like to release," the Australian pressed a red button, "and lift straight up." She handed Muhammed the bottle.

"You may go," Muhammed replied as the jet stopped at the end of the runway.

The woman joined her friends in the cockpit and closed the door.

"Try this eggnog. I find it disgusting, but your people like it," he looked so proud as he held out the bottle.

Stacy held the bottle to her lips as the jet sped down the runway. She lifted it, but the acceleration prevented the liquid from reaching her lips. She tilted higher, but the craft ascended. Stacy tilted higher and felt like she was holding the bottle over her face as the liquid dampened her lips. Fearing the jet would level off and bathe her, she returned the bottle to the cart.

"It is delicious," she lied with a look of discomfort.

She had never enjoyed the drink as a child, but it caused nostalgia. The taste flooded her head with memories of childhood. Her grandparents would host dinners. That was when she was still innocent, untainted by the realities of life. Stacy rarely thought about those times. It had become easier to forget and accept than to rage against the realities of life, but occasionally, she still longed for a life of normalcy, family, and love.

"For you," Muhammed woke Stacy from her thoughts. "Read this. It will tell you how to operate our technology." A binder thudded on the table.

The reading was boring and took several hours. Stacy found it easier to stay awake with regular breaks. She stretched her body against the walls and chair, paced, and used the bathroom for alone time. The technology all seemed simple enough; she needed to ensure there was power and then press the correct buttons.

"Remember," Muhammed warned as Stacy finished her reading. "None of the technology can be captured or lost. If that happens, the Council will conduct a clean-up operation. You will be part of that operation, and you will be used as an example to others. The one thing worse than having bad consequences was being used as an example. Do not lose any equipment, or things worse than your nightmares will haunt your realities."

Stacy's mind scanned her memories for the worst things she had ever experienced. The ceremony in the Atrium, the murder on the boat, the capture by the slave traders, the President of the United States, having nonconsensual plastic surgery, and becoming a whole new woman. She had heard stories of worse horrors, but her brain would not permit her imagination to travel to those places.

"Good to know," she replied. "I will ensure nobody is able to use these, and I will die before they are captured."

Muhammed walked to the rear of the jet.

"Take one for yourself," he lifted a parachute.

Stacy selected one after pretending to know how to inspect them. She let Muhammed help secure it to her body. They put on goggles as they tugged each other's packs to ensure proper fit.

"Hold on," he said as he opened the door. "Look over there," he yelled, pointing out the door. "Do you see that clearing in the desert brush up there?"

Stacy clung to the railing beside the door as she looked for the field.

"I don't see it," she screamed.

"Turn around and look at me. You seem scared," his voice barely audible over the wind and the noise of the engines.

Stacy grabbed the handle with her other hand as she turned to look at him. It was sweaty, and her fingers kept slipping.

"I have never jumped from a plane before," she struggled to be heard.

"I know!" he hollered. "Trust the technology!"

"I do!" As she shook her head, Muhammed kicked her in the sternum.

The parachute's strap cushioned the blow, but not enough to keep her fingers on the handle. She tried to grab for the doorway, as it floated away. Stacy's horror shrieked with every fiber of her being as she plunged toward the ground. After several refills of her lungs and terror-filled minutes, Stacy realized the splendor of the view and the excitement of her current predicament.

She looked up to try to find Muhammed. The plane was a speck in the sky. She was alone. Well, alone with the satellites, but nobody was around to abuse her, correct her, or give her consequences. She was, for the moment, a free woman.

As the tiny hairs on the ground started to grow into winding roads, the parachute opened and pulled her into the sky. The rushing wind slowed, and she took time to enjoy the fresh air. There was a whirling sound behind her, reminding her to open the fan wings.

Stacy pressed a button on her shoulder strap, and two wings with fans appeared behind her. They navigated to the landing spot and then turned to cushion the descent. The landing location was encircled by a thick brush in all directions. No human or animal could be heard, not even the wind permeated the brush.

A second pack landed in the clearing not far away. She finished stuffing the parachute back into the pack before retrieving it. A note on the new pack indicated it was her supplies and gave her a list of mission objectives:

1. Burry the landing gear and mark the stop with eight stacked rocks.
2. Move to the coordinates in the GPS and do not get hit when it falls, you have two days.
3. Identify IR1 and eliminate him.
4. Identify IR22 by finding his Mark of Ghost and eliminate him with extreme hostility for his words and acts of defiance against the Council.
5. Navigate to the extraction coordinates in Ardabil.

Stacy pointed her face at the sky, lifted both hands high in the air, and waived at the satellites. She wasn't sure who was watching but knew they were monitoring every step.

The Rendezvous

Carving a path down the mountain and through the valley would have been easier if the sun wasn't baking her. She had stuffed the chador in her pack, but it didn't prevent the dark sweat lines around her breasts, under her arms, or in the crack of her ass. The breeze cooled and dried intermittently, but that caused the dried salt to chafe.

The pack landed on the ground with a thud. The hike was exhausting. A snake slithered under her bag as she searched for batteries. The ones in her GPS had died.

Stacy raised her machete as she wrapped her fingers around the cloth loop at the top of her sac. As she lifted, she started to hear a deep "thwoop-thwoop-thwoop" approaching. Two black dots were in the distant sky, and they were headed toward her.

"Today is your lucky day," Stacy told the snake as she snatched her back and sprinted to a clumping of bushes.

The shapes became recognizable as Stacy dumped her bag. She could see they were helicopters as she searched through her stash. The gun and rockets on the sides became visible as she lifted a pipe and pressed a button. She could see the outlines of heads hanging out the side, "whoosh," the mirror dome opened.

The pole Stacy was holding had released a glossy cloth that formed a three-foot dome. Stacy could see out, but nobody could see in. The shadow of the rear helicopter passed inches from Stacy's dome. She held her breath as though it would be heard over the noise of the blades. The dust that had filled the area choked her through the hijab when she couldn't hold her breath any longer.

When the helicopters became dots in the distance sky, they hovered as people fell to the ground in straight lines.

"What a curious way and place to commit suicide," she thought to herself. *"I wonder why anyone would fly to the desert to jump to their deaths."*

Stacy changed her GPS batteries and repacked her supplies. Checking the direction of the next stop, she noticed a stop was added. It appeared to be in the direction where the helicopters had hovered. Stacy turned the device off and on several times to ensure it had not malfunctioned. Satisfied the coordinates were not going to change, she started hiking.

"The new stop isn't on the way," she grumbled. "I don't know why you are sending me to a pile of dead bodies," she spoke to the sky.

Stacy stalked the moving destination for hours until it stopped. It was about two miles north. She opened her mirror dome and placed everything other than herself, a bottle of water, and her GPS inside. She covered herself with the chador, not knowing what to expect or how to prepare. She marked a spot 150 paces to the north on her GPS so she could return.

She crouched as she approached the area. She could hear talking, and it wasn't Iranian. It was English. As she crept close, she could see a group of four men standing in a circle, smoking cigarettes and talking.

"Last time I was here, I killed four towel-heads," the man with black hair and his back to Stacy said.

"That's decent," said the one with a shaggy beard. "But you have never lived until you have experienced that Punjab pussy."

"You're an idiot, Smith," laughed the one facing Stacy with a jagged scar on the bridge of his nose. "Punjabis are from India."

The fourth man, the one who had no uniqueness, said something, but Stacy didn't hear. She wanted to move closer while staying hidden. As she backed up to circle to the other side of the brush, a hand tapped her on the shoulder.

It startled her so much that she jumped a foot. A sharp pain struck her side, and she collapsed to the ground, dropping the GPS and water. A man pointing a rifle at her was screaming in a language she didn't understand.

Stacy knew she had to be careful because the one thing more dangerous than a person with a gun was a person with a gun who believed their actions were righteous. She spread her hands wide to her side as she lay flat on her back. The men who had been talking in the circle ran over to see the commotion.

"What did you find, Jones?" The first asked.

"She was spying on us from the bushes, Brooks. This is pretty far from any town. Wonder what she is doing," Jones replied.

"Fucking towel-heads materialize from the ground," said the one with the shaggy beard.

"Calm down with that shit, Smith," chastised jagged scar.

"What the fuck? She knows my name, Wilson," Shaggy Beard pushed Jagged Scar.

"I'm Pratt," the unremarkable man reached out a hand toward Stacy. "Do you speak English?"

Stacy considered grabbing his hand and pulling herself to her feet, but Jones was still pointing the rifle at her head. She also considered speaking to them, but then she would have to explain what an American woman was doing in the middle of the Iranian desert.

She made a bunch of noises with her mouth that she thought sounded like they could be words in another language.

"What the fuck is that? She isn't from around here," Brooks looked irritated and puzzled. "Wilson, do you recognize the dialect?"

"No, it's from the southeast near the border. They have a fucked up language down there that nobody understands," Wilson replied. "What do you want us to do with her?"

"One woman makes you lose all your shit? Bring her to the vehicles and search her," Brooks ordered.

Stacy played as dumb as she felt was safe. She pretended not to understand their words, but when they started pulling her to stand, she complied. She waited until they became pushy before she started walking. She saw Jones pocket her GPS from the corner of her eye. Stacy walked in the wrong direction, and the men threatened to shoot her. Eventually, they corralled her and guided her into a clearing with two old pickup trucks.

"I am going to search you," Smith yelled in her face as they stepped between the trucks. "Do not fight; I am checking to see if you have guns." He made an "L" shape with his hand and bent his pointer finger twice, "Guns, pew-pews, weapons," he yelled.

"She isn't deaf," Wilson interrupted. "Have better noise discipline."

"I'm ready," Jones walked in front of Stacy, waiving his rifle before pointing it at her.

"Okay, if she fights, I will push her away. You know what to do," Smith replied as he stepped closer.

Smith bent Stacy's wrist and elbow, forcing her hand to her neck. He mirrored the action with the other wrist. The pain was sharp, but it stayed in her wrists and was manageable.

"Wilson!" Smith lambasted. "I am not going to hold her all day."

Wilson stepped in front of Stacy and squeezed her forearms, then her biceps and triceps. His hands worked around her collar and then found their way around her neck. He squeezed.

"I could kill you bitch, and nobody would ever know," he whispered.

"Knock it off," Brooks commanded. "This isn't a game. Search her and make sure she isn't hiding anything anywhere. The things I have found in their assholes would surprise you."

"Roger that," Wilson replied as he stepped to Stacy's side and squatted.

In one swift motion, he lifted her garb over her head and wrapped it around Smiths arms. He yanked her leggings and underwear to her knees.

"Fuck, would you look at this," he gasped.

Stacy was not sure of the best way to respond without getting shot, so she remained still. All of the men's eyes were exploring her naked sex with their eyes. She could see each of their pants tighten and decided they seemed attractive enough. She spread her legs and pushed her ass against Smith.

"She wants me to fuck her," Smith smiled.

"She is sexy for a towel head," Wilson smiled as he unbuttoned his pants and pulled out his rod.

"Fuck you, I go first. I am squad leader," Brooks unbuckled his belt, lowering his pants and boxers to his knees.

Smith pushed Stacy towards Brooks. She believed she couldn't let this happen. Stacy thought it would not be believable unless she fought, so she stomped Smith's foot to break free.

"What are you doing? Hold her arms," Brooks yelled. "Bend her over this." He opened a door and slapped the front passenger seat of one of the pickups. "You two spread her ankles," Brooks pointed at Pratt and Wilson.

Pratt peeled Stacy's leggings and underwear away from her legs and bent her leg until her foot touched her ass. Wilson followed Pratt's lead, and they lifted until she was horizontal. Stacy continued to struggle and make noises she thought sounded like a foreign language. The three men forced her chest and abdomen across the bucket seat as her hips hung in the air.

Stacy looked around to find anything she could use to make her escape when the time came. The front seat was empty. There was a wooden box between the back seats. She lifted her head to see inside while she continued to distract the men with her struggling legs. The box contained a handful of fragmentation and percussion grenades, a stack of glow sticks, and what appeared to be road flares. Stacy wondered if Wilson was the one who thought mixing grenades and road flares was a good idea.

"Open her," Brooks said as he approached.

Pratt and Wilson struggled to hold her ankles against her ass with one hand, so Stacy fought less to keep things from getting dangerous. They pried her knees apart with their other hands. Stacy continued to give her best impression of a victim as she enjoyed how the wind cooled and dried her thighs and mound.

"I guess I don't need this," Jones said as he sat in the driver's seat. He placed his rifle on the ground and leaned it against the open door.

Stacy felt pressure against her sex as the fragrance of Jones entered her nostrils. He smelled soapy. She hoped that meant the men had no diseases but supposed she would find out soon enough. Brooks was trying to force his way inside, but she was too dry, and it was starting to hurt, so she permitted herself a single scream of pain.

The men seemed to understand because they each took turns spitting on her sex before Brooks tried again. As he entered, Stacy could understand why he wanted to go first, he wasn't satisfying in girth, was average length, and didn't last long. Despite his quick release, Stacy's legs had already started to fall asleep from being held in their bent position.

Smith was next. He sweated and was greasy. Stacy could feel drips of salty brine smash on her back as he entered. He was much larger in girth and did not take his time to enter. He forced his way in without lubrication, causing a moment of pain that forced Stacy to scream.

As she regained her composure, she remembered she was supposed to be the victim, so she let out a louder, more visceral scream and cried. This seemed to please Smith because he pumped faster. He pulled Stacy from the front seat and plopped himself into the truck. Smith removed Stacy's chador, shirt, and head covering before pulling her onto his lap. As she accepted his endowment, she forgot she was supposed to be crying. He reached back and pushed Jones out of the driver's seat.

Smith grabbed her breasts and lifted them in the air. Stacy understood and slid up his shaft. When he pulled down, she slid down. She looked at the men around the truck and saw Pratt stroking his piece.

As Pratt stepped behind, Stacy knew what was about to happen. He had a longer piece, but it wasn't fat. She knew she could handle it in her ass. Stacy could feel Pratt's naked legs, sex, and chest pressed against her.

"Your ass is mine. I hope you squirm; I love it when you sluts squirm with pain," his breath was hot on her ear.

Pratt stood and ripped Stacy's ass cheeks apart with his hands as she felt his saliva douse her ass hole. Pratt took time bobbing the tip of his member against the sphincter as she rode Smith until her ass accepted his entry. As Stacy felt the tip enter, she could feel her sex grease Wilson's staff. She kind of liked the unusual pleasure of a good-ass fucking if it was done well.

She felt Pratt's hands slide from her ass to her hips and compress. With lightning speed, Pratt coerced her ass to accept his long thin member. She felt a burning explosion electrocute her abdomen. Before she finished her first scream, he had pinned her wrists to her back and coerced several more, deeper advances. The sensation made her stop sliding on Wilson. She wasn't sure how to interpret the sensation because there was pain, but there was also pleasure.

The pain wasn't bad, and the pleasure was new, but Stacy still worried he might injure her enough to prevent mission accomplishment. She fought. She worked to free her hands, but with every squirm, her wrists were bent further, causing more pain. She stomped Pratt's feet and kicked him, but her efforts were curtailed by the other men. The frustration of the moment captured her in a way that no man could, and she cried through the screams.

"Fuck, Pratt. Stop fucking her ass so hard. I can feel your dick pressed against mine," Wilson complained as he pulled Stacy against him.

"Enjoy the ride, bro," Pratt responded as he continued his rapid-fire ride.

Stacy could feel her clit begin to slide against Wilson as Pratt worked. The pleasure was building, and she dug her nails into Pratt's hands as her nipples ground against Wilson's muscular pectorals. Stacy felt fingers from two hands worm into her locks on both sides of her head before pulling her hair. Jones entered her mouth. She could feel him tapping her throat, but she had learned how to subdue her gag reflex.

It wasn't long before Stacy could feel her sex grabbing Wilson and trying to pull him deeper. In response, he pulsated inside and released a massive load of hot liquid that oozed back out down his member, soaking his balls. Pratt finished moments later, and Stacy felt her ass receive his liquid. As he pulled out, Stacy's ass ached.

Jones removed himself from her mouth to let Wilson get up from the vehicle. As Wilson laid Stacy on her back across the seat, Brooks leaned into the truck.

"Jones, make sure you get everyone up in twenty. Do not let her get away. She gets released after the snipe," Brooks commanded.

Knowing she had not been sent to fuck these men, Stacy realized the snipe must be why she was sent. She needed to stop them from completing their mission.

"Got it," Jones responded as he circled the truck.

He pushed into Stacy's raw, sore hole and removed his shirt. He had a five-point mark. Stacy knew the rules and strategized a plan to save herself without breaking the treaty.

It took a while for Stacy to get worked up, but the gentle massaging from Jones's romantic lovemaking caused pleasure to start mounting an assault. Stacy massaged her clitoris as she waited for Jones to finish.

"Listen," Jones whispered as he extracted himself from her throbbing slit.

He pulled a pistol from the holster on his belt.

"I don't know if you can understand me, but make it look good. Not all of us are trying to start a war." He pointed from his mark to her Mark of Ghost.

Stacy was confused and must have looked at Jones like he was crazy. He handed her the GPS he had taken earlier, then pretended to hit himself in the face with the but of the pistol.

Stacy looked around to see if any of the other men were nearby or watching and felt Jones wrap her fingers around the barrel of the gun. As she looked back at him, Jones pulled her to her feet. The weight of the gun was heavier than she imagined as she stood naked and confused. Jones picked up her clothes and handed them to her as he sat in the passenger's seat.

"They are going to wake up soon," he whispered. "Do it."

Stacy pulled on her underwear and pants as she used the GPS to locate the mirror dome's direction.

"Thank you. Turn your face, this is going to hurt," she warned.

Her strike was precise as it cracked against Jones's jaw. He slumped between the seats with a heavy moan, blood puddled. Knowing the commotion would rouse the others, she grabbed a percussion grenade. She started jogging to the edge of the clearing until she noticed Pratt still sleeping.

She crouched and approached him. Stacy raised the gun and fired simultaneously. He awoke, screaming, clinging to his leg as she pulled the pins from the grenade. She tossed it and the gun under the unoccupied truck. She ran as fast as she could away from the men who were trying to discover what was happening.

The grenade exploded, and she wanted to see the damage, but she kept running. The adrenaline must have been coursing because it took her seventeen minutes to find the mirror dome. She crawled under the dome and secured it to the ground as military vehicles emerged from the desert in all directions.

Climactic Events

The wall of fog that rolled from the North ate its way across the landscape under the rising sun. Stacy attempted to reach her destination before she was swallowed, but the bush was too thick. The cloud consumed her, hiding everything beyond her fingertips.

"Fuck you, stupid fucking bush. I fucking hate you," Stacy hissed as she took a step backward, inspecting her arm for gashes.

"What the fuck?" Stacy howled toward the sky that hid behind the low, white ceiling.

A single bright beam of light over her head from the sun was proof the outside world still existed.

"Seriously, three more miles of this shit?" Stacy complained when she consulted the GPS.

The pace slowed under the constant threat of attack from the flora that ripped at Stacy's hands, arms, and legs. The slowed pace and eerie quiet forced Stacy's mind to slow, too. Stacy could not refrain from feeling as though the fog was trying to smother her as she trudged forward.

"Stop it," she ordered, but her brain continued.

Her brain focused on her current existence and friendships. She recounted the time she had spent in the Harem with the girls. She wondered what they were doing and if she had been replaced yet. She hoped her replacement would take care of Pru. Pru always seemed so innocent despite the time she almost killed the French girl during training.

Then Stacy remembered Nancy was supposed to age out that day. What did the Australians mean? If Nancy did get out, where would she go, what would she do? Stacy's brain created a world where she, Nancy, and the other women had managed to escape the society. A life where they were normal women living in a normal city with normal jobs.

Stacy imagined the jobs they would have. She would be a news anchor, Pru would be a kindergarten teacher, Ginny would work with people, and Nancy would be a nun or mayor or something where she could both wield authority and care for people.

But how would they escape the council, and would the council hunt them down and give consequences? What about Muhammed, what if he found out? Would he help or punish?

Stacy's mind continued to explore alternate realities and fantasies as her feet inched toward the destination. An enormous bush rose high and disappeared into white when Stacy was four feet from her final destination. She circled it but could not reach the spot. Stacy decided the middle of the bush must be her final point. It took her an hour with the machete to hack her way to the center. Nothing was there.

Covered in sweat and struggling to catch her breath, Stacy plopped on her bum. She couldn't accept that she had reached the destination and found nothing. There were no sounds, and the fog prevented her ability to see anything.

Suddenly, everything became slow motion as a dark shadow thwapped through the fog over Stacy's head. She tried to spring to her feet, but her legs were stuck. A second shadow followed above. The first altered its trajectory en route for the ground. A wave of heat seared Stacy's face as the sun brightened the cloud that surrounded her. A fireball erupted from where the first shadow had disappeared into the mountainside and engulfed the second shadow.

Stacy tried to sink to the ground, but her body seemed to be suspended in air as the second shadow turned sideways, revealing the silhouette of a helicopter. As Stacy fell, the helicopter pitched. Its rotor dipped to the ground. A frightening chopping pierced the fog.

Stacy did not notice the rock that her shin smashed against when she fell. Her focus was devoured by a dark shadow that grew as it approached. It continued growing until it revealed itself. A broken piece of the rotor blade was headed for her face.

"Fuck," she screamed as the rotor continued to inch towards her.

Her brain imagined the blade slicing through the side of her head, through her eye as it exploded into a cloud of viscous precipitate, crushing a cross-section of her brain and shattering through her skull. The side of her face and ear dangled as she died, watching her brain matter and blood paint the desert floor.

Her mind refocused on the moment as her second leg struck the ground and spiked pain into her hip. The rotor was still limping along. She raised her hands with the hollow hope they would somehow help protect her head.

A gust cooled her neck as she clenched her eyes shut. She had been hit. Stacy lay, covering her head, staring at the ground, and waiting for the pool of blood. She was frozen, and it took several minutes before she felt the burning on her arm.

Stacy rolled to her back in a woozy, shock-filled, out-of-body sensation and lifted her arm. A sliver of metal was protruding from her forearm as it sizzled. Nonchalantly, in her shock, Stacy found her knife, pried the metal from her arm, and dropped the knife and shard to the ground. The wound oozed blood as she wrapped it with a compression bandage.

She turned her head and looked at the fires that were burning through the fog.

"Yep, *this fucking sucks, but almost done. Come on, you got this, find and kill the fuckers,*" her brain tried to motivate her body.

She knew she had a mission to complete and sat up slowly. Her forehead whacked against the rotor blade. It had sliced into the ground where she had sat. The blade was sticking out of the ground like a fencepost. She pressed her hand against her forehead and then looked at her blood-covered fingers.

"You better hope you are already dead," she rose to her feet.

Stacy bounced up and down on her feet while shaking her arms by her sides as she counted to thirty. She needed to get her blood circulating and her adrenaline pumping.

"Okay, here we go, Stacy. Time to get this done so we can go have S'mores with the girls."

She crouched and stalked her way toward the two crashed helicopters. She could hear someone speaking. The voice stopped, and the crackle of a radio replied to the man. As Stacy neared, she passed two bodies, but not before giving each one a swift kick in the crotch to ensure they were gone. She removed a photo from her pocket. Neither was the president. She checked for the Mark of Ghost and found luck to be against her.

Stacy picked up a branch that had been severed during the crash. The outline of the helicopter became visible. The shadow of a man speaking on the radio from the front seat appeared. He was gasping for air between words. She circled to the rear of the helicopter and slunk against its skin.

She poked her head into the opening of the rear and found two more dead men. She crept inside as the pilot cried and begged into the radio. She pressed her back against the wall behind the pilot.

Their backs remained pressed together through the wall as Stacy took three deep breaths. In one swift action, Stacy inserted the branch between the man's chest and chin. She pushed her knees against the wall and pulled with all of her might. She could feel the man's neck collapse as the most horrific gasps of life attrited into silence.

Stacy tossed the branch into the fog as she searched for the Mark of Ghost on the men in the chopper, no luck. It was no surprise that the pilot was a nobody.

Flames continued to rise from the trail of fuel, leading to the other helicopter. Thick smoke clouds darkened the sky above as she decided the best way to approach the wreckage. She knew a twenty-two was far more dangerous than a crying pilot. Pretending she was the kind of ninja she saw in the movies, she made her approach.

Along the way, she found three more bodies. None responded to a groin kick or were her prey. Stacy thought she heard a gargling noise as she pressed her back against the craft. As she peaked into the passenger bay, there sat three men. One towards the middle of the craft had his head slumped and seemed to be watching bubbles form around the item protruding. Broken twigs, dirt, and shrapnel littered the floor. Stacy climbed inside and kneed the first man in the face without response.

"Dead," she whimpered.

The man's cheek caused an unexpected pain, so she decided not to try that again. She grabbed the next man's head and thrust it as hard as she could against the helicopter wall.

"Looks like you are dead, too," she spoke louder.

Stacy approached the bubbler as he strained to look at her.

"Please, I am powerful. Save me, and you will be rewarded," he begged.

"Tell me who you are," Stacy held up the picture of the president. It did not match the man.

"I am nobody, a work of fiction. I am CIA. My people will reward you for saving me," the man replied.

Stacy stepped toward the man and removed the clothes from his body as he resisted.

"Gotcha bitch, let's make this quick," she thought when he was naked, and she found the Mark of Ghost.

"Liar, liar, you broke the rules," Stacy whispered in his ear as she straddled his knees. "Don't worry, I will not punish you for your dishonesty." She searched his pants as the man let his head roll backward.

When Stacy found a pen, she lifted it to the man's eyes.

"You are going to want to watch this." She grabbed his hair and pulled his chin to his chest.

"I always liked playing with bubbles when I was a child. I bet you were the same way." Stacy popped the blood bubbles on his chest with the tip of the pen. "Pop, pop, pop," Stacy chanted as she worked.

"They say I have to torture you, but I am not sure what to do. Pop, pop, pop." She pulled his head back to ensure they were eye-to-eye, "any suggestions?"

The man spat at her, but a single spot of saliva appeared on his lower lip.

"That is rude. I was trying to be polite by asking for your opinion,"

Stacy slapped him in the face. The man slumped his head, but Stacy held it in place.

"Absolutely not, dear sir. You saw fit to disobey the Council. I have been tasked with punishing you. Open,"

Stacy slapped his chin, and he let his jaw droop. She reached down and picked up a piece of wood.

"Bite down on this. It won't help the pain, but it will prevent you from biting so hard you shatter your teeth." She pressed the stick between his lips.

Stacy pulled his head back so it faced the ceiling as she slid forward on his lap. She looked down at his flaccidity then back at his face. She gave him a playful slap.

"Such a waste, you have a pretty nice dick. I know we are kind of in a weird place, but am I sexy? No, actually, don't answer that. If you answer wrong, it will get me mad. Let's get back to what we were doing so I can get out of this fucking desert. Almost forgot to tell you. This part has to do with you not being able to see the power and perfection of the Council. You can't see all they offer, so you don't deserve to see anything. That sounded pretty good, right? It was something about your eyes. I am going to hurt your eyes."

She pressed the tip of the pen against his eye, creating a divot on the surface. He closed his eyes as tears streamed.

"It's okay," Stacy empathized, "I would cry way more than that. Would it help if I played with your dick while I work?"

She licked her hand, reached between her legs, and tugged on his meat. She pressed the pen further through the wrapped eyelids as the man sobbed and shook. She gripped his meat and tugged hard.

"Am I stroking your dick wrong? Focus on the pleasure. Good, I can feel you starting to respond to my hand," he had become erect.

She pulled the pen from his eye and dropped it on the floor.

"Time out. I am going to do something before we continue, but you have to promise not to tell anyone. Do you promise?"

The man shook his head as she removed the laces from his boot. She knelt in front of him and spit on his shrinking meat.

"I need to get this ready for after," she giggled. She filled her mouth to the base and gargled.

He became aroused.

"I didn't believe that would work," she confided as she tied the boot lace around the base of his shaft. "You know, cause the whole you have a giant piece of metal sticking out of your chest, and I am going to torture you thing."

Stacy removed her leggings and underwear, then picked up the pen. She slid onto his lap, massaging her clit with his bound member. When she was aroused, she rocked it inside.

"This is how I am going to be able to make it through the day. I need enjoyment when there is so much horror," she was talking to herself as she lifted and fell on the pleasure stick.

Stacy had not felt or heard his eye rupture, so she reinserted the pen and pressed it further than before. The man bucked as snot ran down his face. His frantic body movements made his member press deep into her and smash her clitoris. Stacy moaned, closing her eyes and forgetting where she was. He pushed her away with his arms, but he had lost strength with his inability to breathe.

She pressed the pen further and started to feel perplexed about when his eye would pop, but even the slightest movement would make him buck pleasure through her clitoris. She wondered if experimenting like this made her a scientist. She estimated how far she had already pushed the pen.

Stacy moved her fingers to the place where his eyelids met the pen shaft. She pressed the pen in further and felt more pleasure between her legs. Careful to hold the place where the shaft crossed the threshold of the lids, she pressed one last time as she felt a series of pleasurable bounces. The resistance behind the pen dissipated. The man was screaming through the wood bit Stacy had placed in his mouth.

As Stacy withdrew the pen, the eye clung to it. The eyeball looked like it would be pulled from the socket, so Stacy released the man's head and used her fingers to keep it in place.

"You can keep it there," Stacy told the man. When the pen was free, she wiped it on the man's cheek before finishing her calculations.

"Looks like almost three-quarters of an inch. The other side will go much faster," she wrapped her fist around the pen and stabbed it into the other eye.

She grabbed his shoulders and held on as she received the ride of her life as the eye erupted. The wood in the man's mouth snapped between both sides of his teeth.

"My god, I bet you can fuck like a champion," Stacy purred, holding his chin as his thrashing weakened. "How fascinating, a violent action causes a violent reaction."

Stacy continued grinding on the man's lap until she couldn't stand looking at the blood bubbles, snot, and eyes. She stood, turned, and reinserted. She pulled one of his legs between hers and ground her clit as she pumped. It took a while, but she was able to achieve victory.

So pleasured by the moment, she lost track of where she was and sat up quickly. Her back struck the shard sticking from the man's chest.

"That fucking hurt," she complained as she turned to look at the man. "Sorry, that was kind of insensitive." His sobbing was inaudible from the collapsed lung.

Stacy stood and removed the lace from his dick. She tossed it out the door as she got dressed. Adjusting her leggings, she walked outside and looked around. Stacy found the right-sized flaming wand. She wrote her name in the air several times before stepping back inside.

"You got me hot and bothered, my turn to return the favor," she forebode as she walked to the man. Stacy held the flaming end towards the man's mouth, "open up." The man turned his head away.

"Listen, your tongue flamed against the Council, so the Council wants flames to find your tongue. Choices and consequences. You know the deal."

Stacy grabbed his hair and pulled his head straight.

"I said open your mouth," she whispered in his ear, still holding the flames close to his orifice.

"Okay then," She straddled his lap without releasing his head or moving the flame. "Last chance, open up. One, two, three," Stacy held the flames to the side of the man's neck, causing him to cry out with pain as his skin melted and the flames died.

The flames had died into Red embers. She moved the hot embers from his neck into his mouth.

The hissing and odor of his burning flesh made Stacy queasy. She stepped outside, looking for something to finish him.

Deciding she could not find anything appropriate, she returned to the man and attempted to remove the stick from his mouth. The flesh inside his mouth had melted to it, causing his head to bob back and forth as she pulled until she held it still with one hand and pried the stick loose with the other. Stacy unbuckled his harness.

"Come on," Stacy pulled his arms.

The thing extending from his chest had nailed him in place.

"Come on," she yelled as she placed a foot on the wall beside the man and pulled.

His body broke free, then stopped. Stacy pulled harder, and with a loud slurp, he flung forward, and Stacy landed on her back with him on top.

"This is getting old," She groaned as she checked her head and body for new wounds.

The dried blood on her forehead and the wound on her arm had not been joined by others. She almost vomited as she stood. A portion of the man's chest still clung to the wall.

A large branch that had pierced through the rear wall of the helicopter. It had the stump of a broken branch that provided its best impression of a had rack with the man's intestines and organs acting as the scarves and hats.

Stacy revisited the bodies, trying to find the president, but was unsuccessful in the thinning fog. The sounds of distant helicopters echoed. Stacy ran into the first helicopter and waited for them to pass. They circled for an hour before leaving. As she watched them through the fog, she noticed a shadow in a tree. It was a body.

Once she was sure the helicopters had departed, Stacy climbed. The body had been skewered on high branches that appeared weak and damaged.

She used her feet to bounce the branches. The first took a long time to break as Stacy had to find the technique. The second was a dead branch that broke easily. The final branch was sagging under the body's weight. As Stacy bounced, the body slipped. Stacy smiled as the body flopped to the desert floor.

Despite some obvious wounds, the body matched the photo. Stacy looked back at the tree and decided stringing him up was too much work. Two branches remained in the man's body. One extended from its entrance in the armpit and out of his back beside the opposite scapula while the other crossed through his hip. Stacy dragged the president into the helicopter and strapped him into a seat after she wrestled the branches from his body.

Avoiding Capture

The sun rose over Ardabil, and Stacy took time to bask. The temperature had lowered the previous evening, and the sun was a welcome friend as she returned her thermals to the pack. The GPS marked a spot located southeast of the city, beside a lake, as her next stop.

With a cursory knowledge of Iranian culture, Stacy decided to stay far outside the city to avoid human contact. She wanted to keep a buffer between her and anyone who might try to question her.

As she approached a field, she could see white balls of cotton floating on the grass. The clouds were grazing under the low-hanging sun without the protection of any dogs or people. Crossing the clearing presented a risk as she could be spotted from a long distance, but there seemed to be nobody to spot her.

Stacy lifted her chador and jogged across the field, hunching low. She must have startled the sheep because they bleated. At first, there was one; then, more joined in until their bleats became a disorganized symphony.

Stacy stopped to stare at the strange choir when she spotted a dark shadow near the edge of the field. Then, another popped up from the grass beside it. Two men were looking around, and Stacy dropped to the ground. Hoping she had not been spotted, she crawled her way over a dirt road on an embankment and lay on the other side.

Stacy peaked over the road after she had decided enough time had passed. The men and sheep had vanished. She hugged the road for several hours without seeing another person until a car passed about a mile ahead on a paved road.

The ground was flat here; there was no place to hide. Stacy quickened her step to rush past the road. The traffic was sparse, and she saw two more cars before she reached the bottom of the embankment that lined the blacktop. As she climbed toward the road, a white car approached. Stacy ran toward the road to try to cross before the white car reached her, but as she stepped onto the highway, a screeching ensued.

Stacy froze like a deer with literal headlights pointed in her direction. The car swerved, and the side mirror slapped her below the ribs. A deep pain filled Stacy as she collapsed.

Pain streaked her side, and the sound of foreign screaming filled her ears as she attempted to stand. Three men were running towards her from the car, arms waiving, car doors remaining open. Stacy did her best to run, but her knees buckled as she stepped forward. The men surrounded her. They first yelled at her, then turned their attention to one another.

Stacy crawled away, but two snatched her under the shoulders while the third lifted her ankles. The searing pain in her hip convinced her not to fight as she watched the road pass under her limp body. The men forced her across the back seat of the car before squashing together in the front seat.

Stacy felt the car make a sharp U-turn and head back toward Ardabil as she wanted to roll over. At the slightest movement, the pain spiked throughout Stacy's body, and her eyes faded into black. In a desperate attempt to see her surroundings and prepare for whatever may come next, Stacy jerked herself to her back. This time, she succumbed to the blackness as she felt the tires humming.

"Hello, Guten Tag, Buenos Dias," a voice greeted Stacy as she opened her eyes.

Everything was blurry, and it took several minutes for her eyes to adjust enough to distinguish the details of the black shadow against the bright light of the window.

"English," Stacy whispered with a dry voice to the woman sitting on the wooden stool.

"Are you CIA?" The woman asked from behind her black face covering.

Stacy looked around to see they were in a clay room. She had been strapped to a medical bed, but they were not in a hospital. A thick cloth hung in the doorway to separate the room from the outside, where she could hear a crowd cheering. Her bag was beside the woman's foot.

"What is the CIA?" Stacy asked, pretending not to know and hoping she would not be associated with the men she had met days earlier.

"Tell me who sent you. Where are you from?" The woman asked as she held a cup to Stacy's mouth. "Drink, you are dehydrated."

Stacy sipped the thick, brown water. It tasted chalky and acidic. "I came here on vacation. I wanted to see the ancient mosque."

Stacy was told all Middle Eastern cities bragged about the age of their mosques, so the lie seemed reasonable.

"Yes, we have the best in Iran. People come from all over the world to see it. What is its name?" The woman probed.

"I cannot remember, the pain is too great," Stacy motioned her chin toward her hip.

"Why do you need this?" The woman pulled the GPS from Stacy's bag.

"I like to hike to see views of the land and one of the best mountains in the region is beside Ardabil. I do not want to get lost," Stacy replied.

"And what is this?" The woman held up the mirror dome staff. "How does it work?"

The woman pressed the button multiple times, but the dome did not open.

"It is an umbrella," Stacy lied. "It must have broken when the car hit me."

The cheering outside the room silenced. The woman placed the staff on the dirt floor and rose. She picked up an AK-47 that had been hidden under Stacy's bed.

Tink, tink, tink. . . BOOM! A grenade had been tossed into the room. A bright flash blinded Stacy, and the boom rendered her deaf. As the blanket of snow covering her eyes thawed, she saw the woman firing the rifle at the door. The woman was running sideways towards the wall, yet she wasn't running. The woman had been frozen like Stacy had been when the helicopter crashed.

The woman glided through the air with a burst of flames erupting from the end of her gun: one, two, three. As the third flame erupted from the barrel, there was an eruption on the side of the woman's forehead, then another in her cheek. Blood sprayed the wall behind the woman as her head jerked and her body arched backward.

Everything returned to normal as the woman landed on the ground. Three women and two men dressed in black entered the room and continued shooting the woman. One of the women approached Stacy.

"Are there any more?" She asked.

"I don't know," she replied. "I just woke up."

"Can you walk?" A man standing over the dead woman asked.

"I hope so," Stacy replied as the woman removed her restraints and helped her to her feet.

"Good," the man said. "Let's move people. We cannot be here when the Iranians send backup."

"The Council sent you pretty quickly," Stacy asserted, feeling relieved that she was being rescued.

Two of the men looked at each other before one responded, "Yes, the Council has been tracking you since the crash. We need to get you to a secure location. You were captured by the Iranian Guard. More will be here soon." The man pointed at one of the women, "Grab her stuff. We need everything."

"The mirror dome," Stacy pointed at the staff.

The two men looked at each other before one placed the staff in the bag and slung it on his back.

"Too much chatter, folks," A woman peeking out of the door whispered. "All clear, let's move."

Stacy was led down a dark clay hallway by the group. On the right was a room with four dead bodies and a tiny television with rabbit ears. There were no windows. Stacy thought the flickering of the fluorescent light seemed to correspond to the static on the screen. She had heard about the council using subtle signals but thought nothing of it.

At the end of the hallway was the bright light of the outside world. As they reached the glow, one of the women and a man crouched and scanned every direction before motioning with their hands.

The group encircled Stacy and pushed her toward a line of three cars in the narrow alley. As a man opened the door and two women pushed Stacy into the middle car, the front car exploded.

"Give me a gun," Stacy screamed, holding out a hand.

"Ambush," yelled the man, "Back inside."

A trail of smoke appeared overhead, and the hallway disappeared behind an explosion and falling debris. The group pulled Stacy from the car.

The two men picked her up and ran down the ally as the others circled and pointed their guns toward the roofs.

"Give me a gun," Stacy implored. "I have completed the training."

"Anybody see him?" Yelled one of the women by the cars.

"I've got nothing," another one yelled back.
Boom!

The rear car exploded under a trail of smoke. Everyone dove to the ground. One of the women was screaming and holding her leg, which had been severed at the knee by a piece of metal that exploded away from the engine.

"Where the fuck are they," a woman yelled as the third started tying a tourniquet on her injured colleague until—

Thwap!

A bullet entered her nose and exploded her head into the dirt. Stacy watched as the woman fell to the ground hard. She wore a look of shock.

"Why was the woman surprised the Iranians would be waiting to kill?" Stacy wondered.

"Fuck you!" The final woman yelled as she emptied her gun towards distant rooftops and backpedaled towards Stacy and the men.

Thwap! Thwap! Thwap!

She somersaulted backward in what Stacy considered to be a ballet decorated by exploding blood, brain, and skull. The beauty of the kill forced Stacy to smile.

The men had reached the street at the far end of the alley when one fell to a knee, releasing Stacy's legs. He looked down and saw most of his leg below the knee was missing. It seemed to be attached to his thigh by stringy red bits of flesh as a pool of blood soaked the ground.

She thought he yelled in a weird language, possibly the one used by the men who had struck her with the car. Her heart sank as she started bouncing on the shoulder of the final rescuer. Had the council's team failed to plan an appropriate rescue?

Thwap!

The man sprang forward as Stacy watched his skull implode. She held her hands backward, but they did not soften the landing. Her tailbone struck the ground hard, and her hip exploded with pain.

She was rolling on her side, whimpering and staring into the eyes of her deceased savior as a silhouette approached and stood above her. It bent down and injected her neck with a burning fluid. The world started fading into darkness, but as it faded, the pain in her body seemed to vanish.

"Sleep, sister," she thought she heard from the silhouette before everything turned to black.

Pulaxo's Final Act

Planning Ahead

"We are learning of some breaking news as we return from the break. Thank you for trusting Conspiracy News Network, your trusted news source," the man on the screen stated as the president, Sam, and the team watched. *"We can confirm that the ultraconservative President of Iran was killed on Thursday in Iran's remote northwest. We are working to get images of the crash, but due to its location and the thick trees and brush in the area, it has been difficult to reach the site. The crash is under investigation but is believed to have resulted from poor visibility due to fog, with the age of the craft being a contributing factor."*

The U.S. president clicked off the television.
"Sam, are they on the line?"

"Yes," Sam replied as he motioned for the team to begin escorting the president to the cabinet room. "They are waiting to brief you."

They walked through the halls, which were quiet despite the frantic staff working to keep things running. As the president passed, everyone seemed to freeze and watch. Something felt different.

The failure of the seals was a well-known secret in the White House, as were their deaths. Everyone couldn't help but wonder if the Iranians had helped the seals to their deaths and if the president had retaliated with a hit on the Iranian president.

The vice president was waiting in the cabinet room when they arrived.

"Was it us?" The vice president stood.

"Don't be stupid. The instability it would cause is too great," the president responded as he found his chair. "What's our play?" He asked to the almost empty room.

"I apologize, I do not understand," a deep voice replied through the phone speaker.

"The Iranians caught our people in the area the day before the crash. What will we do to ensure they know it wasn't us? How can we keep them from retaliating, and how do we ensure they don't let our allies know we sent them money?"

"My recommendation is to do nothing," the voice responded. "They don't want their people to know the 'Axis of Resistance' is taking money from us. It would make their people realize their hypocrisy. Plus, they escorted our people out of the country, so they know it wasn't us."

"Yeah, but our people were torched afterward. Is there any intel on how our people were discovered in Benghazi?" The president contended.

"It looks like there is a leak at State. We do not know the source and are not sure who to trust over there," the voice whispered.

"How sure are we about a leak at the State Department?" The vice president leaned forward.

"We have phone meta between state and hostile factions in the region. We have 85% confidence."

The president snapped his finger at the vice president.

"Get Energy to look into this. We need confirmation from a neutral party. Does any of this come back to me: paying off the Iranians, Benghazi, the dead president?" He questioned.

"You were, officially, not involved in any of the operations nor the negotiations. You approved a package of actions that included both, but they were buried so deep in the text not even the NARA will be able to find them," the voice replied.

"Was it caused by the fog, or did someone assist the crash?" The president sat, "Or was it us?"

"We were not involved officially or unofficially, and we have no chatter from allies or other actors to suggest there was involvement from a third party," the phone spoke.

"The gunfight," a hushed whisper crept through the phone.

"Who's that? What gunfight?" The president demanded.

"Sorry, sir, that was one of our more motivated colonels. When we were scanning the region, we collected intel on a gunfight in a nearby city. Using our time-lapsed satellite feeds, we were able to see some vehicles seemed to have been blown up by RPGs in an alley. There were large dark spots on the ground that the eggheads are calling blood, but I am not convinced. There is a 40% confidence that two local factions had a gunfight in the region, nothing more."

"Is it related to the crash?" The vice president chimed in.

"No, we do not believe that to be the case," returned the voice.

"Steps moving forward?" The president reclaimed the conversation.

"None, sir. We have a bunch of unrelated events and expect no hostile actions directed at us. The Pentagon suggests ignoring the situation and limiting public statements."

"Sounds good. Good work, people, keep me informed." The president pointed at the vice president, who then disconnected the call. "Follow-up with Energy. Make sure they find out if State had a leak. Then, let the Secretary know I am waiting for her resignation."

"Is that necessary?" The vice president rose.

"She is an open wound. We need to get rid of her so we can heal. We need to be focused on the important things. Things like my lunch," the president turned to Sam, "It's lunchtime, right? I'm famished."

"Yes, sir," Sam replied as he opened the door. "Just one more briefing first."

"I will let her know. Oh, and I'll get Energy to investigate," the vice president called as Todd closed the door, following the president.

"I need to step out and make a call," Sam stated as the group entered the Oval Office.

The president raised a thumb as Todd sealed the room. Sam hated himself as he dialed. Valerie had become so excited about having a child.

"Hey," he kept his voice cheery, "how was the appointment?"

"I saw our baby. I will send you the pictures. Do you want to know if we are having a boy or girl?"

The elation in Valerie's voice made Sam teary-eyed as he proceeded with the plan.

"No, don't tell me. I want the surprise. Send pictures so I can show everyone. We are headed to lunch. Did you see the orange juice and prenatal vitamins I left at your place? I had some of the juice. It's super sweet. Make sure you drink some. You need the extra vitamin C."

"That sounds so good. Hold on." Sam could hear Valerie open the fridge and a glass clank on the counter.

"Don't forget the pics," Sam reminded into the phone.

"I'm not stupid. I heard you the first time." Valerie's voice was caustic. "This tastes so disgusting," Valerie coughed into the phone.

"The orange juice?" Sam asked.

"Yeah, I took a swig. It is super gross," the sound of running water could be heard.

"Did you finish the glass?"

"Yep, but I need to wash away the taste," Valerie said before gargling.

He knew that one glass of the orange juice had three doses of mifepristone. Less than half a glass would have worked. Valerie would be destroyed, and the *Pulaxo technique* would reach its apex. She was ripe for the final act. Sam knew the fetus wasn't a baby yet, and he had killed many people, but this felt different. It made him feel dirty and mournful.

"Throw away the orange juice, babe," Sam almost whimpered.

"Why? The taste is because of my hormones," Valerie rebutted.

"We don't want to take the risk. We can get more orange juice. I need to go, it is lunchtime. Send the pictures I want to share. Love you," those words always hurt Sam's heart, but they were more potent when directed at a target.

"Love you, I'm sending them. Have fun at lunch," Valerie blew a kiss into the phone.

"Hey, wait," Sam interjected before Valerie could end the call.

"What is it?" She questioned with a hint of intrigue.

"Can you swing by and pick me up from work tonight? We can have dinner and spend the night together," Sam needed Valerie to agree.

"I can if you let me get a big ass steak and be the little spoon. I need cuddles tonight," Valerie's elation paralleled her ignorance.

"I wouldn't have it any other way. Be here at six." Sam disconnected the call, sickened by the forthcoming trauma, as he dialed another number.

"My job is almost finished." Sam confided into the phone. "I have no idea where I will be sent. Let's get together tomorrow for lunch to say our goodbyes. It looks like I can't keep you. I will keep up the fight on my end if you keep the treaty on yours," another pause.

"Yes, I know. Things are getting dangerous. Make sure you watch your back and be careful who you trust. If your people cannot stop the war, things will get bad, and I don't want anything happening to you."

"I hope so, too," he added.

The thought of having the treaty break down was terrifying. The two most powerful organizations on the planet going to war for control after fifteen hundred years of peace would be catastrophic. Sam took a moment to calm his nerves before dialing the phone.

"The pancake breakfast is tomorrow morning. Let's put on a good show." Sam paused to decide if he should mention the looming war before adding, "They are coming for us. We need to be prepared."

Sam did not expect the sounds that filled his ears.

"Retirement seems quite severe at times as dangerous as these, but I accept whatever is to come," he interrupted.

Staging the Players

"How did the exam go?" Ben asked as the president took a bite from the baked chicken.

"She sent me the sonogram, look," Sam held up his phone. "But, I'm not sure I should be a father."

"I experienced that. But, each time I held mine in the hospital, something changed. When the nurse lets you hold them, and you look down at their tiny, squinty eyes, you feel their eternal love and trust."

"I get that," Sam knew he had to try to be subtle but force the point, "but they are huge financial, emotional, and social burdens. I don't want that. I want freedom."

"So what? Valerie can be difficult, but she doesn't deserve to be a single mother," Ben seemed to be getting upset. "Have you settled on a name?"

Sam took a step away from Ben.

"Valerie has her heart set on naming the baby after her relatives, and I would never make her be a single mother. I am kind of hoping she has a miscarriage or something. Is that bad?"

"Yes, that is evil," Ben scolded.

"I know, never mind. I'm stressed about how a baby will change stuff. Let's forget about this conversation, deal?" Sam held out a hand.

"It's stress?" Ben seemed incredulous.

"I need to get a good night's sleep," Sam extended his hand further.

"Okay, but if you need anything, and I mean anything, come to me. I have kids and know how things can get. Don't ruin your life by being afraid to ask for help," Ben shook Sam's hand.

"What about that helicopter crash?" Sam changed the subject. "Can you believe the Iranian president is dead?"

"We shouldn't be talking about that," Ben moved his eyes toward the president.

"I am under the impression the president already knows. He saw the news and had a meeting with the Pentagon," Sam winked.

"We aren't allowed to comment on that stuff," Ben bulged his eyes.

"No worries, you know we keep it light. Besides, our president is the biggest, baddest, and most powerful on earth. He knows nobody would dare challenge his authority. I was surprised he even asked if the Iranians might try to strike our people," Sam had raised his voice in an attempt to get the president to hear. "It is a good thing the Iranian president was taken out. It will help to remind the rest of the world that at anytime, anywhere, anyone can be removed if they pose a threat to the free world."

"There's chatter over there," bits of potatoes tumbled from the president's mouth as he took another bite. "Is there something I should know?"

"Nothing, sir," Ben replied.

"Sam? Anything from you? I heard something about the Iranians," the president pointed his fork.

"Nothing important. I was saying it was a good thing the Iranian president was taken out," Sam provoked.

"You were in the room. There is nothing to indicate he was targeted. Why would you believe anything different," the expression on the president's face mirrored his reaction to the moment he received the Harem's invitation; he wondered what was going on.

"Nothing specifically. You are such a powerful leader that it would make sense for someone to take out an enemy of yours in the hopes it would win your favor," Sam rationalized.

"Take out an enemy for me?" The president mirrored. "Without my permission?"

"Yes, to win favor or even to be given the chance to take the power that is available for the grabbing."

"That is interesting. Who would be trying to win my favor and trying to grab power in Iran? Are there any specific groups or names that might be associated with your theory?" The president continued his interrogation with a modest grin.

"I have no idea. It is my imagination running wild. I haven't got much sleep since Val and I found out we are pregnant." Sam held up his phone screen, "She sent me photos of the baby."

"I thought you were talking about... Never mind that. Bring the phone, my eyes are terrible," the president's mood lightened.

Sam held the phone over the president's food as he stuffed his mouth with a fork full of green beans. The president tipped his forehead toward the phone and seemed to be studying the picture while he chomped.

"I see the head," the president coughed as he turned his head sideways. "Do you know if you are having a boy or a girl?"

"I'm not sure," Sam put the phone in his pocket.

"Which do you want?" The president wiped the leftovers from the corners of his mouth.

"I am not sure I want either," the point had to be implanted in enough people to be plausible. "They are autocrats, and I like freedom."

"What's the wife say about your concerns?" the president stood, "Let's walk and talk."

"I have not told her I don't want kids. Everything is happening too fast. She has been erratic, emotional, and unpredictable," Sam lied.

"I remember those days. There were tears and late-night meals," the president slowed his pace. "It all calms down, and you settle into a routine. Before you know it, the kids are headed to college."

"I hope she stops sneaking around with other men and throwing plates at me," Sam looked at the carpet, frowning.

The president stopped walking and stepped close to Sam's face, "You knew who she was when you got involved. Remember the first time you watched me play with her on my desk? If you cannot love her for who she is, then suck it up and fake it for the kids. That's what I do for the kids and voters. That part about throwing things at you, that shit is hilarious. I would love to see a tiny Asian throwing plates at a big, strong man like you. I would die from laughter." The president subdued his giggles as he walked.

"She needs to see someone. She started to become crazy," Sam wasn't sure if he was planting the seeds correctly.

"My wife is the same way. Did I ever tell you about the time she hit me with a hammer because I offered to get Ninny Pelogi a drink during the caucus? Wives, hell, all women, get crazy occasionally. It happens to most during their teens, settles to once a month for most of their lives, then they have the hourly crazies through menopause, and when things settle down, you die. It's the circle of life."

"And I'm trying to be the fucked up one?" Sam's brain was in disbelief at the alleged wisdom. *"Good job on electing an upstanding and inclusive president, America."*

"Hopefully, she is going through a phase like that," Sam opened the door to the Oval Office. "You have a meeting in eighteen minutes. You are going to be briefed by the Secretary of the Interior."

"I am going to do you a favor," the president walked to the desk and scrawled something on the corner of a piece of paper. Tearing the scribble from the rest of the classified document, he carried on, "Take this; it is the number of the doctor my wife uses. Have Valerie tell him I recommended she be seen. If there are any issues, this doctor will help. He is one of the best in the world. As the president, I should know I am the biggest, baddest, and most powerful on earth," he alluded to Sam's earlier comments.

Sam slipped the scrap into his pocket, "I appreciate your support."

"Sam," the president's voice followed him to his spot.

"Yes?"

"I will be asking the doctor if he received a call from you. I expect to hear updates," the president sat and read the torn document.

Treachery

"How are you feeling?" Sam sounded sincere as he greeted Valerie outside the president's Study. Valerie's work clothes were tighter than usual, but the pregnancy was not obvious.

"I was feeling pretty good this morning, But in the past couple of hours, I have been bloated and sore. I might need a laxative," Valerie replied. "Why did you want me to come inside?"

"Come with me," Sam turned and strode to the work area as Valerie followed. He stepped into Deloris's workspace, "Is the V.P. gone?"

"Yeah, why?" She asked while she typed on her laptop.

"I need to borrow a room for 10 minutes. Valerie and I need to talk," Sam stepped to the side so Deloris could see Valerie.

"Yay!" Deloris screeched and clapped her hands together. "I heard we are going to have a young Sam joining us. You must be so excited."

"I wasn't at first, but Sam has been so great. I don't know what I did to deserve him, but things are good," Valerie placed a hand on her belly.

"Thanks, Deloris," Sam interrupted. "Shall we?" He placed a hand on Valeries back and held out an arm.

"Don't get caught," Deloris warned. "Nobody is supposed to be in there."

"We will be quick. Thank you," Sam smiled as he followed Valerie. They walked in silence until Sam sealed them in the office.

"What did you want to talk about, love?" Valery intertwined the fingers of her hands and held them to her chest as she leaned against Sam, looking up into his eyes with a schoolgirl grin.

"I heard chocolate is good for pregnant women," Sam pulled a foil-wrapped candy from his pocket. "Ben brought them in. His wife is too good for them."

"I can't ruin my diet," Valerie pushed his hand away.

"Just one to celebrate the sonogram can't hurt," Sam insisted.

He needed Valerie to eat the chocolate to get her dose of misoprostol. The *Pulaxo Technique* hung in the balance. Sam unwrapped the chocolate and held it in his flat hand.

"Okay, but one," Valerie scarfed down the chocolate so quickly that Sam was convinced she didn't chew it.

She did not taste it because the misoprostol was intolerable. Sam's playful and kind demeanor became dark and rigid as he stepped around Valerie and walked to the desk.

"Come," he ordered.

"Sam, what's wrong?" Valerie expressed concern as she stepped forward.

"Come," Sam snapped his finger and pointed at the floor between his feet.

Valerie approached nervously, "Did I do something wrong?"

"How can you ask that? You are a racist whore." Sam kept his voice cold and emotionless despite the tremendous pain and anxiety he felt at what he needed to do.

"You said you loved me," Valerie's eyes teared.

"Your tears mean nothing. Stop your shit," Sam barked.

"Why are you doing this?" Valerie wiped her eyes and took a deep breath as she shook.

"You have served your purpose. You are a pregnant whore who is useless. A fat pregnant prostitute has no value when it comes to national security. Don't you understand? You were a tool. Now, you are a broken tool," Sam could see the spark of anger begin smoldering behind Valerie's eyes.

"You used me?" She snarled.

"No more than the president, the agents who double stuffed you, or the fake dignitaries who got you pregnant," Sam jabbed.

"Fake dignitaries?" Valerie raised her voice.

"That's right, you got all those pretty little holes stuffed by three fake warlords so I could watch you be humiliated," Sam bellowed with feigned laughter. "Now, bend over and let me take another turn." He grabbed Valerie, picked her up, and bent her over the side of the desk.

"No, fuck you, I hate you," Valerie shouted and fought. "Look what you made me do," she pointed at her abdomen.

"That's right, struggle whore," Sam hissed as he held her down with one hand and exposed her holes with the other.

"You are hurting me," she screamed.

"*This is too much. I have to stop. She doesn't deserve this,*" Sam's heart was shattering. "*Fuck, it's either her or me. I am sorry, Valerie, but I am not brave enough to face the consequences.*"

"Lay there and take it. Pretend I am the president, and I am dangling a promotion in front of your face," Sam forced her knees apart.

He could tell Valerie was in full panic mode, which meant they had reached the final act of their argument. He lowered his pants and pressed his sex against her asshole, leaned over, mimicked her dead father's voice, and whispered, "Just pretend I am your father. Take it like you did when you came home from college that Christmas."

Valerie grabbed things from the desk and hit Sam: the phone, a picture frame, and an acrylic souvenir box with a baseball. Nothing seemed to be working, and it was clear Valerie's frustration and rage were increasing.

"That's right bitch. Your sweet ass is daddy's," Sam whispered in her ear as he swayed his hips and forced the tip inward.

Valerie reached her peak. She grabbed the desk lamp, and Sam loosened his grip to let her roll. As she rolled, Sam pulled up his pants and prepared for the strike. The lampshade smashed against his cheek, jerking his head to the side.

Sam threw himself on the floor to make it look good. Valerie jumped off the desk, pulled up her pants, and ran sobbing from the room. The strike made him woozy, but he managed to find the exit.

He had three missed calls from Sarah, and his phone was buzzing as he reached Valerie's street.

"Hey," Sam answered. "Are we still having lunch tomorrow?"

"I heard what happened. They followed her and are sending a full team in twenty-seven hours," She sounded frightened.

"Wait, they followed who?" Sam had to be careful not to reveal anything.

"The girl from Ardabil. They know what your people did in Iran, and they are pissed," the words chilled Sam. His plans for Valerie reached a new level of insignificance and regret.

"I have no idea what you are talking about," Sam hid his panic. "I am sure whoever was in Armenia, did you say Armenia or Argon?"

Sarah lowered her voice, "One of our extraction teams was ambushed. They will be arriving in twenty-seven hours. This is a war neither of us wants. I have to go."

"So, no lunch tomorrow?" Sam persisted.

"Goodbye, I hope we find each other on the other side. I still plan on keeping you," She whispered.

"And I, you," Sam replied. "Will I see you at lunch?"

"I am not part of the team, but I have to go. Bye." Sarah ended the call.

Sam dialed the phone, "I am finishing *Pulaxo* this evening, but we have a problem. The war has begun, and the Harem will be hit in twenty-seven hours. Save as many as you can."

Sam walked to Valerie's home, knowing she would not be there. The night air was cool and crisp, with a slight breeze that rattled the dry, dead leaves. The production he had orchestrated earlier would force her to spend time watching old westerns with her mother before she settled down and returned.

As he approached the building, he removed the phone from his pocket and dialed.

"Do we have one? Good, bring it in," Sam hesitated before opening the door.

It would be the last time he would use the spare key Valerie had given him. A black SUV stopped in the street. A well-dressed, nondescript middle-aged man with a moderate build removed a large suitcase from the trunk.

"Sam?" He called from the sidewalk.

"That's me, how can I help you?" Sam returned.

"Didn't the airline contact you? We are supposed to return your luggage," the man lowered the suitcase to the sidewalk and pulled a clipboard from the front seat.

"Yes, perfect," Sam trotted to the man.

"Sign here," the clipboard was presented.

"Here we go," Sam pretended to sign the blank page.

The man examined the blank sheet of paper.

"Everything seems to be in order. Thank you for flying Hoopla Airlines." The man then lowered his voice, "The cloned phone is inside," before speeding away.

The package was heavier than Sam expected, but it did not take long to drag it to the bathroom. Sam reached down to open it and stopped. He walked to Valerie's bedroom and retrieved her spare revolver. He opened it to make sure it was loaded and returned to the bathroom with one of her pillows.

He placed the pillow in the sink with the revolver on top. He could feel the nervousness growing as he walked to the bedroom to see the clock, forgetting about his phone. Time was moving too quickly, and Valerie could return in forty minutes. He had to finish in thirty minutes or less.

As he paced back into the bathroom, he felt the urge to urinate. After relieving himself, he unzipped the suitcase. His hands had begun to tremble, and he had to pee. He was able to squeeze out four drips. He finished unzipping the suitcase, and a naked man flopped to the floor. He had to pee. Sam couldn't help but stare at the man's face as he struggled to release any drops; their faces were identical. He laid the suitcase outside the bathroom.

Sam knew what he was receiving and had trained many times for this moment, but now that it had arrived, it felt overwhelming. The man staring up at him lay motionless despite being unrestrained.

Sam used the clothes he was wearing to dress the naked body, leaving all of his possessions in the pockets except for the phone. Sam found the phone in the suitcase, switched the SIM cards with his phone, and placed it in the breast pocket of the man.

"I have to pee again?" Sam whined, half to himself and half to his onlooker. After several moments, he squeezed out a single drip. He turned his attention back to the man, "We must hurry. Your drugs metabolize quickly, and if you struggle, that could leave unwanted DNA lying around."

Sam lifted the man into the tub. He held the gun with his finger on the trigger as he used his free hand to wrap the pillow around it. He pressed the gun to the man's chest and squeezed.

"Stop," he whispered to himself. "What are you doing?" Sam addressed the man, "I apologize." A tear formed in the man's eye and rolled down his cheek.

"Stop that. I am not sorry for killing you, that would be silly. I am sorry that I almost did it without preparing correctly. It's best not to get caught," he declared as he placed the pillow and pistol on the toilet.

Sam selected a hand towel and a bath towel.

"These look appropriate." Sam walked to the kitchen, retrieved three fresh trash bags, and checked the time. Valerie could be back in fifteen minutes.

"We must speed things up," Sam told the paralyzed victim.

He hugged the man under his arms and lifted. Sam wrangled the man onto the sink. He used his head to hold the body up. He sandwiched the pillow between the muzzle and the man's chest as he wrenched it taught around the weapon. It took a couple of tries to get the man to balance on the tip of the barrel. Sam bent his knees, turned his head, closed his eyes, and fired one shot.

The mirror shattered, green mouthwash cascaded into the sink. Sam dropped the pillow at the high side of the tub and used the hand towel to cover the wound. The blood soaked through quickly. Sam grabbed the bath towel, balled it, and pressed it against the wound as he moved the man into the tub. He kept the towels pressed against the opening. He was careful to keep the draining blood away from the pillow and pistol.

As the man cried his last tears, Sam pulled the pillow and revolver from beneath his head. He sank the revolver in the toilet and flushed to wash away all forensics. He placed the pillow in a trash bag and sat the bag in the suitcase. Sam opened both unused trash bags and placed them on the toilet. He washed each foot in the sink and stepped into each bag, tied them to his legs, and stepped out of the bathroom while avoiding all blood.

He found another towel and knelt outside the bathroom door. He made sweeping motions to spread the blood to hide his footprints. The blood had already started getting sticky, but when he was satisfied with the work, he tossed the towel into the tub over the blood-soaked corpse.

Sam removed the trash bags and placed them in the suitcase before he walked to Valerie's room and found some of his dirty clothes in the hamper. He dressed, grabbed the suitcase, and headed to the alley across the street. The crisp night had descended into a full chill when Valerie's car made its appearance.

"I'm sorry, this is a consequence nobody deserves, especially not you," Sam whispered as he dialed his phone.

"911, what is the nature of your emergency?" the phone asked.

"I heard loud arguing and what sounded like a gunshot," Sam told a story and watched Valerie sit in her vehicle crying.

He couldn't stop himself from wanting to take his life. He reached for the suitcase and unzipped it before he remembered he left the revolver in the toilet. He knew spending significant time with targets would cause a level of empathy that could risk the higher purpose, but he was not prepared for this.

As Valerie waddled to her door, sirens were approaching. Sam's heart raced as the sirens got louder because Valerie was moving so slowly. The sirens were blocks away as Valerie pulled out her keys. She was struggling with the lock as the sirens were about to round the corner. She stepped over the threshold as the first police car appeared at the end of the street.

Sam backed further into the darkness as the cruiser rolled to a stop. The light in Valerie's kitchen flicked on. A second car appeared. Police walked to Valerie's door with their hands on their guns and knocked. It took her a while to answer, but when she did, Sam could see she had never stopped crying before getting out of her vehicle.

She invited the police inside. The windows illuminated. When the window in the hall outside the bathroom lit up, Sam turned and disappeared into the far reaches of his dark path.

Opportunistic Exits

Time to Break Away

Bzz, Bzz, Bzz. Alya rolled over and reached for her missing lover, ignoring her phone.

"TaVi," she called, disoriented and still unaccustomed to living with someone. "TaVi, where are you?" She called more loudly, enjoying the feel of expensive silk against her naked body.

The realization that her phone was still buzzing created a panic. Alya shot up in her bed.

"Yes," she answered.

"The general will be returning, so we need to keep this brief. You are being recalled. Your time in Russia is done," an electronic voice informed.

"She is passionate about me," Alya replied. She wanted to add, *'and I can no longer live without her,'* but instead continued, "She will use the power of Russia to find me."

"Silly girl, you are not the first twenty-two that has been extracted. You will be retrieved within the week."

As the phone disconnected, the sound of the lock in the front door clicked. A profound sadness claimed her morning as she thought about a life without TaVi.

Alya slapped her phone back in its spot, lay on her side, and pulled the blankets up to her face. As she closed her eyes, the scent of fresh pierogi pranced around the room and pirouetted into her nostrils.

"Are you awake, my love?" Talia called.

The crackling of a paper sack in the kitchen was followed by footsteps approaching the room. Talia knocked on the door and then cracked it open.

"I have brought you treats, my sweet Alya," she spoke softly.

Alya rolled on her back and stretched her arms wide. She rubbed her eyes as she faked a yawn, trying to hide her despair.

"You treat me too well, TaVi. What have I done to deserve you?"

"You are my prize. I keep you happy so you stay beautiful," Talia smirked as she dove onto the bed beside Alya. "Before you get your treat, I get mine."

"Yes, TaVi, I will get the straps," Alya rolled her eyes as she spun sideways and sat with her feed off the bed.

"Not today," Talia pulled Alya backward, forcing her flat on her back and kissing her.

When their lips were freed, Alya questioned, "Wait, TaVi, I have earned…"

"This is a special occasion," Talia interrupted. "I have news, but first, we make love and eat treats."

Alya pulled her down for another kiss as she swung her torso alongside Talia. Talia stepped her knees between Alya's legs as their tongues touched. Alya was fighting her emotions and trying to enjoy the moment, but the words of the electronic voice dominated her thoughts. She felt the pre-tear stinging attack her eyes.

"I'm ready for the machine, TaVi," Alya whispered.

"Not today, I want to taste you," Talia whispered in her ear.

Talia's kisses felt good as they walked across her cheek, down her neck, and hiked the ridge to her shoulder. Alya couldn't help but notice Talia smelled nice, but there was something unusual in her hair this morning, something smokey. Alya had hated the smell of cigar smoke since her second experience at the Harem. She guided Talia much further south with forceful hands.

"Don't rush it," Talia warned. "I let you have control; I can take it away."

"Yes, TaVi," Alya moved her hands to her sides.

"Don't do that," Talia placed Alya's hands back on her shoulders. "Just take your time and enjoy the gift."

Talia held both of Alya's hips and kissed the upper bluff of the hip, skiing her lips into the ravine. Alya always had a strong sexual sensitivity trapped in the ravine where her hip, thigh, and pubis met. Somehow, Talia had discovered it and often stimulated the region to the great satisfaction of Alya. Even now, as Talia kissed, Alya could feel honeydew on her lips, her hips rolled backward to raise her sex into the air.

Alya guided Talia's lips toward her sex, but Talia swerved and made her way to the inside of the hip. Alya's breath quickened as she curled her knees, trying to force Talia to stop teasing. Talia evaded and nibbled her way from the underside of Alya's belly button on a path into the ravine.

Alya braided her fingers in Talia's hair and pushed, but Talia was too powerful. Talia removed Alya's hands and intertwined their fingers, but Alya pulled her hands back as Talia continued kissing down her pubis.

Alya's hips rocked by themselves as Alya accepted that she still had no control when TaVi was involved. Her fingers found silk as her hips continued to yearn for the tender kisses of her first true love.

"Ask me nicely," Talia whispered as her lips reached the boundary between foreplay and fulfillment.

"TaVi," Alya lifted her head and pleaded with her eyes.

"Ask me nicely," Talia bit the periphery.

"Please, TaVi. Please, I need you," Alya acquiesced.

Talia pressed her hands against Alya's sides near her breasts and slid them down as she continued to kiss and nibble the crest. Her hands slipped to Alya's belly button and continued south. They departed around Talia's face and rested between Alya's thighs; her index fingers pressed against Alya's labia major.

Talia pressed her hands into Alya's thighs to open the outer labia as she extended her tongue. Talia's tongue felt rough but was exciting as it landed on Alya's clitoris, forcing her to moan. Alya rocked her hips, and Talia pressed down harder as she used her tongue.

Alya grabbed TaVi's head and, this time, would not let go. She pulled Talia against her sex and ground. Talia's hands still held her majors open, and Alya could feel her clitoris being stimulated by Talia's mouth while Talia's chin stoked her minora, once even sliding between them. After half a dozen strokes, Talia broke free.

"Calm," Talia soothed.

She inserted three fingers into Alya and kissed her clitoris. The way Talia played her clitoris like a balalaika always drove Alya insane. Alya released a primal guttural reverberation of carnal euphoria that caused her fear. Never before had she experienced such a lack of control of her faculties, and the vulnerability was frightening. The vocal ejaculation was an unwilling confirmation that she no longer retained free will.

"You're being such a good girl," Talia whispered as she continued her torture.

That compliment, one that would seem so insignificant or condescending to others, was rare to the ears of Alya, and it caused her to spiral. Her entire body descended into sexual madness, agony, bliss, and exhaustion.

As Talia rose and walked across the room, Alya lay naked on her side, shivering, enjoying the moment as she had been ordered. She felt Talia return to the bed and plopped something behind her. Talia lay in front of her, face-to-face.

"Hey," she whispered as she stroked Alya's hair. "Are you ready to take your turn?"

"My turn?" Alya was confused.

"Yes, you have earned your chance to pleasure me. Do you have the strength?" Talia continued stroking as she kissed Alya. A sudden rush of energy filled Alya.

"I'm ready, TaVi." She rolled over to look at the item Talia had dropped on the bed.

It was a leather harness with a short, fat, phallic pleasure rod. Talia stood and walked around the bed. She picked up the device and held it.

"Put your legs in," Talia instructed.

Alya stepped into the harness and raised it to her waist. The rod and waistband drooped to her knee.

"Turn around," Talia directed.

As she tightened the straps, Alya stroked her new appendage. It felt good in her hand. She felt powerful. While many of the Harem beauties had opportunities to take the role of a man, that was one experience that had always eluded her.

"Turn," Talia instructed.

Alya continued stroking the shaft as she faced Talia. Talia squirted lubricant on the member, then crawled onto the edge of the bed and opened herself for Alya.

"Start gently, then prove you have earned this opportunity," Talia suggested.

"Yes, TaVi," Alya said as she slapped Talia's ass hard, causing her hand to sting.

A bright red handprint stared at Alya as Talia turned and gave a devilish smile.

"Yes, punish me for making you wait so long," she exclaimed as she shook her ass side-to-side.

Alya slapped the other cheek harder with her other hand, causing that hand to go numb.

"Yes!" Talia screamed.

Talia spread herself open wider. Alya considered giving Talia another spank, but her hands were stinging, and it seemed Talia wanted to be filled. Alya grabbed Talia's hips and pivoted them backward over the edge of the bed. Alya held Talia's hip with her hand as she rubbed the tip of the mast against Talia's vulva. Talia bounced on the tip, working it inside as Alya held both hips.

When the tip had worked its way past Talia's minora, Alya thrust hard. Talia screamed and grabbed a pillow. She laid her face into the pillow as Alya pulled her onto the appendage. Alya could feel Talia begin to flatten and squirm away, so she yanked Talia back onto her knees and walked her to the edge of the bed. To ensure Talia couldn't escape, Alya grabbed Talia's hair.

"No escaping, TaVi," she ordered as she pulled.

Talia stood on her knees until Alya pushed her down and pulled her hair. Talia's back arched.

"Yes," Talia squealed.

"No talking, TaVi," Alya pushed Talia's face into the pillow as she used her free hand to pull Talia down on her appendage.

"And call me..." Alya couldn't think of anything and started getting embarrassed, so she grabbed both of Talia's hips and punished Talia for her embarrassment.

Talia rolled on her side, so Alya used the roll to her advantage. She pushed Talia onto her back and stepped over the lower leg. Placing one foot on the bed, Alya started pounding down into Talia, using the bed as a sexual springboard.

Talia inched away, so Alya hugged Talia's raised leg and pulled her to the edge, holding her in place as she trampolined. Talia was holding her hands over her face and singing old Russian prayers, which Alya found distracting at first, but somehow, they morphed into something erotic the more Alya worked.

Alya rose both of Talia's legs over her shoulders as she climbed on the bed. Alya planked over Talia's curled body and thrust. She was surprised at the difficulty of holding this pose, but she resolved to keep pumping for at least five minutes.

Talia clenched Alya's thighs as she drove the mast deep inside her tunnel. Talia kept trying to slide her legs off Alya's shoulders, but Alya forced them back into position each time. As the end of the five minutes approached, the thrusting had become lazier, and Alya was glad to turn Talia on her side.

Alya sat on her legs as she scooted into Talia. This position was much easier and explained why so many of her past penetrators had used it to finish. Alya dipped her hips and rubbed her clitoris and vulva against Talia's lower thigh. It was exciting, but she knew she wouldn't be able to finish. As she looked into Talia's eyes, she realized she was the one who wasn't going to finish.

Talia was huffing gratitudes and compliments as she finished and pulled Alya to her face for a kiss. Alya decided she wasn't done and rolled Talia on her back. She laid between Talia's legs, kissing her as she inserted into her. Talia moaned in exhaustion as she accepted the girth. Moments later, she finished and pushed Alya off. Talia rolled on her stomach.

"You're not done, TaVi," Alya declared.

"I am raw," Talia said, for the first time revealing a vulnerable side to Alya.

"That's okay, TaVi," Alya said as she squirted lube on Talia's ass. "You have other holes."

"Wait," Talia said as Alya laid on her back, but it was too late.

Alya was spreading her ass and worming inside.

"Fuck," Talia screamed into the pillow.

Alya enjoyed making Talia scream in both pleasure and pain but was sure to be careful to keep from causing the wrong kind of pain. She started thrusting between Talia's cheeks. The bed had spring. Each time she thrust, the bed would respond by thrusting the pair into the air. The trampoline effect was almost as fun as Talia's squeals.

Despite her excitement at the opportunity, Alya was becoming tired quickly. The thrusts became weaker, the bounces shallower, and the sweat more greasy. It was not long before she had enough energy to lay on Talia's back and rock her hips against Talia's ass. Alya enjoyed that for a few minutes before she realized neither of them could be getting any pleasure from the movements, so she stopped. She enjoyed the human contact with her lover, knowing it would soon be gone.

"Five minutes," Talia whispered.

"TaVi?" Alya asked.

"In five minutes, we will go eat pierogi, and I got your favorite fruit."

Alya kissed Talia's neck and gave one final, shallow thrust, causing Talia to give one final squeal.

"Yes, TaVi, my love," Alya answered.

Alya was the first off the bed. She removed the harness and placed it in the bathroom before returning. Talia was rolling to the edge, rubbing her ass where Alya's handprints remained. As they reached the kitchen, Talia grabbed Alya's wrist and turned her around. She pulled their naked bodies together and kissed her more passionately and deeply than ever before.

"I wish I had given you the opportunity sooner," she professed. "Now, sit."

Alya sat as Talia served the breakfast. They weren't warm like Alya preferred, but given the circumstances, she was delighted to eat cold pierogi.

"Thank you, TaVi," Alya nibbled as she spun her stool back and forth.

As she watched Talia eat, she remembered her earlier phone call, and the despair returned.

"What's wrong?" Talia inquired as she ate.

"Just enjoying how perfect this is and wondering if it will last," Alya answered. "I know you will get tired of me, promise you will remember me."

"I could never tire of you," Talia consoled as her demeanor transformed from loving to menacing

"My people have questioned General Klopvor about his loyalties at great length. He insists his intentions have always been pure and has no ambitions above his place. I know you have expressed concern, but I cannot find anything." Talia placed another pierogi in front of Alya, "Eat and tell me your thoughts."

"The president was poisoned, and someone had to do it. It makes sense that it would be someone close to him whom he trusts. General Klopvor is his closest ally. I thought it made sense," horror was not taking its time to wash over Alya. She thought disappearing may not be the worst option.

"Yes, it must be someone close to the president. It has to be someone he trusts. They say women are the most likely to use poison. Do you know any women close to the president whom he trusts?"

Talia's eyes were imbuing Alya's soul with the accusations. Alya knew her move was the one that had proved to be a true friend throughout the years.

"Please, TaVi, it could not be me," she cried and begged.

Talia laughed ferociously.

"Nobody ever accused you, my love. Come here and settle down. You are safe in my arms."

As they embraced, something felt different within Alya. She knew Talia was smart enough to know she was the culprit and was a proud Russian general. She had to disappear. Love could never exist. Not for her, not in this life, not in this world.

Pompous Returns

"Should we check on him?" Griforiy whispered from the other side of the table.

"We protect, not question," Alya advised, but she, too, was concerned.

The way Talia pranced around the room, whispering in the ears of Generals and Politicians between glances, hinted at the truth. Alya's eyes averted to General Klopvor's empty seat.

Everyone faced the dining hall entrance and silenced as the lights dimmed. The doors opened to reveal a handful of well-dressed men. One held a silk bag that resembled a Russian flag. Something heavy inside made it droop. As they parted, Alya's heart thumped against her ribcage. Her breathing howled through her nasal passage as her lungs expanded and collapsed in rhythmic dramatics. She clasped her hands behind her back as a dampness cooled her palms.

General Klopvor hobbled in the spotlight. He had grown thin and pale. His uniform sagged from the wrinkles that once held his jovial demeanor. The general kept his eyes on the floor as one of the men helped him. A thunderous clapping filled the room. Talia intercepted him and whispered something in his ear, which caused the broken general to stop and look at the stage. He held a hand above his eyes to shield them from the spotlight as he shook his head from side to side.

Alya glared at the general with her most intimidating facial expression. The general returned the glare until Talia whispered something in his ear. The general was lowered into his chair with assistance from two escorts as the lights returned to normal brightness and the spotlight disappeared. The silk bag was placed on the table in front of the general's plate. It remained tied. The contents were hidden from the world, and more importantly, in Alya's mind, the contents were a secret from her. The clapping continued for several minutes before the crowd mingled.

The murmuring suffocated Alya. She could feel sweat beading on her head as group after group approached the general, whispering, joking, laughing. Alya believed that several had even looked at her from the corners of their eyes. She clasped her hands tighter and fought to keep her breathing steady as her lungs hyperventilated. The lights dimmed, the spotlight on the entrance. Everyone stood in silence.

The doors opened to reveal the Russian president. A booming applause shook the room as he entered with a smile and waived. He stopped to shake several hands on his way to his seat at the table on the raised platform. As he passed Alya, he stopped.

"Has the traitor been found? Answer as you seat me," he whispered.

He turned and waved at the crowd as Alya walked behind the table and pulled his chair back. The spotlight stopped below Alya's mouth as the Russian president sat.

"I have had no updates. It could be anyone in this room," her voice trembled.

The president continued to waive as he replied, "Sit, you will test my food and drink. You could have killed me in the hospital. You are the single person that remains worthy of trust."

"Thank you," Alya's fight for control over her faculties won the war.

"No," he replied. "Do not thank me for the truth, sit. What is in the silk sitting before General Klopvor?"

"The item is a surprise to me," Alya gulped. "I have learned he has been proven to be faithful to the Motherland and yourself. I do not anticipate it to be something of concern."

"He has proven to be faithful?" The president raised an eyebrow.

"I have heard rumors that he has been questioned about his loyalties and been found to have steadfast support for your leadership," Alya informed.

"He seems nervous. Watch him to ensure his nerves are not secret malice," the president ordered.

"I will be watching him all evening," Alya confirmed as she waived Griforiy over. "See what General Klopvor has in the bag," she delegated.

The applause stopped when Alya sat beside the president. Everyone whispered as they kept their eyes on the table. Alya let her eyes wander to TaVi, who sat motionless and emotionless. Whispering filled the room until the Russian president stood. He placed his full champagne flute in front of Alya.

"Russia has claimed great victories. Tonight, we celebrate our strength and the strength of our agreements with China. I am working to secure agreements with North Korea. They should be finalized soon. Both the Chinese and North Koreans have recognized the might of the Russians and are desperate for our partnership. Many of the greatest Russians in this room have worked to help them overcome their intellectual disabilities to realize the motherland is the land of strength, intelligence, wealth, and resistance," he toasted.

Alya watched Griforiy crouch and whisper to one of the general's companions as she sipped from the champagne flute. As the president finished his speech, Alya placed the flute in his hand. He raised the glass to the crowd as Griforiy scurried behind Alya, crouching.

The room cheered, "Za vashe zdorov'ye!"

"It's an expensive bottle of the president's favorite liquor," Griforiy squeaked.

"What is the president's favorite liquor?" Alya challenged.

"They didn't tell me, but they let me feel the bottle through the silk. It's heavy and feels like glass," Griforiy mimicked, feeling a bottle with his hands.

"You are as helpful as a hawk hunting for mushrooms," Alya groaned. "Go back to your spot and stay vigilant."

Griforiy nodded and crawled as he passed behind the table, ensuring he refrained from taking the attention of the guests away from the president. Alya smirked at how stupid he was most of the time, yet he was smart enough to stay out of the spotlight. Talia stood.

"The Motherland is the most powerful force on the planet. I am its humble servant, the daughter of a long line of business owners who have resisted the temptations of all who might oppose your leadership. There is no force stronger than love, and my love," Talia glanced at Alya, then back to the president, "has become indestructible."

"Can we trust her?" The president asked as Talia continued.

"She is a fierce ally and defender of the Russian leadership. Like all clever Russian leaders, she has used sex and blackmail to ascend. She is a new general and has no history, which suggests she is a threat. She knows nothing of your recent vacation," Alya reported.

When Talia was finished, another man stood. He wore a fine business suit and was one of the president's staunchest, non-military supporters. He pontificated in great detail about the meaning of the newfound agreements, economic prosperity, and overcoming the West.

"He loves the attention. Any news on his loyalties?" The president inquired as Alya was mid-yawn.

Alya shook her head with embarrassment.

"The civilians are engrossed with battling each other for wealth. They seem to miss the nuances of who is leading the country as long as their accounts continue to fatten," he advised.

Another general rose and gave a long-winded speech as the food flowed into the room. Everyone took their seats with all attention on the Russian president's table. Despite the large number of workers zipping plates around the room, it took several minutes for the Russian president to receive his meal. He insisted on being the last to receive a plate to ensure his meal was still hot when he ate.

Everyone in the room watched, waiting for him to eat so they, too, had permission to feast. The president waited for all of the workers to retreat from the hall before he pushed his plate in front of Alya. The spotlight cooked Alya's brow as she looked down at the meat, gravy-covered potatoes, and carrot slices. The room was silent until someone's stomach urged her along with a deep growl.

Alya took the fork in her hand and looked to the crowd. The light was too bright, and she could see outlines. Several people were standing on their chairs to ensure she ate.

Alya dipped the fork into the potatoes and gravy. They were better than the ones her grandmother made when she was young. She almost took a second bite before remembering her surroundings. She poked a carrot and ate it. Alya thought the crunch in the center was a funny surprise and smiled.

Alya picked up the knife in her free hand and looked at the president. She knew she could do it, and nobody could stop her. She saw Griforiy beyond the far edge of the table and shook her head at his innocence and gullibility before looking back at the crowd.

Alya knew TaVi was going to hate her forever after that night. Her heart twinged with pain. She searched for TaVi through the spotlight and found the outline of her empty seat. Alya returned her attention to the plate and sliced a piece of meat.

The inside was well done like the president liked. He was terrified about parasites and always required his food to be cooked until it was tough. She thought he believed eating tough meat somehow strengthened him. Her jaw muscles were sore by the time she finished chewing. She swallowed the stiff leather and sipped the president's water.

"Everything seems to be to your liking, Mr. President," she whispered.

The president stood as he moved the plate in front of himself.

"Please, dine. The food is delicious."

An orchestra of flatware clanking against porcelain, open-mouth chewing, and slurping erupted.

"You serve me well," the president stated as he sat. Alya rose to take her spot beside the table, but the president stopped her, "We still have more speeches. You have more drinking to do. Plus, dessert will be served. You know how much I like the taste of sweet things."

A Drink to Remember

Guests meandered about the room as they finished their meals. The Russian president was methodical in his consumption: potatoes, scan the room with his eyes, meat, scan the room, two slices of carrot, scan the room, repeat. Occasionally, he would whisper questions about specific guests to Alya, who would provide updates on the level of risk they posed and their weaknesses.

"Someone needs to speak with you." Alya heard. She looked around, "Back here." Griforiy had crawled behind the president.

"Go away," she replied from the side of her mouth.

"What's this?" The president demanded.

"General Vilonka has requested her. She says it is an urgent matter," Griforiy didn't realize the president was not speaking to him.

"It's nothing," Alya minimized the president's attention.

"Go. You said she is a new general. Maybe she knows things. Find out if we should conduct a full interview with her," the president pointed his steak knife.

Alya rose and kicked Griforiy in the side.

"Get back in position," she scolded.

Alya scanned the room as she stepped off the platform, unable to locate TaVi. She hunted, prowling from front to back, until she reached the far wall. TaVi was nowhere to be found, so Alya took the opportunity to empty her bladder.

Before she urinated, she checked the restroom for TaVi. She was alone. It felt eerie. As she drained, she thought she heard a noise.

"TaVi, are you here?" She called out.

There was no response. As she wiped, for a moment, she thought she heard a moan. Alya searched the bathroom again, but there was nobody. When she finished washing her hands, she thought she heard another moan and looked around as the hairs on her neck rose.

Alya noticed a vent over a toilet when she looked up. She looked into the vent by standing on the toilet. There was another room on the other side of the wall. In the hall, she discovered the men's bathroom was the other room. Alya opened the door. She could not see anyone from her position, so she stepped inside and crouched.

The feet of a man were under the furthest stall. Alya rose, prepared to leave, and then she heard another moan.

"TaVi, you can do better," a deep voice said.

Alya covered her mouth with her hand and ran from the room. As she ran, the door slammed. She fixed her make-up to hide the tears before reentering the dining hall. She took a deep breath and strode to the president's side.

"Did the general have any updates I should know?" The waiting president asked.

"No," Alya felt anger that Talia could betray her in such a way.

"Talia wants to be with a man. She must know I am the traitor and is trying to save herself but with a man?" Alya's mind spiraled.

"She is playing Russian politics," Alya fought the tears.

"If she is free from disease, I might have to mentor her in the ways of Russian politics. She said her love of Russia is very strong, maybe I should feel how strong," the president smiled as he stood. "Bring in the dessert!"

Alya curled her hand around the knife on the table while she imagined plunging it into his belly and spilling his bowels. She placed the knife on his plate as he sat and waved over a waiter.

"If you do not want to be punished, I suggest you clear this table before the dessert arrives," Alya urged.

The crowd returned to their seats as the lights flickered to indicate dessert was being served.

General Klopvor rose with the assistance of his groupies as the crowd hushed.

"This has been a wonderful feast," He yelled to quiet the persisting undertones as the staff distributed plates of Ptichye Moloko.

"It is said that French chefs worked with the kings and queens of the motherland to achieve something that could not be attained. Something so magnificent that no place on earth could deny Russian superiority or contest the elegance and enchantment of the motherland. It took more than one hundred years for the recipe to perfect into what has been set before you. It represents the unattainable strength, sophistication, and power of the Russian people, the Russian nobility, and the Russian leadership. As you savor every bite of this impossible dessert, remember it is the epitome of Russian superiority; yet, it pales in comparison to the perfection, strength, power, dedication, wisdom, and leadership of the greatest Russian," the general pointed at the Russian president. "Join me in celebrating the greatest Russian, who can never be bested, challenged, or questioned."

The general led the clapping as the room joined. It took several minutes for the room to begin to break the applause. Alya found herself wondering why the general had given such a display if Talia had already found him to be innocent and let her eyes wander to Talia's seat. She must have still been pleasing the man in the bathroom because her seat was empty, and her dinner was untouched.

"I like him," the president whispered.

"I have worked with the saucier to select this evening's dessert as a show of my love of the motherland and our ferocious leader. I have," the general continued as he pointed to the silk sac, "the finest liquor that money can purchase and that the saucier has assured me pairs with the dessert. Please," he pointed at one of his helpers, "bring it to the president. Let him inspect it and be the first to open it. There is no perfection greater than the pairing of this liquor with our Ptichye Moloko. As such, nobody deserves to experience the heaven making notes of this combination before our enduring hero."

As the helper walked toward the stage, Alya leaped to her feed, and Griforiy hurled himself from the stage toward the advancing silk. The man stopped, holding out the treasure toward Griforiy, who became motionless.

"Hand it to me, Griforiy," Alya demanded as she approached. Griforiy took the bag with one hand. Without changing position, he reached under his armpit and handed it to Alya. She unwrapped the bottle and handed the sac back to Griforiy, who ensured it made its way back to the general.

Alya held the bottle in the spotlight as she approached the president. She couldn't see anything in the liquid, so she placed it beside the president's dessert. She reoccupied her place at the president's side.

"Open it," the president commanded.

Alya had not planned on this gift or this moment, but here it stood. This gift was meant for the president, but she would pirate the opportunity and make it a gift for herself. It was her chance. She didn't want, but needed, to erase TaVi's earlier intrusion from the president's mind, complete her extraction within the next two days, and make sure she never saw the traitorous face of General Talia Vilonka for the rest of her life.

Alya's hand shook as she moved the bottle in front of her. She opened it and let its perfume grace her nostrils. There was no hint of poison. It was moved in front of the president, who waved the aroma towards his face with several hand rolls. When he was satisfied, he stood.

"It is not known that ptichye moloko is my favorite. General Klopvor, you have outdone yourself. Being the 'greatest Russian' is unattainable, and I am too humble to claim such a title, but I thank you for your kind words."

Alya slipped a jell capsule from her pocket and crushed one end as the president spoke.

"I have enjoyed the fragrance of your gift, and it is one of the best I have ever inhaled. I must let my tester," he motioned toward Alya, "prove it to be safe, but I look forward to delighting in this fine gift."

Alya poured the alcohol into a glass and then used sleight of hand to dump the contents of the capsule into the bottle.

"General, you have always managed to work wonders, and I look forward to your continued service to the motherland. Don't let me stop anyone from enjoying this great treat; eat!" The president clapped toward the general.

Alya removed a second capsule from her pocket as the president clapped. Her eyes scanned the room, stopping to watch General Klopvor laughing with the guests that gathered around his table. They seemed to be congratulating and competing for his attention and favor. She continued scanning and stopped at TaVi's table to find it empty as she pretended to cough. She slipped both the empty capsule and the new pill between her cheek and upper teeth.

Her mouth was dry from the excitement. The pill started to burn as it glued itself to the inside of her cheek. Alya clenched her jaw as a hole was seared. The Russian president finished waving to his fans and sat. He returned the bottle to its home beside his dessert as he pointed at Alya's glass. She raised the glass, and the guests copied with their champagne flutes. They honored the president.

"I must act. My time has come," thought Alya. *"It's my finale. I better make it look good because extractions are not supposed to have an audience. There's no going back. Is she still fucking? What the fuck, she can't even be here for my end? Calm, she doesn't know, and I don't want that traitor here anyway. She is a liar and hates me. Plus, she is disgusting, she chooses to fuck men. Okay, here I go before the tablet melts."*

Her mind would not stop racing, and she knew there was no going back. Alya drew a long, slow breath and made herself calm. She looked at TaVi's table; she still hadn't returned. It was unsurprising, given the night's previous events, but still made Alya's heart twinge.

"I love you," Alya mouthed to TaVi's empty chair.

She pulled the glass to her lips and crushed the jell-coated capsule between her teeth. She pretended to sip the liquor. She swished the sweet drink in her teeth until the jell coatings and the pill's contents were dissolved. She spit the entire contents of her mouth back into the glass without letting anyone notice. When her mouth was empty, Alya exaggerated a swallow.

Alya dropped the glass on the table as she sprang to her feet, clutching her neck with one hand. She strangled herself so the veins would jut from her forehead and her face would crimson. With her free hand, she withdrew a chalky tablet from her pocket. She coughed and covered her mouth with the hand that concealed the tablet.

As the tablet entered her mouth, it foamed and dissolved. The light started fading from her eyes as the Russian president's face contorted into horror. He was whisked away. She felt her legs fail as she collapsed to the floor. Her body was numb, and the room narrowed into tiny circles.

TaVi had returned and was waving her arms as she knelt beside Alya. Her face and neck were red, her stockings torn. As the light slipped away, Alya could see TaVi yelling something in her face as she shook her shoulders, but all sound had already faded.

Heartbreak Railways

"She's coming around," the words sounded far away. "You gave us quite a scare." A woman was beside Alya. A single lamp on a table in the corner of the room.

"Acetaminophen," Alya whined. Pain ripped through her stomach as she sat up.

"Slow," the woman urged as she placed a hand behind Alya's neck and arm as supports. "Lean your back against the wall. I will get you medicine."

Alya closed her eyes as she dragged her legs over the side of the cot. The room caused nausea as it spun. The cold air felt good on her shins. Alya felt herself below the heavy blanket. She was naked, and her body was a furnace.

"Go," Alya whimpered, not looking to see if the woman was still present.

Something touched her shoulder, and Alya raised a hand. Her fingers curled around a heavy cup as she raised her other hand. Two pills rolled into her palm. Alya rolled the pills onto her tongue and then gulped the water. One of the pills felt like it was stuck in her throat, so she chugged the rest. Her tongue was swollen with dehydration.

"Get some rest," the voice said as it took the drink and guided Alya's head back to the pillow. "You are still recovering."

Alya did not resist. The weight of the blanket's embrace felt soothing as Alya rolled on her side and enjoyed slumber's quiet companionship.

"She is waking," a young voice sprang forth with the unadulterated joy of youthful ignorance.

"Quiet, she does not need your yelling," the voice from before scolded. "Go, get water and the medicine."

"I was only—" the youth rebutted.

"The medicine," the older one snapped her finger.

Alya opened her eyes. The stomach pain had subsided, and the room had stopped spinning.

"Tell me how I arrived," Alya's throat ached from its recent drought. Her swollen tongue was heavy, and speaking was difficult.

"Take your time. You need water and food. You have been recovering for five days. You put on quite a show, do you know that?"

"Tell me," Alya massaged her throat as pain tugged at her vocal cords.

"We collected you from the coroner's. It caused us a headache. The president had saturated all routes out of Moscow with secret police and investigators. We had to risk our whole operation to get you to St. Petersburg. This is our most secret place. After you leave, we will have to burn it to the ground," the woman seemed more interested in complaining than explaining.

"Can I come in?" A young woman was peaking through the doorway beside the lamp and table. "I have water and food."

Alya waved to her, but she did not budge.

"Don't be shy. Our guest needs to drink," the older woman approved her entrance.

"Thank you," Alya's voice scratched as she was handed a wooden board that held a stone cup, sliced bread, and a potato. "I do not understand the potato."

"We had extra, they are my favorite," the youth admitted.

"Go," the older woman pointed to the door while struggling to withhold laughter.

"Thank you," Alya whispered. "I love potatoes. You did good."

"You're welcome," the youth replied before sticking her tongue out at the other woman.

The other woman stomped a foot toward the youth, who took the action as a sign she needed to run from the room.

"My sister," the woman explained. "She has not learned how to keep herself."

"She reminds me of my sisters. We had the best times when I was…" Alya's voice trailed while she thought about the eights and nines she had known when she was a Harem Beauty and started nibbling on the bread and sipping the water. "I was younger. You said the president had shut down Moscow."

"Yes," the woman sat on the wood floor across the room from Alya. "You made quite a scene. They have used incredible resources to cover up the evening, but there are rumors. Do you remember what happened?"

"I was betrayed," Alya still forced her raspy voice to penetrate the pain. "I mean, I was supposed to exit, but not the way I did."

"Why did you use arsenic and nightshade? Did you use two because the president might have made himself immune to one?"

"What are you talking about?" Alya was confused. The Society never mixed poisons. It would be a signature that could be used to identify their actions.

"I have a cousin in the army. He said General Vilonka went crazy when you died. Her brutality and restraint were unleashed when the president put her in charge of investigating your death. My cousin said she found two poisons in both your glass and the alcohol bottle."

"She isn't that bad," Alya croaked as she poked the potato with a finger. It was still steamy. She lifted it and took a large bite.

"I heard that when the medics were removing your body, the general, Vilonka, I mean, forced a gun from a guard and started shooting General Klopvor's escorts. One survived, and he escaped. He disappeared that night, and nobody knows where he went. Some have said General Vilonka captured him and is interrogating him in a warehouse."

"*TaVi*," Alya's brain sighed. It was her hope that her love was safe, even if she was an enemy. She was retreating into her sadness and couldn't prevent it.

"I am sorry, I didn't mean to upset you," the woman looked concerned.

"The matters of Russia are no longer my concern. I have been extracted," Alya hardened her emotions. She felt that getting out of Russia would help the healing. "When do I move again?"

"We transport for the SoG all the time. We can leave when you are ready," the woman stood.

Alya placed the board beside her and sprang to her feet. All the blood and life drained from her head, the room swirled, and the wood floor rose to greet Alya's face.

"She's awake," the youth's voice seemed less jovial. She was sitting on the floor writing in a notebook as Alya sat up. "You broke your wrist," the youth pointed at Alya's arm.

"I thought you were transporters," Alya investigated the messy-looking cast.

"We know how to treat wounds. People get hurt all the time," the youth responded as she continued writing. "Do you know how to spell 'indeterminant?' I have to write a report on the value of living in the city versus the country, and my opinion is that it is indeterminate."

"I don't write without my phone," Alya was embarrassed. "Let me check to see how it is spelled. Where have you placed my belongings?"

"We transport people, not things," the youth replied as the older woman entered the room with food. "You don't have things anymore."

"The phone is property of the Society. It must be handled in a specific way," Alya was aggravated by the response despite knowing the young woman was being honest and was correct.

"We destroyed everything in the kiln," the older woman interrupted. "My sister doesn't understand the consequences, but I do. I take all complaints about our operations." The woman turned to her sister, "Go do your schoolwork in the other room."

"You told me to watch her," the youth whined.

"You are done. School is your priority. You cannot be a nurse with bad grades."

"Wait," Alya stopped the youth. "Your sister is not wrong. Listen to her. She is making great sacrifices to take care of you. I wish I had a sister like yours when I was your age."

"Okay," the youth grumbled. "It's not fair."

"Hold on," Alya stopped the youth. "You are still young and do not understand how unfair things are. The most powerful people in the world tried to kill me for doing my job and protecting the Russian people. I have lost many sisters, friends, and lovers," Alya's mind raced through the faces of all the Harem girls she had loved, then froze on TaVi. "There is no shame in working to earn a life as a nurse where you can save people without losing the ones you love. Go, do as your sister says, and study harder than all other

Russians. Be the best nurse so your sister's life and efforts are not wasted."

"Yes, ma'am," the youth's head sunk as she dragged her feet from the room.

"You shouldn't lecture her," the older sister grimaced. "We are not like you. Yes, I take these jobs to support her, but she doesn't need to know I am in danger. She needs to know she is loved and that there are no worries about money."

"I apologize, you are correct," Alya pulled the food tray. "I am hungry, and I should have said nothing. You are the boss here, and this is your operation."

"We will leave in two days," the woman replied as she released the tray. "Until then, please keep your stories away from her ears. She needs to focus on school, not some exciting life as whatever you are."

"It is horror, betrayal, and loneliness, not excitement," Alya corrected as the woman abandoned her to her loneliness.

When her belly filled, it made her eyes heavy. She placed the tray on the floor and laid her head on the pillow to rest.

"I received the highest grade in my class," the youth's eyes sparkled as they hovered over Alya's face. "Did I do a good job?"

"You didn't brush your teeth today," Alya groaned as she awoke.

"Please don't tell my sister. I forgot, and by the time I remembered, I was already late for school," the girl took two steps backward.

"Your secret is safe with me as long as you promise to start making it to school on time," Alya rubbed her eyes as she rose.

"Shh," the girl whispered as her sister entered.

"It's moving day," the elder sister greeted. "What are you two whispering about?"

"I was telling her about my grades," the youth had a giant fake grin.

"Yes, and I was telling her how proud everyone should be that she is doing so well," Alya supported the youth.

"Are you well enough to travel?" The older sister asked.

"Yes, sore though," Alya lifted her cast. "It is a short drive to Finland."

"Even better, we aren't driving," the younger sister beamed with joy.

"Go," the older sister shooed the girl from the room.

"Driving is standard," Alya was confused.

"Yes, but things have been so tight that we must go by train," the elder sister shrugged. "You will need to borrow my documents. We have hair dye and scissors in the bathroom."

"My hair is shorter than yours," Alya stood.

"But my hair is shorter than the wig," the sister rebutted. "We need to dye the wig. It was expensive, but we need real human hair, so the dye works."

"If you have heels and we tape my chest, it might fool some folks," Alya pressed her breasts against her ribs.

"My younger sister will drive you to the train and send you off," the woman continued.

"No," Alya rejected the idea. "She cannot be put in danger. You must drive me."

"I am too old. They will know I am not her," the woman replied.

"You are a neighbor helping out a neighbor. They will know nothing. Leave your sister where it is safe. She will not come," Alya insisted.

"You need a shower," the woman pursed her lips as though she was deep in thought. "Follow me, I have soap."

Alya did not mind being naked around strangers and thought nothing of it since they were all women and there had been no sexuality displayed. Her skin felt tight, but walking was gratifying.

The apartment had three rooms: the bedroom where Alya had been recovering on the cot, the bathroom, and the kitchen with a square table where the younger sister was writing in a notebook. The floor in the kitchen had two sleeping bags and a single pillow.

"This is a clean towel. You can use the soap in the shower to wash yourself. I have provided you a pair of my pants and a shirt on the sink. I have one pair of heels, but they should work if your feet can fit," the woman closed the bathroom door.

The ride to the train station was short but filled with silence. The elder sister parked at the far end of the lot.

"Here is your traveling package," she handed Alya a cloth bag.

Alya untied the dainty strings and dumped the contents on the seat between them. There was a phone, a switchblade, the train ticket, and a roll of cash in various currencies.

"Take this," Alya removed a couple of bills from the roll for herself and handed the rest to the sister. "Make sure she finishes nursing school."

"I can't," the sister pushed the roll away.

"Take it. Spend a little at a time to cover your bills, or save it for when she needs it later. It is your good consequence for being an invaluable transporter."

"This is too much," the resistance persisted.

"Not accepting this generosity might be rude. You know about consequences, and I am sure you would rather not have bad ones," Alya tucked the roll into the woman's pocket.

"Thank you," the woman stared at the steering wheel, motionless even after Alya walked to the station.

Alya's muscles were still sore and weak. They fought against her with every step, but she managed to survive the journey to the bench on the platform. She compared the time on the phone with the time on the train ticket. The train would be arriving in nine minutes. Alya scanned the crowd and decided she was safe enough to rest her eyes for a moment. She set a five-minute timer on her phone and let her eyes close. She felt someone sit on the bench beside her but ignored it.

"It is time to come with me," a stern voice spoke from the other side of the bench. "Do not make a scene. I have my pistol, and it will respond to any threat."

Alya leaned forward and opened her eyes to look at the ground. Beside her feet were a pair of new, white sneakers. Her eyes lifted to the olive ankles, then traced the seam of the maroon yoga pants to the most beautiful set of hips. Her eyes continued their voyage until she locked eyes with the black-haired, brown-eyed beauty.

"I've missed you, TaVi," Alya struggled to not hug her former lover, who had dark bags under her eyes. "How did you find me?"

"Stand up, this is not the time for questions," there was a cold ruthlessness in her accent. Something was there that was not there before, but Alya could not identify the change.

"Yes, TaVi," Alya obeyed.

"Stop it. Do not call me that. Not after what you did," Talia growled.

A tall, handsome man with muscles bulging from every part of his body walked toward them, waving.

"Hey! I have been looking all over for you. Where have you been, my dearest wife?" The man called.

Talia and Alya both looked at each other in confusion as the man grabbed Alya by the shoulders and kissed her cheek.

"Who is your friend?" He asked.

Talia pulled her hand from her pocket, revealing her pistol, "Leave us."

"That's pretty," the man grabbed Talia's wrist. "But I don't know you. It's time for you to go away."

Alya grabbed the man to help TaVi, but she was still too weak. He shrugged her away and ripped the gun from TaVi's hand. He bear-hugged TaVi.

"God, I have missed you," he professed as he lifted her. TaVi kicked the man in the crotch, but he laughed and said, "I sure am glad I am wearing my cup, you have strong legs."

"Alya," TaVi gasped as the man walked toward the building.

TaVi managed to squirm an arm free and grabbed the corner of the building, clinging for life, horrific hysteria on her face. She kept her head in view until the man's hand reached from behind the building, grabbed her neck, and yanked her out of site.

Alya shuffled her way toward the commotion as she heard struggling, grunting, and a plea. The man emerged with blood-soaked hands.

"We need to go before they find her," he said, approaching. She ran to the stopping train but could not breathe.

"Hey you, halt," yelled a police officer as the man stepped beside Alya. "Stop!"

The man spun around as he pulled TaVi's gun from his pocket. He fired as Alya dropped. She hit the platform's surface with crushing pain. 'Bang, crack. Bang, bang, bang, crack, bang, crack.' Alya crawled to the train as the man fell to a knee.

"Help me," he gasped as he reached a hand toward Alya.

As his arm extended, Alya noticed an obvious tattoo on his forearm, it was a five-point star. Alya turned and continued crawling to the train. As she reached the entrance, a conductor pulled her inside.

"Good thing you dropped. They fired over your head. Don't worry about your ticket, find a seat, and we can settle things once I make sure everyone on the train is safe," he guided her into a sitting car.

As the train pulled away from the station, Alya collapsed in a chair, curled her knees to her chest, and hugged. She sobbed and couldn't keep herself from making some noise. As passengers searched for available seats, they gave her looks of pity but said nothing. She watched through the tears as the police beat and shackled the man before they flung his bleeding body into a van.

Alya's pocket vibrated as the station disappeared. She was sobbing and rocking herself so that she almost did not notice. She answered in time.

"Do not exit the train. We are sending a full extraction team. The transporter has been compromised. The fives have started the war," the voice was exotic but welcoming.

"They killed TaVi," Alya wiped her tears. "They deserve the worst consequences we can imagine."

"You have been selected. You will be diverted and updated."

"Wait," Alya was forcing her emotions into submission. "You said the transporter was compromised. We need to extract them."

"There is no 'them.' Our transporters are single-unit operators, and you know they are expendable."

"No," Alya rejected the answer. "I mean, yes, you are correct about those things, but she has a sister. Her sister is studying to be a nurse. She's a healer. We have to protect her." There were several minutes of silence, "I am still here," Alya confirmed.

"Stand by," the voice remained silent for several more minutes. "Do you have confirmation on the sister?"

"Yes, I met her," Alya replied. "She is bright and happy and doesn't know our horrors."

"Standby," this pause was much shorter. "Do not worry yourself about Russian matters. You have been extracted." Another silence, "We will put the sisters under observation and remote safety protocols."

"I need to heal before I war, but I am ready to level cities," Alya snarled.

When the call disconnected, Alya couldn't fight the tears anymore. As the train clacked on the tracks, Alya swayed from side to side, hugging her legs with her tear-dripping face pressed against her knees. Her mind was replaying TaVi's face as it was forced behind the building. The horror in TaVi's eyes and the hand squeezing TaVi's neck as she pleaded for Alya.

"Why did I let myself become too weak to save my love?"

Retirement

Uninvited Guests

Muhammed placed the phone on the receiver and walked to the large glass doors. He knew a flurry of activity was underway to prepare for the day. The compound grounds were calm, motionless to the eye, but he was aware that it was being prepared. He strained to discern the workers from their surroundings but, after several minutes, knew he would never see those who chose to remain unseen.

As his anticipation and nerves grew, Muhammed resolved to settle himself and made his way to 'Pleasurable Choices.' The bar was always well-stocked. Muhammed always considered alcohol abhorrent and didn't mind seeing it destroyed, but the cherry nectar was the pinnacle of perfection.

Muhammed poured himself a shot and slammed it like he was a rough-and-tumble cowboy from an old John Wayne film. The kind he had seen when he was a boy at his aunt's. He poured one more shot.

"It seems this planet isn't big enough for both of us..." his voice trailed as he stared at an invisible foe, "for both of our futures." He gulped the shot and slammed the glass on the bar. "It's almost high noon, partner."

A man was standing in the circle beside a wooden crate as Muhammed entered the Atrium holding a bag. The gold necklace glinted in the sun that streamed through the glass ceiling. The maroon tracksuit was an odd sight in the Harem, but Muhammed seemed unfazed.

"They are dropping four miles to the west," the man announced as he pressed a hand to his ear. "They will be here within the hour. Tell me you have secured the beauties and have activated the nines."

"We are ready. I have brought you a mask," Muhammed lifted the bag. "I did not see your people preparing the grounds."

"They saw you take your time searching for them. How was the cherry nectar?" The man smiled as Muhammed descended the steps and stepped into the center of the room. "It's good to see you, old friend," the man held out an arm.

Muhammed grabbed the man's forearm, pulled him, and gave him an embrace.

"Too long! How have things been on the subcontinent?"

"Controlling Mungra has been a sweet gig. He is pretty emotional, but he has become paranoid. I am sure you heard about the kill squads," the man stepped back and sat on the edge of one of the cushions.

Muhammed followed the lead of his long-lost friend and sat. If he was going to be retired, there was no person more soothing and comforting.

"I have heard," Muhammed acknowledged, "it seems many of the leaders have increased their paranoia. Did you hear about the Brazilians?"

"Meh, they aren't that important yet. It's a shame about the Harem, though," the man looked around the room. "This place is heaven. The lodge has made huge upgrades, but it is nothing like this."

"Have you been to the lodge recently?" Muhammed was surprised at the comment because he had not heard about the Indians visiting the Lodge.

"About a year ago. Indian leadership prefers the spitting cobra over the rabbit hole," the man laughed, "but he's not alone."

"That loses something in translation," Muhammed responded with an eye twinkle. "But yes, many prefer the cobra. I am sure you have heard discussions pertaining to replacements and relocation."

"You know I cannot tell you about things that will happen after your retirement. I heard you started the promotion of a new member. Tell me about her," the man lay on his back, his feet still on the floor.

Muhammed walked to the man's cushion, circled it, and laid on his back. The two men lay with their heads side-by-side.

"She is capable and strong, but let's not talk about that. Let's focus on what is to come," he let the guest know.

"You still command this place," the man sighed and wiped his face, "at least for now. Tell me what we should focus on."

"Nothing, let's say nothing. People who speak too much often say nothing anyway. Try to remember when we were in our cage together and the first time you experienced a guest. That night, we all spent the night in silence. We were strong because we were together, and no words were needed. Let's honor that moment," Muhammed could feel himself get lost in his feelings as he closed his eyes.

As his eyes moistened, fingers found the top of his head. They walked to the side, circled his ear two times, then journeyed to his cheek. They were replaced by a palm as lips pressed against Muhammed's other cheek.

"I remember, and I am here to return the favor. I requested to be the one. You are not alone," the man consoled.

The men waited for the future to arrive, even after the first screams sounded from the compound walls, they lay motionless. As the men covered their eyes with their arms, glass showered.

"It is time," Muhammed stated with some disappointment.

"At your leisure," the man replied as they both stood.

Muhammed walked to the bag and removed two gas masks. He tossed one to the man.

"Your people have 45 seconds." Muhammed ran to the cage doors at the top of the room and shouted, "Press it!"

"Masks on," the man said as he pressed his finger to his ear.

Muhammed pulled his mask over his face as he ran down the steps and joined the man in the center of the room. The man opened the crate, handed Muhammed an MP-5, and took the other for himself. Muhammed selected six magazines and two grenades from the crate and lined his waist while the man filled his pockets. Dozens more magazines remained untouched.

"To the cage doors," Muhammed pointed as he lifted one side of the crate.

"Move," the man yelled as he grabbed the other side of the crate and ran. A pastel yellow smoke seeped into the room.

As the men reached the top of the steps, screams became louder, and a helicopter passed overhead. There was a loud explosion followed by an even louder grinding of metal.

Another helicopter hovered above the Atrium's shattered dome. Shattering glass streamed from the panes that had evaded previous attacks. Ropes penetrated the sanctuary. Muhammed and the man readied their weapons.

The doors to the hallway flung open. Two blood-soaked men in black military uniforms entered and shot. Muhammed and the man dove to the floor and returned fire.

Four men carrying swords ran through the open doors. The first swordsman lopped off the head of one of the gun toters with a strong chop but was riddled with bullets by the other. The second swordsman moved toward the gunman and was dispatched. The third swordsman fared no better but did dance to his death as the bullets manipulated his movements. As the final swordsman approached, the man seemed to run out of bullets and pulled out his sidearm. He wasn't quick enough, and a sword was chopped deep into his neck as he fell to the floor, his hand spasmed, shooting the swordsman in the foot.

The swordsman fell to his knee on the man's chest as he wriggled his sword free. As he struggled to his feet, bodies slid down the ropes in the middle of the room. The swordsman hobbled to the open doors and pulled them shut as the descending bodies initiated a barrage of bullets.

Muhammed looked at his friend and signaled he was unharmed. The man rolled on his side to show Muhammed a blood spot on his upper arm before indicating he was unharmed. Muhammed held up three fingers, then two, then one.

The men rolled onto their knees and fired at the descending men. One of the men fell to the ground with a thud while the others returned fire. As they reached the ground, the man beside Muhammed threw a grenade into the circle. The men scattered, but the grenade was effective.

Blood filled the circle as bodies twitched. The two men circled the top of the Atrium, shooting each of the bodies to ensure the trespassers were inanimate before they stepped through the doors to the cages. Several dead nines and many military bodies dotted the hallways. All of the cage doors appeared secured, so the men made their way back to the Atrium and refilled their ammunition.

They worked until a loud banging sounded at the door to the cages. The men dove behind the bodies of the intruders and aimed at the door as it opened.

A Lithuanian and French Harem nine peaked into the room. Blood dripped from their masks, swords, and clothes as they entered. They made hand signals and circled the top of the Atrium. Muhammed and the man stood.

"Come," Muhammed waived them down. "Give us your report."

"Six have fallen: Thailand, India, Togo, Netherlands, Paraguay, and Canada," the Lithuanian was emotional.

"Your team has lost many," Muhammed assumed because the woman standing before him was not the senior Lithuanian.

"We lost three. We ordered our junior to protect our beauty and helped save the African hallway. Several intruders were able to make entry into fifteen different cages. My sisters fought valiantly, and many lives were saved before they succumbed."

"They will be honored," the man standing beside Muhammed assured.

"Give your report," Muhammed turned to the French protector.

"We have lost one," her accent was thick, and the mask made it almost impossible to understand her words. "We did not know the strength of the invasion, so we kept two protectors with our beauty. We defended our hallway because our duty is to our beauty. We acted as support for the others who were racing to be the first to fight the invaders. We ensured no trespassers made it beyond the Netherlands. No team was able to defend the Netherlands, and many teams were obliterated while trying."

"It is impressive that your team had no losses," the man said with a hint of disbelief.

"That is not correct," the French girl replied, knowing he had not heard what she said. "I apologize for causing confusion. We have lost one. When we were fighting to save the Netherlands, an invader caught us by surprise by scaling the outside wall."

"She will be honored," the man replied. "Go, continue to defend the cages. We," he motioned toward Muhammed, "have more work to do before the Harem is secured."

Both women looked to Muhammed for guidance. He shook his head, "He will be leading the Harem until a permanent twenty-two is selected. Go, continue to serve. Both of your teams are honored throughout the society. Your lost sisters will be honored, and you will be receiving great consequences for being among the best within the society. Let me honor you with my deep gratitude for having the opportunity to know you." Muhammed knelt and bowed before the women.

The woman seemed to be in a state of shock at Muhammed's words and actions. They looked at each other and removed their gas masks.

The French woman crouched and touched Muhammed's head, "It is we who have been honored to have had the opportunity to be led by a man such as you."

The Lithuanian sat cross-legged and added, "We cannot voice the immense gratitude we have for your leadership through all of the horrors this world has to offer. You can never be replaced, but we will honor your loss and continue our devotion to this society and our place in it."

"Well said," the man standing beside Muhammed removed his mask. "Now, please do as he had asked and defend the cages. The attack may not be finished."

The women ascended the steps, turning to look at Muhammed one last time before encasing themselves in their new reality.

"Report," the man said as he held a finger in his ear. "Secure the area to receive us."

The man crouched and placed a hand on Muhammed's back.

"They are gone. It is time to proceed," he prompted.

Muhammad knew his friend hadn't realized he was sobbing. His entire body shook with adrenaline and remorse. Muhammed was dismantled by the thought he was entering a new era, an era where he no longer served the Harem, A reality where he no longer protected the girls from the harsh realities and ruthlessness of the rule followers.

"Come," the man's voice softened as Muhammed lifted his face and exposed the tears that were collecting inside the mask. "Take off your mask. We are the deepest of friends. I am here to make the transition less painful, not more."

"I am sure you know what a war with the fives means for the world," Muhammed stripped the mask away. "The entire world is going to enter a period of darkness that most histories have not recorded. The society will be so tied up that we cannot help the inhabitants."

"I know, the closest thing recorded was the Dark Ages, but there is no other way. We cannot save others if we do not save ourselves," the man's reply was tender.

"The beauties will be sacrificed," Muhammed replied. "I have worked so hard."

"Which is why you have been selected," the man interrupted. "We will take care of what you have built. Your legacy is not wasted. There is no bad blood between you and the council, but we both know this is the way things must be." The man held a finger to his ear before yelling, "Come in!"

The doors to the hallway opened. Two blood-soaked swordsmen entered.

"We are finished with it, you can proceed when ready," one briefed.

Private Party

"It's bigger than I imagined," the man said as they entered the office. "It's hard to believe this is the original Atrium. I can't imagine all the beauties fitting in here."

"There were a lot less then," Muhammed reminisced. "In those days, we had room for women to represent all skin tones and body shapes, not every country."

"Bring us drinks," the man pressed a finger to his ear as the pair walked to the sofa.

Returning his attention to Muhammed, "I suspect the selectees will be focused on overcoming their traumas given the recent and current events. Your protégé may even be hostile; I have told everyone to capture her on-site and notify me. We should take time to relax before they arrive."

"Tell me what you have in mind," Muhammed smiled as he reclined with his hand under his head. His torso pointed at the man while his bent legs split the sofa in half.

"Earlier, you asked me to remember our time in the Lodge. I remember the times and often look back with great excitement. I was hoping you would be willing to relive one of my favorite memories before we…" The man looked at the floor with dead eyes, and he seemed to be fighting some internal battle over his ability to continue. "Before we put on a production for the selectees and, I have to retire you."

Muhammed straightened his legs. He placed one in the man's lap and the other behind the man's back. A swordsman entered with a tray filled with nectars and juices from the room of 'Pleasurable Choices' and placed it on the desk.

"Tell me your preferences so I may serve you one last time," the man said as he arranged the various beverages.

Muhammed and his friend looked at each other and cackled.

"Go," the man instructed. "If you stay, you may be offering juices that are not found in those bottles."

"But he looks so fun…" Muhammed raised his eyebrows with a smile as the swordsman made a polite retreat.

"I know what you like," the man held Muhammed's ankle with one hand as he slid the other up Muhammed's leg.

"This is such a fucked up day," Muhammed snickered. "We might as well relive the glory days before we need to get back to work."

Muhammed sat up when the man's hand kneaded the inside of his thigh. His scrotum started rubbing side-to-side as his member stiffened.

"It's good to see some things haven't changed," the man said as he lifted Muhammed's garbs over the erection. "You always were easy to get started. Lay back."

The man turned toward Muhammed, got on his hands and knees on the sofa, and pressed Muhammed's chest to make him lie.

"It has been so long," Muhammed confessed.

"Relax and enjoy brother," the man stroked down Muhammed's body and rested his hand in the crease of Muhammed's hip.

Muhammed placed both of his hands behind his head and closed his eyes as saliva dripped from the man's mouth and covered the head of his uncircumcised manhood. A hand wrapped around the neck and pulled the foreskin back as another drip covered the tip.

Muhammed took a deep breath as he felt the hand begin to massage up and down. It pulled his balls away from his thighs then guided them back into position as the nerves tingled. Muhammed rotated his knees outward, causing his legs to spread. The hand understood and pressed further into his balls.

The hand remained motionless for a moment then Muhammed felt a warm, moist sensation engulf his head and work its way down the shaft. At first, there was scratching from teeth, but lips were curled.

As the lips reached the base of his manhood, Muhammed could feel the throat of his friend grabbing the top of his rod, massaging. As the lips worked their way up the rod, the cool air of the room tingled the damp staff.

"Mmm," Muhammed purred, causing the lips to entomb his member.

As Muhammed enjoyed the moment, he let his mind begin to wander. He imagined he was back at the Lodge, and they were in their cage. He could almost smell the lamb his brothers were preparing in the courtyard. Life was simpler then, everyone knew their purpose, knew the rules, and knew when they were going to die. While lost in memories, Muhammed lifted his hips as the lips reached his base.

As he continued to imagine being that young and enjoying his brother, Jane walked into the fantasy. She was wearing nothing.

"*What are you doing here?*" He asked.

"*You have been a naughty boy, and I am here to teach you a lesson,*" a leather paddle appeared in her hand, and thigh-high leather boots appeared on her legs.

Muhammed opened his eyes and watched the man gulp his mast.

"*Why did she show up?*" He wondered to himself as he placed a hand on the man's head and held himself deep inside the mouth until the man gagged.

"mmmmm, yes," Muhammed moaned, "You have always known how to get me going."

The man slipped the member out of his mouth and stroked it with his hands as he leaned forward and kissed Muhammed. Muhammed held the man's head, keeping their lips pressed together as he sat up.

"Take off your pants," Muhammed whispered. "It's time."

The man stood beside the sofa and removed his boots and pants. Muhammed used both hands to yank down the man's underwear by the seams.

"The agave nectar," Muhammed pointed at the desk.

The man waddled to the desk with his underwear wrapped around his knees before he seemed to realize the ridiculousness of the moment. He turned to Muhammed, blushing, and removed the underwear before returning. He stood before Muhammed, drizzling and massaging his limp member and scrotum with the nectar.

Muhammed pushed the bottle away as he leaned forward and guided the flaccid form into his salivating mouth. The nectar was sweet and had washed away the day's work. Muhammed twirled his tongue around the tip as it plumped. As the slender serpent grew and slid to Muhammed's throat, he grabbed the man's hips and pulled. He could feel the saliva seeping from the corner of his mouth. The man's scrotum patted Muhammed's chin.

Muhammed closed his eyes and fantasized as he slurped. He returned to his cage in the lodge. The day was bright. He felt a deep sense of companionship and love wash over him. He was lying with the man, his brother in arms, in the bed, and they were cuddling.

Jane appeared. This time, she was wearing a large strap-on. The whip was gone, but she still wore the same large leather boots and, this time had matching gloves that were form-fitting all the way to her elbow.

"You have been a bad boy, you must be punished," she had a devilish grin.

The next moment, everything was different. Muhammed's friend had disappeared. The sky outside the window was dark. Muhammed was kneeling on the bed, wearing pantyhose, and his wrists were chained to an iron headboard.

"Time for you to take it like a real man," Jane whispered in his ear as she ripped the pantyhose that covered his ass. She pressed the tip of the dildo against his anus.

"Call me Stacy, bitch," She moaned as she forced her way inside.

Muhammed opened his eyes and pulled away from his friend.

"Fuck me," he smiled into his friend's eyes.

"You are in a mood," the man said as he kissed Muhammed's forehead. "The last time I remember you asking to bottom was the day your Mayan friend aged out."

"I am having a weird day," Muhammed stood and removed his clothes.

"These are weird times," the man said as he tossed his shirt on the floor.

Muhammed moved a pillow to the arm of the sofa and leaned across it.

"This is a good position," he commented.

His toes barely reached the floor when the man pushed his shoulders into the cushion, standing behind him with the agave nectar.

"Bottoms up," the man said as he drizzled the nectar over Muhammed's ass. The juice was cold but stimulating. As it tickled its way down the crevice, He could feel his staff begin to petrify.

Muhammed reached back and pulled his ass cheeks wide.

"Start gently," he requested.

The man pressed his tip against Muhammed's sphincter and pushed firmly. Muhammed grunted as the man pulled back and pressed. After several firm presses, the man had worked his tip inside and rocked. Muhammed felt the man grab his hips and begin penetrating deeper. With each thrust, Muhammed held back his pleasure, but it grew louder.

Muhammed imagined as the man thumped, the swing of their scrotums becoming synchronized. This time, Stacy was waiting. Muhammed found himself chained like before, wearing ripped pantyhose, with Stacy behind him. The large strap-on a menacing threat.

"Why do you keep disappearing?" Stacy asked. "This is what you want. *This is your fantasy. You dirty little slut,"* Stacy forced the dildo into Muhammed and grabbed his hips.

"Wait," Muhammed gasped.

"There's no waiting," Stacy replied as she thrust deep inside, causing pangs of pleasurable pain to erupt.

Stacy stepped one foot over Muhammed's body and placed it beside him. The other foot behind his ass. Her legs squeezed him as she withdrew her fantastic appendage. As she plunged, her knees bent, and the weight of her vigor made Muhammed sink into the mattress with a yelp.

After several plunges, Muhammed could feel Stacy wrap her fingers around his love. She fucked him slower as she massaged his member. She knelt behind him and laid on his back. Muhammed had never understood or appreciated breasts, but hers seemed somehow erotic as they pressed against his back. As she continued to pump into him and stroke his flesh.

"*Finish for me before I return to the Harem,*" she coaxed.

"*Why are you here?*" Muhammed asked.

"*Because you want me, silly,*" Stacy giggled.

There was a bright flash, and Muhammed found he was lying on his back, his arms free. He was fondling Stacy's breasts as her sex worked his manhood.

"*Get me pregnant. Cum deep inside me. I know you want to fill me with your babies,*" her voice was honey as she leaned forward and kissed him passionately.

As her tongue filled his mouth, Muhammed wanted the moment to last but could feel his love begin to spasm.

He returned to the sofa from his fantasy. His friend was milking him while penetrating. Muhammed could feel his hot liquid shoot on both the sofa and his abdomen as the man's meat pulsated. The man pressed deep into Muhammed and released his liquid love.

"Just like old times in the cages," the man huffed as he pulled out. "It doesn't get any better than this."

"No, I could not imagine anything more gratifying," Muhammed smiled as they smooched.

"Unfortunately, all good things must come to an end," the man said as he collected his clothes. "It appears I am needed elsewhere," he pointed at his ear as he pulled his shirt over his head.

"Just when I found wonderland," Muhammed was sardonic.

"I will have the lads bring you to the workroom for your retirement."

The man pressed a finger against his ear as he pulled on his underwear and pants.

"Report on the status of the workroom," he demanded.

"Yep," Muhammed spoke to himself while the man was preoccupied with his events. "This fantasy is what dreams are made from."

"Good, send two lads to escort our guest. He is waiting."

The man returned his attention to Muhammed as he tied his boots, "I will meet you there soon. You will be safe until I arrive." The man kissed Muhammed. "You can still back out of retirement."

"No, this is what needs to be done to save the future," Muhammed's head rejected the man's statement.

"Still," the man walked to the door. "Your new girl is going to lose her shit when I kill you." He exited the room as two swordsmen entered.

Ceremonial Displays

The room of 'Fulfilled Desires' had almost no modifications. Muhammed considered it a proper workroom as he surveyed the changes. In the open space, on the marble floor in front of the giant glass doors, sat a chair. Beneath the chair was a large metal bin. There was a table and waste bin beside the chair. On the table sat an assortment of jars, a roll of aluminum foil, and medical utensils.

"I was informed the workroom had been prepared," Muhammed's skeptical voice was directed at the taller swordsman.

"These are the specifications that were provided," the figure replied. "The practitioner will be in and can answer any questions you have about today's retirement."

"I suspect you know the rules. I have no questions, just answers," Muhammed chastised as he thought, "*arrogant shit.*"

"Indeed, my apologies. Please sit, I would be happy to get you ready for the retirement."

"No," Muhammed rebuffed the offer. "I will enjoy standing in the light," He walked into the dust, dancing in the rays of sunshine near the windows, "until the host returns. There is no need to rush."

"As you wish," the swordsman replied. "We will be by the doors if you need anything. Also, please don't run; it makes things so much worse."

"Run," Muhammed scoffed. He wanted to educate the young man but decided the few minutes he had remaining were better spent soaking in his final memories of the Harem. "Take your places by the door. I will wait in the light."

"I apologize," Muhammed's old friend announced as he entered the room, carrying a crystal of liquor and two shot glasses. "It seems your protege has returned. She was upset that we had arrived and assumed control of the Harem. She killed several of our people before we subdued her."

"She should remain unharmed," Muhammed replied without diverting his eyes from the sun-soaked garden beyond the glass.

"All choices have consequences, even hers," the man's tone stiffened. "However, considering what she is about to see and the fact the council has marked her for future use, I am sure her actions have already been weighed."

"I have delayed this long enough," Muhammed walked to the chair and sat. He could see the leather straps coiled beneath his throne. "We should begin."

The two swordsmen walked toward Muhammed.

"No!" shouted the man. "I will prepare him. He is one of the last kings among us. Nobody is to touch him but me," he commanded as he stepped into the bucket that defined the work area's perimeter.

"First, we drink." The man handed Muhammed a glass.

"You know I do not drink," Muhammed replied.

"Nonsense," the man brushed off the assertion. "Killing a few brain cells and numbing your senses for your retirement always helps alleviate the discomfort. You have been labeled as expendable and no longer have any value, that is more than enough extra pain."

The man moved his pupils to the corner of his eyes, referencing the swordsmen by the door. Muhammed gave the man a puzzled look.

"Relax," he continued as he filled both shot glasses. "We do this together. I need something to calm my nerves, and I do not drink alone. Start sipping, and don't offend your host." The man side-eyed the swordsmen.

Muhammed knew the retirement would be painful, and his friend was trying to help. Plus, it would force his friend to be more brutal and violent during the ceremony if the swordsmen thought he had been disrespectful.

"Okay," Muhammed said. "I shall honor my host with a drink."

Muhammed gagged and sputtered as the alcohol seared his throat. The swordsmen broke into thunderous, uncontrollable laughter and were shouted out of the room by the man.

"Have another," the man refilled the glasses. "This one is to honor the council."

Muhammed coughed and sputtered, but there was less burning.

"Now, one for the Harem," the glasses were refilled. This time, Muhammed managed to drink the shot without the fireworks.

"Last one. Let's honor those who have come before us and who will survive us," the men gulped the shots. The man took the glass from Muhammed. He sat the glasses and crystal near the door where the swordsmen had been watching and returned to Muhammed's side. The man pressed his finger to his ear, "Tell me when the package is prepared. Then I will start."

"Life used to be simple in those days," Muhammed slurred.

"I am assuming you mean at the Lodge," the man replied.

"Yes, remember when all we had to do was serve the guests and protect each other. All the rules existed, sure, but only a handful were relevant."

"Yes," the man set a hand on Muhammed's

shoulder and squeezed. "Life was short and simple. Even the consequences were simple. If we served well, we were treated well, if we didn't, death was quick. None of this nasty retirement business."

"I know I have made mistakes," Muhammed felt no obligation to maintain decorum. "But you know something, I have no regrets. I have always acted in the best interest of the council, and even though I did things my way, I progressed the society."

"Do not forget why we are here and what we are doing. You have reached levels of honor that almost no one in history has mirrored. All who know you love and respect you." The man crouched and whispered in Muhammed's ear. "You were chosen because you have accomplished things that nobody else believed possible, you are eternal."

Muhammed heard the words, but his brain did not process the meaning. The alcohol had taken over.

"I know I have been weak. I shouldn't have brought her in, brought her up, promoted her; however you want to say it, but it was for the good of the entire Society of Ghost. She is superior, and we should embrace her power," Muhammed rambled.

"It seems the alcohol has taken over. I will not start unless you are sure about this."

"Do it," Muhammed drooled.

The man stepped in front of Muhammed.

"You know the rules." He raised his voice and spoke with a deep authority. "We are not deciders. We are implementors. We do not get to change our role as we see fit. It is not our prerogative to do as we please. The council has ordered your consequences, and they must be carried out." The man circled Muhammed and crouched in the bucket. "I will make this as quick as I can," the man whispered as he bound Muhammed's wrists, forearms, ankles, and knees to the wood. He stepped out of the bucket, "This is your party. How should we begin, acid, pliers, or knife?"

"Pliers," Muhammed's head drooped as he drooled.

The man lifted a pair of lineman's from the table and tussled Muhammed's hair.

"I am sorry, old friend, but I need to make this look good," he mumbled.

Muhammed grunted something non-comprehensible as the man gripped his pointer finger between the first and second knuckles. With a swift jerk, he pulled it backward, ripping off the skin. Muhammed shrieked in pain. A loud bang reverberated from the mirror on the far wall.

"Report," the man said as he pressed his finger to his ear. "Is the package secured, can I continue?"

"Ow," Muhammed sobbed. "Why are you trying to hurt me?"

"Fuck," the man gasped when he saw Muhammed's hand.

The areas where he had squeezed was shredded flesh with pinholes of blood seeping to the surface.

"I am so sorry, but I have to try again."

He stepped a foot across Muhammed's arm so the hand was between his legs, grabbed the oozing skinless digit, squeezed the lineman's handle with both hands and yanked with all his might. This time, the finger dislocated. Muhammed shrieked as his sobbing became vehement. The man grabbed the middle finger and repeated. He continued the process until all ten fingers had been completed.

Muhammed was begging by the time the man started snapping the finger's lower joints. Once all of Muhammed's fingers dangled limply, like knotted string flapping in the wind, the man returned the pliers to the table.

He secured a cotton ball in five of the six medical clamps and snapped his fingers several times in front of Muhammed's snot-riddled, sobbing, agony-filled face.

"Acid or knife?" He asked.

"Acid," Muhammed choked through the heaves.

Contributing to his suffering was the weight of the people he had slain who decided to fill his thoughts. A muffled screaming whispered from the mirror.

"Don't punish her. She is new. Let her release her rage when you are finished," he slurred.

"She is a twenty-two, she decides the consequences of the nines who are restraining her. Rules are rules," the man replied without moving his lips.

It almost appeared as though Muhammed smiled at the words.

"I am going to clean your face first so you do not get infected. I have been told this can help keep the burning down."

The man put on latex gloves and picked up a straight razor. He dipped his hand into a jar filled with white cream and spread it across Muhammed's face. It smelled like menthol. He shaved, revealing for the first time since entering the society, Muhammed's cheeks, lips, and chin. He removed the gloves and dropped them in the bucket before dawning a new pair. He dipped one of the cotton balls into a glass jar filled with clear liquid.

The cotton ball stung as it wiped across Muhammed's cheeks, nose, and chin. The smell burned his nose, made him cough, and turned his face red. Muhammed's nose stopped draining as he shook his head, trying to expel the fumes from his nostrils.

"The foil will ensure we do not drip anywhere without knowing," the man lifted the roll and wrapped Muhammed's from shoulder to knee.

"Here comes the hard part," the man stated as he dipped a cotton ball into a jar containing orange liquid. "I will be wiping fast. Try not to move so I do not get your eyes or nose."

He pressed the soaked cotton clamp against Muhammed's cheek, painting the entire canvas down the jawline to the chin. He lifted the cotton and repeated the process on the other side.

Muhammed's skin had already started bubbling and melting as the man dropped the clamp in the bucket. His eyes grew wide, and he grabbed the last two clamps. He dunked the clamps in the opaque white liquid in the final jar and wiped the liquid on Muhammed's disappearing flesh. The man appeared to be growing frantic as he dropped the clamps in the bucket and lifted the jar. He splashed the liquid against Muhammed's face until it was empty.

"Holy shit," the man pressed his forearm to his forehead. "That was scary. Don't ever do that."

Muhammed tried to speak, but his face was too rigid with pain. He couldn't move his mouth, and the sound that emerged was a low, deep moan from the base of his vocal cords that didn't seem to escape his throat.

"Don't talk, focus on breathing and staying awake," the man urged as he removed the foil, crushed it into a ball, and placed it inside the bucket below the chair.

He removed his gloves and walked behind Muhammed to set them in the bucket, away from everything else. Muhammed tried again but was unable to communicate.

"We have the knife," the man bellowed as he stepped in front of Muhammed and lifted the remaining clamp and the knife.

He cut away Muhammed's clothes. Muhammed sat naked, floundering in agony and humiliated.

"You are being retired. No, not longer are permitted to hold the Mark of Ghost. As we finish our ceremony, I must ensure it is removed and can never be restored."

The man sliced a circle around the mark. He clamped one edge of the epidermal patch and pealed. When the skin started to rip and stick to muscle, the man used the knife to ensure the integrity of the patch, even after Muhammed lost consciousness. Once the patch had been separated from Muhammed's still frame, the man held it in the air.

"He has been retired. It is done," his voice trumpeted.

He plunged the knife into Muhammed's side below the ribs on the left, then the right. As guttural, ancient war cries penetrated the mirror. Four swordsmen entered the room as the man stepped out of the bucket.

"There better be a good reason for this interruption," the man warned.

"He's in the front room," one of the swordsmen responded.

"Move the package to the secondary workroom," the man held his ear to speak.

He turned his attention back to the swordsmen, "It is your job to ensure nobody enters this room or touches the body. I will return to make certain his remains are incinerated."

Breaking In

Nasir

The heat pulled her from the deep dream that made her grin and moan unintelligibly. Before her eyes opened, she could feel the humidity drowning her every breath. Her muscles were stiff, and an airplane buckle was digging into her hip.

When she opened her eyes, she found herself in a jet fuselage. She raised her head over the seats to peek around. It was too dark to see anything except the light shining through the open door of the craft.

"Hello," she called into the darkness. Stacy reached for the window shade and lifted, then paused.

"Better not, I do not know who is waiting. Don't want to let them know I am awake."

Stacy inched her way down the aisle, trying to find any surprises before they found her. When she reached the edge of the light, she sat against the bathroom door to let her eyes adjust.

"Why was I left alone in the dark, abandoned?" She wondered as she looked into the darkness.

Once objects took form through the open door, Stacy rose. The emergency slide had been prepared. She clung to the side of the doorway, hanging her body out, to look around. There was nobody, she was alone.

"Is this part of the mission?" she wondered.

In the distance, an airport building looked promising, but there were no hangars, no other planes, and no sign of life or the Society.

She pulled herself back into the plane, stepped back, then sprang forward. As she sailed through the air, she yelled, "cannonball." She rolled as she landed. Stacy spread her arms and legs wide to steady her descent.

"That was pretty fun," Stacy recounted, "but it looks like too much work to climb back up. Plus, it's hot as shit." She looked to the sky and yelled, "Where the fuck am I?"

With no response, Stacy walked to the building in the distance. The pavement burned her heels through her shoes as she walked, so she zig-zagged from dirt patch to dirt patch.

The building had one room, and it was empty, except for a white wooden box with the name "Jane" painted on the side. There was one place she had been assigned that name, and it wasn't as a twenty-two. She tugged at her hair as she ground the toe of her shoe on the floor.

Stacy worried this was a trap and scanned the room for any obvious signs of surveillance. She crouched and waddled to a window, looking in all directions.

"*Fuck,*" she thought, "*nothing I can do. Whatever happens, happens.*"

Stacy waddled back to the box. The white paint was recent and made the lid stick. The hinges creaked as she lifted the lid.

"*Paint on a pig,*" her brain laughed.

Inside, Stacy found a note on rice paper, a nine's outfit and sword, and a pistol with two rounds. The note read:

> THE HAREM IS UNDER SIEGE. PROTECT IT AND RECEIVE GOOD CONSEQUENCES. SAVE IT AND BE REWARDED. IT IS LOCATED 49 KILOMETERS WEST.
>
> THE WAR HAS BEGUN.

Stacy remained crouched as she changed into the outfit and stuck the pistol in the waist of her panties. She strapped the sword outside her outfit and ate the rice paper. She waddled back to the window and looked out, still nothing, but she thought she heard something.

"*Just the wind,*" she thought after waiting for several minutes and seeing no movement. She stood and walked outside to look at her shadow.

"*Okay, west is above my shadow, so it must be that way.*" She held an arm in front of her to find something to walk toward in the distance. "That was a sound," but she didn't know what caused it.

Another sound screeched, it was tires. Stacy ran back into the building and crouched by the window. A bright orange Maserati's tires squealed as it drifted onto the airport runway. The driver spun the car in circles, raced from end to end, and sped around an invisible obstacle course, making the engine squeal as the tires smoke.

Stacy had seen enough, and the smell of the burning rubber was making her queasy. She stepped outside and walked to the car as it continued screaming and smoking. The driver didn't seem to notice, even after he parked and stepped outside to smoke. Stacy pulled her arm inside her garments and retrieved the pistol as she neared the car. The driver was leaning against it and admiring the passenger jet.

Stacy walked around the Maserati, keeping the pistol pointed at the man's head. As she rounded the engine, he noticed her out of the corner of his eye and jumped from the surprise. The cigarette fell from his mouth as he raised his hands and said something in Arabic.

"Keys," Stacy yelled, ensuring to enunciate.

"Okay," he replied in a thick accent. "They are in the car, but I am going with you, babe. Americans like to be called. 'babe,' right?" He stared at the gun while his voice quaked. "This is my dad's car. He will kill me if he knows I was racing it."

Stacy wondered if the man knew what was happening.

"You aren't going to kill me, are you? Who are you, and why are you here? Nobody ever comes here. Is that your jet? It's nice. I have cigarettes, do you like cigarettes?" He fumbled as he pulled the pack from his pocket and dropped it.

"Tell me your name," Stacy replied.

"I am Nasir," the man squeaked. "It's hot, can I have my water when you leave?"

"You will drive me," Stacy replied as she glanced at the car. She wasn't sure she would be able to make it out of the airport with a manual transmission.

Nasir relaxed as he slipped the cigarettes back into his pocket and leaned his back against the car.

"Okay, where are we going babe? I will drive you anywhere, but we have plenty of privacy."

Stacy pointed the gun into the air and fired a round. "The next one is for you."

"Right," Nasir stood and walked to the driver's door. "Business before pleasure."

"Wait," Stacy commanded. "I get in first, then you."

"After you, my queen," Nasir smiled as he jogged around the car and opened the door. "Someone as beautiful as you deserves to be treated as the desert flower that you are."

"Thank you, Nasir," Stacy stroked her hand down his chest while keeping her finger on the trigger with the other.

It was clear he was aroused. His manhood looked better than average; however, Stacy had orders. She lowered herself backward until her bum found the seat.

"Now go, get in and drive me west."

"West?" Nasir looked puzzled. "There's nothing out there but empty desert for thousands of kilometers. No, you want east, towards the city."

"I said west," Stacy repeated as she swung her legs into the car.

"As you wish, my queen," Nasir performed an extravagant bow as he closed the door.

As Nasir pulled out of the airport and drove west on a thin, one-lane road.

"You can put the gun away. The most I would do is fall in love with you and try to impress you with my money, hoping you would marry me and give me a family," his voice was soft.

Stacy placed the gun on the floor.

"You wouldn't want to fuck me for fun?" She asked as she grabbed his still erect member.

"Yes, of course," Nasir straightened in his seat. "You Americans are so straightforward."

"If you are a good boy, I might let you fuck me. We are going to my house, and if nobody is home, you can come inside," she teased as she stroked a few times before reclaiming her hand.

"Don't stop, that felt so good," Nasir relaxed.

"Be a good boy and drive," Stacy purred.

"Okay, but I hope you like music?" Nasir clicked on the radio.

"I love music. Stay on this road. We won't be able to miss my place."

"This is so exciting," Nasir exclaimed. "Nobody is going to believe this story. A sexy American took me hostage and brought me to her secret mansion for a wild night of passion."

"That is an exciting story," Stacy smiled. "I would love that to come true for you."

"Listen," Nasir placed a hand on Stacy's thigh. "There is nothing, and I mean nothing, you could do that would make me reject a night with you."

Stacy returned his hand and stroked his member a couple more times.

"I guess we'll find out," she purred.

Nasir pushed the car to reach its top speed. It was twenty-two minutes before the compound came into sight.

"Slow down," Stacy advised as she searched the surrounding desert. "If anyone is home, we need to sneak in before we can play."

There was a bend in the road as it reached the compound wall. Stacy could see the gate was open.

"Stop!" She exclaimed. She couldn't let an innocent be murdered.

Nasir pressed the brakes hard. The tires screeched as the pair flew forward in their restraints.

As their bodies were pulled back into their seats, a man with a sword raised above his head ran into the driveway, inside the compound walls, before crumpling to the ground in a hail of popping.

Fear smacked Stacy across the face with the reality of the situation: the Harem was being dismantled, and everyone who made their way inside was going to die. She looked at Nasir and could see the adrenaline begin to take over as his breathing became heavy and his jaw clenched. She opened her door and slid into a couch in an instant.

"Hey," she called to Nasir as he squeezed the life from the steering wheel without response. "Hey, babe, look at me," Stacy leaned into the car and yanked on his dick hard. It seemed to do the trick, and Nasir turned his head.

"Listen," Stacy said. "You can come inside if you want, but you should try to get out alive."

"Yeah," Nasir whispered as he looked through the compound walls. "Yeah, fuck this. My boss would kill me if he knew I took a car."

"Nasir," Stacy snapped her fingers by his cheek. "Get out of here!"

"I'm going to die, aren't I?" He asked.

"I promise you, if you make it out alive, I will find you, and I will fuck you better than you can imagine. Go!" Stacy yelled.

She slammed the door and ran toward the compound wall. She crouched with her back against it as she watched Nasir spin the car in a cloud of smoke.

Puh-Keww

The rear window of the Maserati shattered as the car spun to a stop. Stacy strained her eyes as she searched for signs of life inside the dark vehicle.

Puh-keww... dink!

A grey spot appeared as paint flew from the car, followed by screaming in Arabic as the tires smoked and the car shot down the road.

Puh-keww

The car kept rocketing as Stacy crept to the compound entrance.

Puh-keww... crunch!

Some of the wall above Stacy's head tumbled and dusted her with pebbles and shrapnel. Stacy dropped flat to the ground and slithered into the compound, hiding between the bushes and the inside of the wall, wondering if it was too late.

Sword Dancing

The wood chip mulch was much softer than she had imagined. Her knees were leaving a trail of divots as the trimmed bushes scraped her side. She worked her way toward the Arboretum parking lot. Every few yards, she stopped to peek through the hedges, searching for signs of Harem life.

The first time she stopped, she watched the dead swordsman's blood pool in the driveway as several men lined up outside the main door. They wore black military uniforms, carried machine guns, and were not invited. One of their friends lay not far from the swordsman on the grass. His abdomen had been sliced open, and a pile of sausage links had spilled out.

The second time Stacy stopped was when she got stuck on a protruding branch. She struggled to free herself until several intruders vaulted over the wall in front of her. She froze and held her breath, fearing she would die, stuck in the bushes, impotent to assist, but they crouched and walked toward the doors to "Pleasurable Choices."

Stacy worked her fingers in the bush and cloth quickly, struggling against the relentless grasp of the wood. As she continued to fight for freedom, she watched the men line up beside one of the large glass doors. The first man opened the door as the other men ran inside in what appeared to be magic, a hoard of swordsmen swarmed from all directions. Some ran across the grass, some hurdled garden bushes, some sprinted across the marble patio, some appeared from nowhere inside the room, and some poured in from neighboring rooms. Stacy suspected they had located and used the hidden Harem hallways and tunnels.

The guns fired, swordsmen fell, but the finale was unavoidable. The intruders were hacked to pieces in a grotesque ballet of blood, bodies, and bullets. It was the most wonderful, mesmerizing, and brutal thing Stacy had ever seen. The swordsmen seemed to have a deep rage that did not subside even as the lifeless bodies fell to the marble, one still firing its weapon.

Snap, snap, snap

Bits of the wall rained down on Stacy's head. Deciding it was time to force her freedom, she used both hands to snap the branch. When she looked at the battle scene, all the bodies and swordsmen had vanished, pools of blood remained.

The final time Stacy stopped, she could see the wall of the Arboretum. A man with a gun raised was standing outside with his back to the corner. Stacy knew she would need to run across the open parking lot and grass to end him before he had a chance to make a sound. It was almost thirty yards, so she needed to wait for the perfect moment.

The man was speaking into a radio, but his voice did not carry, and the words were faint. He looked disinterested in the events that were transpiring and let his gun fall and hang by some form of harness. He pulled a pack of cigarettes from beneath his vest. After he lit a cigarette, he held it with his lips as he opened his pants and urinated. He flicked the ash from the cigarette with one hand and held his drain pipe in the other.

Stacy knew this was her chance. The bushes etched her face as she flew through them. The man was so focused on watching his stream that he didn't notice her running across the parking lot. Stacy pulled her sword loose and sprinted as the man lifted his eyes as she entered the grass. They grew wide as he shook his member, as though he was trying to release the last drops.

He dropped himself and his cigarette, He flailed his hands, trying to aim his gun, but was too late. Stacy's sword struck with precision. It entered the base of his neck, under the Adam's apple. The man lifted the gun, but Stacy forced the barrel to his side as he squeezed the trigger. Dirt exploded from the grass as the man's magazine emptied.

Stacy examined the look on the man's face. It was not horror or pain; it was surprise. As she tried to pull the sword out of the man's neck, she realized it was stuck. She braced her back leg on the flat, dry grass as she kicked the man in the chest. He stumbled backward and fell on the bush. His body landed on the wood chips against the wall, with his feet sticking into the air.

Stacy crawled to the body and pulled the legs down. She dug a hole in the chips below his throat and sliced his arteries. As the hole filled and overflowed, she liberated his radio and crawled into the Arboretum. A swordsman had been waiting.

Stacy stood on the cobblestones and motioned for the swordsman to lead her inside. He remained motionless, staring at her in the cool, dark forest. She took a step to the side to circle him and proceed. He pointed his sword at her. Then, he swung. Stacy flipped her sword in her grip. The back rested against her forearm as she rolled away from his attack.

"Stop," she whispered. "I am here to help."

The swordsman swung. She held up her arm to block. The swords clanked loudly. Hers pounded her muscle. Stacy looked around to see if anyone had heard. Nobody was approaching. The swordsman swung. Another loud clank. Her arm sang.

"Last chance," Stacy warned as she circled him.

The cobblestones were rounded at the top and needed to be replaced but provided excellent footholds. The swordsman swung. Stacy bent low, compressed her legs, and exploded forward. She parried. The blade's edge sliced to the spine as she sailed past. She used her momentum to return to a standing position behind the man. As he turned, internals protruded.

"Stop!" Stacy commanded. "You are injured, and I need to be on my way."

The man looked at his stomach and then at Stacy. His arms wobbled as he raised the sword above his head. The action stretched his middle, what was protruding, dangled.

"Okay," Stacy replied. "It was an honor, and you will die with dignity."

She raised her sword parallel to the ground. Spinning in a circle, she punched the edge into his chest, slicing his heart in half.

Stacy used a hand to help the man keep the sword raised as she guided his body to the floor. His face had no emotion. A single tear rolled from the corner of his eye.

"I am sure you were quite the character. I would have respected you, and we might have been friends," she eulogized, using her fingers to close his eyes. "Now, I must get into the Harem."

Stacy jogged, believing any other intruders, swordsman or otherwise, would have heard the commotion. She was wrong. As she ran from the jungle into the coniferous forest, where the Arboretum entrance faced the Harem, two more swordsmen leaped from behind trees. The one on the left was taller and chubbier.

"Really?" She exasperated. "Look, one of your guys is dead back there. You might want to grab the body and let me pass. I didn't want to kill him, but he wouldn't let me pass."

The men lifted their swords.

"For Fucks sake," Stacy growled. "I don't have time for this. Please let me pass, and you can kill all the other people you see."

The taller one turned and side-stepped forward.

"Hey, tubby, have you seen fat fencers? Turning sideways does not make your belly smaller," Stacy's anger was taking over as she watched the shorter one start to circle. "I see you, little guy," her voice a low growl.

She stepped toward the tall man, and he thrust. Stacy held her sword as she spun. The swords clanked. As she stepped forward, the man overrose his wild slash. Stacy turned her sword parallel to the floor. The swords clanked as she felt a burning in the rear of her shoulder. She looked back, the tip of the short man's sword had reached her, leaving a shallow laceration.

"I was being nice," she explained through a roll that ended with the edge of her sword severing the tendons behind the tall man's knee.

She used her weight to roll into a kneeling position. He fumbled as he lost control, using his sword as a cane to keep from losing all balance.

The short swordsman had circled and was approaching from Stacy's back. This time, she was waiting. She spun on one knee. As she deflected his attack, her sword vibrated pain into her hand. She rose to her feet and thrust. He dodged. He slashed, and she dove behind a tree. She poked her head out to see where he stood. He slashed, causing bark to spray.

Stacy looked around, then up. There was a branch, but it was in the short man's view. She stuck her head into danger on the opposite side of the tree, and the man thrust, almost striking her face. She looked, he was circling that side. He swiped at her head. Another spritz of bark sprayed the air.

Stacy stepped under the branch and jumped. She pulled herself into the tree. Stacy skipped to another branch as the man entered view. He continued circling, looking for her. As he passed, Stacy dropped flat to the ground behind him. He spun with a slash that passed over her. He had spun so hard that he couldn't stop.

As he spun, she rocketed to her feet. She held her blade in both hands with the sharp edge facing her. Stacy lowered the blade over his spinning head and found his neck. She jerked it as hard as her muscles would permit. The blade sliced through his soft tissue and ground on bone. His spinning stopped. His body became limp as his weight fell to the ground. She stepped back, releasing the sword and raising her hands. She didn't want to cut herself.

"That's what you get for poking me without permission, asshole," she ridiculed as she stepped on the dying face and retrieved her sword.

The other swordsman was still struggling to stand as Stacy approached. She stopped two meters away in case he wanted to attempt one last valiant effort.

"Your war is not with me. Remember, I let you live. I must get inside. Point to any more swordsmen that are hiding in the Arboretum so I can avoid them and be on my way."

The man let his body drop to the floor and struggled to lift his sword above his chest. Stacy walked to him and pulled the sword from his hands.

"No, your consequence is that you must live with this. You do not choose your fate." She hurled the sword through the trees.

Stacy found herself kneeling beside the door, searching the garden for any more dangers. The swordsmen were a problem, but not the enemy. She couldn't see any threats, so she prowled her way to the edge of the Harem and rested her back to the wall of the cages.

Sisterhood

Stacy tried to sneak into the cages to find her sisters, but the door was locked. Jumping, she grabbed the top of the wall. The edges of her gored shoulder wound ripped. She looked over the wall as she pulled. Five dead intruders scattered the lawn. Six protectors lay near, or on top of, them. Stacy swung a leg over and sat up.

Puh-keww . . . snap!

An invisible assailant whizzed by her head. She tumbled to the ground and landed on a dead nine. The blood-soaked her arm. Stacy lay silent, her brain cursing the sniper, as she looked into the cage. Another dead intruder lay under a swordsman.

Stacy sat with her knees bent. She dusted her hands on her sides and rose. Searching through the large glass doors revealed no additional secrets.

Examining the dead nine revealed the flag of India. This must be the Asian hallway. Feeling bad for the Indians was easy, but their deaths were not unexpected, they had always been among the weakest.

Stacy opened the door and stepped inside. The perfumed smoke burned her senses. A noise from the closet caught her off guard. Crouched, she unsheathed her sword, rounded the bed, and crossed the hand-made rug.

It sounded like moaning. Stacy's heartbeat her ribs as she swallowed her fear. The tall walls stood over her, watching like judging giants as she reached out her hand. The gold knob turned. The 'click' sent a shock of fear up her arm.

It was fifteen seconds before she cracked the door. The closet was too dark to see inside. Stacy threw the door open and ran to the bed, waiting for something, anything, to happen.

Moaning made its way from the closet. Stacy crouched and inched forward, sword ready. When she reached the opening, she stopped, held her breath, and leaped inside.

Nobody was there. Stacy stood, took a deep breath, and flicked on the light. She had never been in this closet. All the clothes were majestic. There were pinks, purples, bright greens, and blues. There was a wall of saris that had come from her fantasies.

As Stacy admired the collection, she heard a murmur. It made its way from the formal dresses. She crouched to look under the clothes and saw no feet. She readied her sword and advanced. Reaching the dresses, she yanked them aside. The sword thrust, stopping before piercing the face of the Indian eight. She had several bubbling bullet holes in her chest.

She tried to speak from behind closed eyes, but no words came out. She had been hidden on a shelf, most likely when the assault got underway. Stacy turned and walked to the opposite wall. Light streaked through the shadows when she pulled the clothes away. Stacy turned to look at the eight as her pity grew. She sheathed her sword.

"I will be back. I am sorry your nines did not do their job."

She walked to the dead intruder in the main room. Rolling the body over, she tried to release the gun, but it was stuck. Cursing, she stomped on the dead chest and face. She felt the nose break, then the jaw, then the cheek. As her blind rage started to dissipate, she noticed the sidearm. She freed it from the holster and returned to the closet.

"I am sorry, you do not deserve this. Nobody does," she held the gun to the woman's forehead and squeezed the trigger.

Her ears were deafened as she dropped the gun and exited the closet. She was greeted by half a dozen nines with drawn swords. Surprisingly, they were joined by several eights who also carried swords. They circled her as she removed her sheath, sword still inserted, and let it slip to the floor. She removed her head covering.

"Stop!" A familiar voice yelled. "It's Stacy!"

Orla pummeled her way into the circle and swept Stacy off the floor with an embrace.

"Thank god you are home," Orla rejoiced.

"I am sorry it took so long to find my way home," Stacy felt tears beginning to stream.

"She was too far gone, I had to end her pain," She pointed toward the closet.

"We know," Orla consoled as she lowered Stacy. "We have lost nines. It's bad."

Stacy's heart fell into her stomach.

"What about mine? Where's Pru, Ginny, Nancy, and Bea?"

She tried to run from the room, but Orla held her back.

"No, where are my sisters?" Stacy screamed as she wrestled to free herself. "Let me go! Where are my sisters?"

"Stop," Orla hugged Stacy. "It's okay. Listen to the sound of my voice. I am here, and you are home."

Orla continued squeezing as Stacy fought. Too overwhelmed with emotion, fatigued from the day, and injured, Stacy could not break the embrace. She let herself collapse and continued crying and begging for her sisters.

Orla said something to one of the nines in an Asian language. The nine disappeared and reappeared a few minutes later. Orla took a report.

"Someone is here to see you. It's too dangerous to leave this room, so we had to sneak her in. When you are ready, I will let you go," Orla released her hold.

Stacy wiped her eyes as a blood-soaked nine entered. The American flag visible through the thick red sap. It crouched at the edge of the circle.

"Stacy," the voice had lost its joy, its youth, its innocence.

"Pru?" Stacy whispered.

"They said you betrayed us," Prudence removed her head covering. "The swordsmen are supposed to kill you the moment they see you. I told them I would never believe it." Prudence sat on her bum, patting her lap. "Can we cuddle for a while? I miss cuddling with you."

Stacy crawled to her Harem sister, laid her head in Pru's lap, and closed her eyes.

Pru stroked Stacy's hair as she spoke to Orla, "Get someone to bandage her shoulder, and do not let the boys know."

Orla nodded and instructed the Asian nines. Moments later, another blood-soaked nine entered carrying a blue plastic container. The nine knelt behind Stacy and gave Prudence a long, silent stare.

"She didn't do it," Prudence mouthed. "You know her."

The nine worked quickly. First, cutting away the surrounding clothing, then cleaning and bandaging.

"It's done," the voice whispered.

"Why didn't you say hi, Bea," Stacy asked without opening her eyes.

"It's your fault," Beatrice accused as she stood.

"I would never hurt my sisters or the Harem," Stacy sat up in disbelief at the accusation.

"Not this, Stacy. Nancy is gone, and you didn't stop it. She's dead because she turned twenty-six, and you didn't stop it, and you could have stopped it, and you didn't." Beatrice's face twisted with rage as tears matted her lashes. "It's all your fault, and you should have done something, and I hate you and—"

"Stop!" Prudence shouted. "Stop that. We are all in the same boat. That doesn't help."

Bea ran from the room as Stacy responded. Stacy's eyes watered as she realized Beatrice was correct. She was a twenty-two, she could have stopped it. She should have done more, but the Australians promised Nancy would be safe. She wiped her eyes and stood.

"Where are the Australians?" She asked. "They have some explaining to do."

"We cannot walk there," Pru replied. "The halls are still swarming with swordsmen, and there are too many. They will kill us if they catch us protecting you.

"Fine," Stacy retorted as she reaffixed her head covering. "Then I will go by myself. Make sure Bea is waiting for my arrival."

Prudence gave Stacy an odd look of skepticism, then said, "Orla, tell the Asians to swarm us so Stacy isn't spotted. We are going to the Australian's cage."

"That's at the end of the Pacifica hallway. You'll never make it," Orla exclaimed.

"Do it!" Stacy commanded. "I need to give consequences."

Orla barked orders in an Asian language. The message was translated into several other languages until everyone in the room understood the mission: Make it to the Australian's room without dying.

Stacy crouched in the center of the huddle as the group exited. They walked through the spokes with their swords drawn. Prudence had not exaggerated. There were four swordsmen lining every cage door. Stacy wondered if anyone had remained to defend the Lodge.

As they reached the entrance to the Pacifica hallway, all of the swordsmen collapsed into an ocean around the group. Their swords providing a menacing threat to every life. A mysterious man descended the staircase and yelled something that halted the attack.

"Jane," the man called. "I know you are in the group. Please do not let all of your companions be chopped away like weeds from the garden. We have no ill will toward them, and they will remain safe so long as you make good choices."

"Jane's not the enemy. She is one of us. If you are going to take her, you have to take all of us."

Orla yelled something in an Asian language, and the nines took a step toward the swordsmen.

"Stop!" Stacy shouted, Orla echoing in a translated language. "I am here. You know the rules. You cannot lie."

"I know the rules?" the man mocked. "Tell all your companions to take a knee. I want to see you as you surrender." The swordsmen parted as the man approached.

"Do it, Orla," Stacy ordered.

All the women took a knee, and Stacy removed her head covering.

"Good girl, this next bit may be uncomfortable," the man said something to the swordsmen. A group weaved through the kneelers and bound Stacy with chains.

"You will wait for me in your cage, Jane," the man said as the majority of the swordsmen returned to their previous positions.

The group that bound Stacy carried her to the American cage, dropping her inside.

Distress Undressed

"Stacy?" The voice had weathered. "We couldn't protect Nancy. We tried, but..." Ginny faded into despair.

"Hey, I am here to make things right," Stacy smiled while struggling against the weight of her shackles.

Ginny helped lift her to a more comfortable position. The cage door opened as Ginny spoke.

"Leave us," the unknown man commanded.

Ginny looked at Stacy cross-eyed before she strode from the apartment. The look filled Stacy with comfort and calmed her nerves. It reminded Stacy that her sisters were still part of her, and she a part of them.

Like Nancy had said, "*Stacy, we love you. You are our sister, no matter what you are doing or where you find yourself.*"

As she focused on those words, Stacy could not restrain her desire to see Nancy, to hold her, to hug her, to cuddle. She even wouldn't mind Nancy getting temperamental and bitchy. She missed *mama-bear*.

The smell of sulfur and body odor ripped Nancy from Stacy's mind and returned her to the man standing over her. She knew that if she was free, the swordsmen would die, then this man, then the Australians for failing Nancy.

The man crouched while ensuring he was beyond her reach. He seemed to know she wouldn't hesitate to give him a swift foot to the face.

"Jane," he shook his head. "You are not an authorized twenty-two. You are a rogue eight. You are a Harem beauty and have stepped beyond your authority and position. I apologize that you have been misled, but you made the choice to accept the unauthorized promotion and assignments. I do not exceed my position or authority, so I have no other choice than to give you your consequences." The man stood and faced the hall, "I am headed to the workroom. Take her to observe."

Both horror and relief washed over Stacy. She knew the man could not lie because of the rules, but she also knew the types of consequences that would be provided for such transgressions. Fearing unimaginable torture, Stacy did not resist as the men carried her from the room.

Nines and beauties alike amassed in the hallways to watch as she was carried in a procession of swordsmen. The Lithuanians and her sisters caught her eye as they unsheathed. Stacy crossed her eyes and stared at them until they smiled and understood.

Stacy forced a smile in an attempt to somehow say, "I love you, be safe, survive."

The men carried her to a dark room she had never noticed. It was quite large and had a window facing the 'Fulfilled Desires' room. A triangle of light covered a chair in front of the window as the door closed. The men were gentle as they sat her in the chair.

"The package is prepared," a shrill voice said to an invisible listener. Stacy looked around, but there was blackness and the window.

"Watch," a hand appeared from the dark and pointed through the window.

A man was sitting in a chair facing the garden. Stacy studied the man's head, but it could be anyone. He appeared to be bound to the chair, which was in a large mettle bin. Stacy wondered if there was water in the bin. She thought it looked like the man was in an electric chair, but there were no wires, just a table with some glass jars and a pair of pliers.

The unknown man from before stepped into the bin and crouched before lifting the pliers. Stacy could feel her heart start to race as she leaned forward. She wondered if the man was going to pull teeth like they did in movies. She leaned to see who was sitting in the chair as the unknown man gripped a finger of the hostage and yanked. The bound man turned his head as he screamed in agony.

"Dear *god,*" Stacy's mind became frantic as she leaped to the window.

Smashing the cuffs and chains against it, she whaled, "Stop! This is too much!"

What seemed like a thousand hands yanked her from the window. Stacy used all her might to thrash and rebel against the darkness, but it forced her back into the chair. Hands pulled her hair, clasped her face, and forced her eyelids open.

"Yes, we have restrained her," the voice spoke.

"I am going to kill you all," Stacy growled through the jaw they held shut.

A hand slapped flat against the front of her face, splintering paint through her nose and into her eyes and brain.

"Whoever did that is going to suffer the most," she continued her threats as tears streamed.

They forced her to watch as the unknown man broke every joint in Muhammed's hands.

"No!" Stacy focused on squeezing the scream from every part of her body as the unknown man spoke to Muhammed.

He was placing a hand on a medical clamp. The flat hand met her face. Stacy wiggled her nose in an attempt to see if it was pain or broken.

"You will drown in your brain juice. Muhammed taught me that one," she growled.

The hand returned, and Stacy thought she felt the bridge of her nose shift. The man shaved Muhammed and wiped his face with something from one of the jars. He finished by waterboarding Muhammed with a white liquid.

Stacy could feel her urine release as Muhammed revealed the side of his face. It was blistered and melting. Vomit burned her throat as it sprayed through her teeth, lips, and the fingers holding her mouth.

Stacy strained with all her might to stand. She hovered several inches above the chair before she was forced to splash into her puddle. The smell of her urine grew noticeable as she watched the man lift a knife. He cut away Muhammed's clothes, peeled the skin and mark off of Muhammed's naked body, and stabbed Muhammed multiple times before returning the knife to the table.

The hands released Stacy as she slid from the chair and collapsed on the floor. She permitted herself to mourn because she knew the freedom would not last long and her retribution would be swift.

"Stand," the voice penetrated the darkness as the door at the end of the room opened. "You are being moved to the office."

Even if Stacy wanted to stand, she was too weak. She had used all her strength to try to reach Muhammed and thought she might have pulled several muscles in the process.

"Fuck you," she spit at the invisible offenders.

"Drag her," the voice prompted the swordsmen.

A large group of swordsmen, nines, and eights had gathered in the hallway when they heard the screaming. They stared as she was dragged past. Her assailants took the long way to the office to ensure everyone got a good look at her urine-soaked clothes.

As she was dragged, the wet cloth on her ass felt freezing, they had succeeded in humiliating her, but she vowed to have the final retribution. She couldn't believe she had pissed herself.

"*Melting flesh is too much, it's way worse than melting a man's mouth shut,*" she rationalized but knew her urine was from something much deeper.

She focused on her breathing and slowing heart to calm her nerves. Like many, Muhammed was gone, and there was nothing she could do but avenge the transgression. When they entered the office, Stacy was half expecting him to be standing there, explaining what she saw was fake, a test. Instead, the room contained her and the five swordsmen. They cut away her clothes before pushing her onto the sofa. Seconds later, the unknown man entered. His face revealed his surprise as he looked at her, then the swordsmen.

"She's naked?" he pointed at her sex, directing the question to the swordsman who had taken a position behind the desk.

"She pissed herself," the man said in the peculiar voice that had been lurking in the dark.

"That was some scary shit," the unknown man replied. "I pissed myself." He turned to Stacy, "I am assuming you prefer to be clothed."

"Either way, I am going to kill them and you," she wiped her face with her forearm.

"Maybe them, after our discussion, but I am much too important for you to kill," the man motioned towards the swordsmen, who looked at each other nervously. "But, what I am hearing is that you have no clothing preference. I see your nose is bleeding. It may be broken." He turned to the swordsmen, "Someone needs to explain that."

"She was being too loud," a tall, feeble-minded-sounding one stated. "I was trying to get her to be quiet so you could finish."

"I didn't know you had been given the authority to give consequences," the man responded rhetorically.

As the tall one responded, the unknown man turned to Stacy.

"I am going to have your shackles removed. They are so barbaric; you understand why they were necessary."

"Clothed," Stacy held her chin high.

"I didn't hear you," he responded.

"I prefer to be clothed," her voice more decisive.

"Go to her cage and get some," the man was pointing to a stout swordsman with golden eyebrows.

"Yoga pants and a T. Tell the girls it is for me, they will know which ones to get," Stacy interrupted. She wanted to send everyone a signal that she was safe.

"Okay," the unknown man continued with slight annoyance in his voice, "get some yoga pants and a T." The stout blond raced from the room as the unknown man pointed at the tall one, "unshackle her."

Stacy spread her legs in the face of the man as he let her ankle chains clang to the floor. She laid back on the sofa and raised her hands above her head. He climbed on top of her and reached for her wrists as planned.

"You are my special friend," she arched her back and pressed her tits against him. "Unlock me, and we can play."

A sloppy grin soaked his face as he fumbled with the keys, the tip of his excitement poking outward. As the irons fell over the sofa and clanked to the floor, Stacy grabbed his face with both hands and bucked her head against his nose. He sneezed, spattering blood across her face and shoulders. Stacy rolled him to the floor and climbed on top as he clutched his gushing nostrils.

"Stop," the unknown man pulled her by the shoulders and tossed her back on the sofa. "Our discussion is not over."

He kicked the tall one in the side.

"You should know better. Get back over there."

"Tell me more about the discussion," Stacy was calm.

"I am waiting for your clothes," the man replied.

"No need. I requested those so my girls wouldn't storm in and kill everyone," Stacy smiled.

"That was a good choice by our newest twenty-two," the man returned the smile.

"You said I was rogue," Stacy was so confused.

"You were, but you aren't. Your punishment was to watch the retirement ceremony," the man nodded his head with raised eyebrows.

"I am hearing that I will be in charge," Stacy felt elation and couldn't wait to start making improvements to the Harem.

"Absolutely not," the man's words beat the joy from her heart. "The replacement is in the other room. You will get to hear him address all of the Harem staff in a few minutes."

"You intend to make me operational. I can handle that as long as my girls are kept safe," she negotiated.

"You saw the retirement ceremony. It's either promotion or retirement. Let me know your choice," the man sat on the desk.

"That isn't a choice," Stacy rebutted.

"Yes, it is, you just do not like the options," he corrected.

"Clearly, promotion is the only option," she tugged her hair. "I am already trained."

"Not correctly, you will be retrained, and you will relearn all of the rules, techniques, and technologies."

"I was already on a mission," she bragged.

"I saw," he applauded. "It was impressive for someone who hasn't been trained until you got hit by a car in the middle of an abandoned desert road, captured by the local government, almost kidnapped by the fives, and then were used to lead the fives to the Harem."

"I was unaware of some of those things," Stacy frowned and examined the patterns on the floor. "I assume people died because of me."

"Stand outside until I call you," he addressed the swordsmen.

Once they were gone, he approached Stacy.

"That is a good assumption; however, the fives have already captured several of our people and are holding them in unknown locations. They would have found this place either way."

"Muhammed was retired because of my failures, at least, that is what I assume," Stacy used her finger to draw circles on her knee.

"No, we are implementing the FOWLERI protocol. You have been chosen," the man whispered.

"FOWLERI protocol?" Stacy looked at the man in disbelief.

"Yes, you are going to act as an overt twenty-two, but you will be reporting to the council. Saying even this much is a risk. You will be briefed in a more secure location." The man rose and yelled, "Come back!"

The swordsmen returned.

"Where the hell are her clothes?" The unknown man growled as he broke the rules.

"I have them," the blond held up a stack of garments.

"Tell me if you want to take a sword or have one given to you for the next bit," the man directed the words at Stacy.

"Put my clothes on the desk and hand me your sword," Stacy pointed at the tall one who looked at the unknown man.

"I don't know why you are looking at me. A twenty-two gave you an order. The rest of you, give me your swords. You are about to make the sweetest kind of love."

As the unknown man exited the office and closed the door, a symphony of pleas and screaming resounded throughout the Harem.

The Layover

Speedy Relocation

"How was the flight?" Asked the driver.

"I didn't realize how long we would be in the air, and the landing was rough," grumbled the passenger.

"I am sure a man like you has handled worse," the driver seemed to be hinting at a secret knowledge. "Are you here for business or pleasure?"

"I am not sure. I suppose business, but it will be pleasurable," Sam was noncommittal.

As the car departed the airport, the driver continued the inquisition, "It's hot today. Will you relax and enjoy the heat?"

"I apologize," Sam replied, "but after the long flight, I need a few minutes to relax in silence. It helps me rejuvenate. I hope you don't mind."

"No problem," the driver smiled. "I can wake you when we arrive."

Sam hadn't meant to drift to sleep, but in the next moment, the driver's voice was bringing him back to life.

"We will need to drive fast through this part. It may be bumpy. The sniper has not been removed yet."

The engine of the car revved as the desert sped past. Through the windshield, Sam could see the compound wall, an oasis beckoning. As the walls of the compound grew, so did Sam's concern. There was a bend in the road before the wall, and they were traveling over 225 KMH.

"Umm…" Sam pointed at the nearing bend, but the driver seemed unfazed. "You may need to slow down," Sam asserted, only to be greeted by more silence. "Hey!" Sam shouted as they were at the corner. "Stop!" Sam shouted as he grabbed the seatbelt and strapped in.

As his belt clicked, the tires screeched, and the car started turning sideways. Smoke and the smell of burning filled the air. The compound entrance started on one side, but as the car screamed, it circled.

With another screech of the tires, the entrance to the compound swerved to the front of the car and swallowed it without a scratch. Once inside the walls, Sam could feel the seatbelt pulling his chest and torso.

Sam took half a second to reposition himself in his seat. About to let his thoughts be known, he realized the driver was speaking.

"I apologize for any discomfort. Earlier, there was an incident. Please make your way to the first room and wait to be greeted." The car stopped at the entrance.

"You seem to know what you are doing, I suppose you drove reasonably," Sam opened the door.

Sam saw several men with swords. They wore the same outfits as the driver and reminded him of his days as a nine. The ones in the garden were pulling a military corpse from a bush. The deep cut in the throat ripped as they carried it toward a building that was billowing smoke.

"Did my driver have his sword, and what are they burning? It smells like death," Sam's mind wandered.

Remembering where he was, he realized death itself was being burned.

"You have arrived!" an unknown man called from the Harem entrance. "Come, you must witness the retired leader for the record. Tell me the name you have chosen, and do not say 'Muhammed,' or I will have to retire you, too."

"I am Jacque," Sam replied. "I have always found it exotic and intriguing."

"Wow, that says a lot, Jacque. I've never heard a French name called 'exotic,' I suppose it's a matter of perspective," the man held a hand out.

"I agree," Sam performed the secret shake. As they passed through "Pleasurable Choices," Sam admired the wide selection of refreshments.

A gaggle of swordsmen were huddled against the far wall.

"This is where guests choose which beauty or beauties they want, and then the women will entertain them in this room," the unknown man pushed open ornate doors to reveal a large marble room.

The swordsmen filed in and dotted the perimeter. A man's body was strapped to a chair in a metal bucket facing the garden.

"This is the room of 'Fulfilled Desires.' As you can see, there is a magnificent view, minus Muhammed. The guests are permitted to take the beauties into the garden. Please inspect the body."

Sam walked to Muhammed and crouched.

"I suppose I am checking to see if he is dead. Hand me a pair of gloves," he looked at the man with doubt.

He pulled the gloves over his fingers.

"He has lost blood," Sam looked up at the man. "I can't imagine anyone could survive this level of damage. I can't find a pulse. He has to be dead. We should move him to the kiln so the beauties don't see. They could revolt."

"Speak louder," the unknown man commanded. "Is he alive or dead?"

"He is dead. We need to burn the body before the beauties see," he matched the unknown man's volume.

"Let's hurry then. You need to address the beauties to see if they accept you," the unknown man unstrapped the restraints.

Sam followed his lead as they carried Muhammed's lifeless body to the kiln. The fire was raging, but nobody seemed to be tending it as they entered.

"Wait outside, make sure none of the beauties peak in the windows or see. I will put him in the kiln," the man guided Sam to the door, locking it as Sam stepped into the garden.

"Tour the grounds. I have an appointment in the office." The man stated as he rejoined Sam. "Please meet me at the top of the cage steps in thirty minutes."

"Seems easy enough," Sam replied as he pointed to the other building in the garden. "That looks interesting."

"That's the Arboretum. Time has been put into creating a true oasis. The most amazing waterfall is in the desert section."

"I might take a look," Sam was intrigued by the thought of a desert waterfall. "I have not received the limits as they pertain to the beauties."

"Because you set the limits. You are in charge. I should warn you, though, I know you used the *Pulaxo Technique.* You might not want to let the beauties or nines know, and you may want to be friendlier to them. They outnumber you, and a revolt would not end well."

"Understood," Sam took the warning seriously, knowing he would enforce the rules, nothing more or less.

"If there is nothing else, I will see you in thirty minutes."

The man crossed the garden.

"It's an honor to serve," Sam yelled to the man's back as he basked in the light.

Taking Inventory

A wailing from the Harem sparked intrigue. The Arboretum was impressive, but he had seen many plants throughout his lifetime. Sam made his way toward the room where Muhammed had been presented. Several mercenary and swordsmen bodies dotted the path. The number of swordsmen who charged into death's eternal embrace was shocking.

"The council could have let them use their guns," he used a foot to roll one of the bodies. *"That had to hurt,"* the pureed face of a swordsman didn't refute the assertion. *"Better him than me."*

As he reached the end of the hall, Sam peeked through the office door. Five dead swordsmen appeared to be staged in sexual positions. The most artistic pair was created using a tall man and a pale man. The pale one's member had been removed and placed in his mouth. The tall one's head was pinned to the pale man's bloody stump with a sword.

"Fucking artists," he shook his head as he continued toward his pedestal.

Crossing the Atrium took more energy than anticipated. The steps burned his thighs and tightened his chest. He focused on deep breathing and took a minute before opening the door.

"Perfect timing," the unknown man was waiting. "I recently arrived, too."

The top of the spiral staircase was more revealing than expected, Sam felt naked. Hallways from every naturally populated continent drained swordsmen and Harem women into the giant room. Everyone stared up to him. He could feel his throat dry, his forehead burn, and his toe begin to tap inside his shoe.

"It is no secret that your house was attacked. As a result, the twenty-two stationed here has been retired. Those of you who know Jane," the man pointed an open palm toward Stacy, who was near the 'North America' hallway, "and for those that do not know Jane, please see her if you have questions."

Sam thought it odd to recommend they ask questions as it was against the rules, but he was not in a position to challenge.

"I have with me Jacque. He will be the interim leader of the Harem. Give him your loyalty, respect, and love. He has been chosen because he has proven he can serve the counsel and those he has been tasked to protect with great dedication and ferocity." The unknown man turned to Sam, "It's your turn."

"Thank you," Sam's voice cracked under the pressure. "As you heard, I am Jacque," he overcompensated and was yelling. "I cannot express how honored I am to be placed in a position of such trust and responsibility, I do not believe I deserve it, but accept it with humility."

He relaxed as he continued.

"Today, many of our brothers from the lodge perished, we can never repay that debt. We saw our losses, too. Each one of those losses will be avenged. You have my word as a noble twenty-two of the Society of Ghost. We will avenge every drop of blood, every scratch, every tear, every pain inflicted upon us today. Our society will remain a secret from the world, but it will be seared into the nightmares of all who dare to cause us harm or break treaties."

Sam jumped backward as he was startled by the cheer that erupted. It was so unexpected and truly uncharacteristic of society members.

"Keep going." The unknown man urged and placed a hand on his shoulder.

"I thank you for showing me love in this moment of despair. Your fallen brothers and sisters will be handled with the utmost respect. Navajo, Apache, and Cherokee Harem nines, please step forward," Sam paused as the group formed at the bottom of the staircase. "These will be the ones responsible for caring for our fallen. I do not know who carried the responsibility before, but it is theirs. I have grown to cherish and respect their traditions, and know they will honor those we love in a way that none can find inappropriate.

"The kiln is already burning, but do not enter until I authorize it," he addressed the women at the bottom of the steps.

He turned his attention back to the hoard, "Nobody is to enter the kiln. Anyone who is seen near it or its windows will receive the most brutal consequences."

The room broke into chatter, but Sam was not finished speaking.

"Speaking of consequences," he continued. "I am by the book. Brush up on the rules if needed. I am tolerant, but repeated offenses receive increased consequences. If you act in accordance with the rules, you will have long, happy tenures. Any concerns you have should be voiced."

A nine raised her hand.

"Just shout," he pointed at the woman.

"I heard you used the *Pulaxo Technique,* and I don't know what that means. I assume it is a consequence for breaking the rules, but I am not sure if it is a good or bad one," she hollered.

Sam winced at the words. How had it been spread around already?

"Tell me where you heard that rumor," Sam demanded.

"It is not a rumor if it is true," the unknown man interjected.

Sam gave the unknown man a scowl, "Yes, I did use that technique. No, it is not a consequence. You do not need to worry yourselves about the techniques twenty-twos use on their missions."

"You didn't say what it was," Stacy yelled. "I can tell them if you prefer."

Sam felt his face flush with rage and embarrassment.

"I knew you were ballsy when I recommended you for promotion," he replied.

"The *Pulaxo Technique* is a way for twenty-twos to exit their assignments. It involves tricking a woman into getting pregnant by an enemy. Then, the goal is to make her want to keep the baby. Of course, this conflict makes it easier to make her seem crazy, which is also important. When she reaches the deepest levels of emotion, you force her to have a miscarriage, which will send her into a psychological spiral. It makes framing her easier when the time comes to fake your death."

The room was frozen by his words. Sam noticed even his breathing had ceased as he waited for something, anything to start time.

"We all do things to further the goals," the whisper from the unknown man swept through every ear in the room. "It is not the job of Harem or Lodge members to judge no matter the circumstances. Jane is a new twenty-two, so she is different. She can challenge and judge, but do not forget she has earned her promotion."

"Yes, my speech may have carried on long enough," Sam was desperate to get out of the spotlight. "We will avenge every wrong that we have suffered, but first, we must heal. Harem sisters and

Lodge brothers, please work together to collect, count, and prepare our fallen family. Jane, please join me in the Office when we are done."

"I have no secrets from my sisters," Jane yelled. "We can speak."

"Your sisters are not permitted to be present. I recommend they stay to ensure they are following the rules," Sam glared at Stacy. "Be there in ten minutes. I know you believe you have already been promoted, but I was tasked with giving final approval."

"I remember you," Stacy replied. "I know you."

"Keep your place," the unknown man warned. "Jacque is doing his job. I expect you to be in the office for your interview."

Stacy hugged each of her American sisters and whispered promises in their ears. All the Harem women lined up to honor her and encourage her as she walked toward the spiral staircase. The Lithuanians and French women were the final groups.

"We can kill them," the Lithuanians whispered.

"Or we can make you disappear like the others," the French whispered.

"No," Stacy replied. "No matter what happens, make sure my girls survive and get them out."

"We will have to ensure he doesn't find the tunnels," a French girl whispered. "He will be watching everything. Every breath will be checked with his book of rules."

"I know," Stacy confirmed. "Just promise me you will do whatever it takes."

"We have always had your back," a Lithuanian hugged Stacy. "You are one of the good ones."

"You are all a bunch of bitches," Stacy laughed. "You are trying to make me cry, and it isn't funny."

"Poor American girl is going to cry," teased a French girl who pretended to rub her eyes with closed fists. "Be strong, protect your sisters yourself. You are strong enough to make it through anything. We watched you with the president. We know who he is, too. He has nothing on you."

"God," Stacy grabbed the girl and squeezed. "You fucking suck."

She wiped her face on the girl's shoulder before she let go and climbed towards her promotion.

Embracing Family

"After you," Sam opened the door to the Atrium.

The walk was short, but it took an eternity. He was tasked with pushing the line without crossing it, which required a level of precision he had not mastered. He knew Stacy was still recovering, but testing all promotions was vital. Sam searched for a way to avoid the orders.

As she opened the door to the office, he stopped her.

"There has been a change of plans. We will be conducting the interview in the pink room," he nodded when she gave him an odd look.

"I have never heard of the pink room," Stacy turned, looking confused. "Lead the way."

Sam faced the wall and glided his palms along the center. He knew the reader was somewhere, but the unknown man wasn't specific about where. As his hand made a sweeping circular pattern, he felt a spot that was different. It wasn't as smooth or cold. He pressed his hand stiffly. A wave of light passed beneath his fingers and palm.

A blue light appeared in the ball beside his hand. With his eye to the light, a whirling filled the hall. From floor to ceiling, the center third of the wall slid backward two feet. It was the coolest thing he had ever seen, but he didn't know what to do next. There didn't seem to be an opening.

Sam paced along the recessed wall, studying for any clues. He could feel his embarrassment grow as Stacy watched. The unknown man had not said anything about this.

"It's broken. We might need to conduct the interview in the office after all," he grumped.

"We could try standing there," Stacy pointed to an area behind the part of the wall that had not moved. "Maybe when this closes, that area will be safe."

"Or, this wall could crush us, and we could die," Sam replied, examining the spot. It did look big enough for the both of them if they squeezed.

"Everyone dies, at least if we die like this, it will be an incredible story," Stacy grabbed Sam's hand and pulled him into place. "We need to smoosh.".

Sam placed his feet outside of hers and pressed forward. Her body warmed him, and her smells were exciting. As he compressed their bodies, his blood started flowing. He could feel his heart beating against hers. The fake wall entombed their discomfort as he became aware her nipples were buried in his chest. The warmth, her scent, the closeness made his member begin to firm.

"Your turn for an idea, big boy," Stacy whispered in the darkness.

"Don't mind my hands. I am going to feel for a knob or something."

The narrowness of the compartment prevented his arms from raising.

"New plan. You feel for a way out behind me, and I will feel behind you."

"I can feel you already," Stacy used her pubis to apply pressure to his member. "Let's get out of here."

Sam used his hands to feel the walls beside them as Stacy mimicked. There was nothing. He slid his hands behind her thighs, working upward. As his hands reached her ass, he thought he felt her rock into them, so he squeezed.

"What the fuck was that?" She demanded.

"I'm sorry, I thought you pressed your ass into my hands," he replied.

"I did not. If you wanted to grope me, you didn't have to trap me in this creepy box," she admonished. "I knew something was up when you pressed your dick against me."

"Stop," Sam replied in a harsh tone. "I have something."

He felt a round wooden disk.

"Yeah, me trapped in a box with your dick against me and a handful of my ass," she continued.

Sam leaned forward, squeezing the breath from both of their bodies before he jerked backward, keeping the disk against Stacy's ass. The wall beside them split in two and flung open. Silks and laces draped from the ceiling creating a patchwork of colors separated by arches of semi-opaque fabrics.

"You are welcome," Sam huffed as he leaned Stacy against the wall and scooted around her. "Now, control yourself and come here for the interview."

Sam scrutinized the candle-lit room. In the center was a round, concave bed. Sam snickered at the raised edge because it reminded him of pizza crust that was too puffy.

"I get weird in small spaces," Stacy confided as she stepped into the room. "I don't think it is claustrophobia, but maybe it is. I'm not a doctor; I pretend to be one sexually."

"Don't worry about it," Sam barely heard her words as he circled the bed, looking at all the things that surrounded it. "I never would have expected to find a writing desk. We don't write anything. I wonder if he was writing a memoir or something, but then again, who could read it without being murdered."

"I don't think—" Stacy protested.

"Ignore that. It looks like there is a seat over there," Sam had almost forgotten she was there. He pointed to a leather armchair in the corner. "I never cared for the feel of leather, but if it would make you comfortable..."

"The bed looks comfy," Stacy used a hand to vault her body onto the bed. "Holy shit..." She pointed at the ceiling.

Sam looked up, "The stuff hanging from the ceiling does give it an interesting look."

"No," Stacy rolled to her knees and crawled to him. She grabbed his hand and toppled him into the bowl.

"Now look who is doing the groping," he smiled as she lost her balance and her hand pressed into his manhood.

"Seriously?" she looked at him with what appeared to be disgust. "Look at the ceiling," she pushed him onto his back and flopped beside him.

"I am supposed to torture you to see if you will break," he stated as he moved his eyes from her face to the ceiling. "Holy shit," he gasped. "We can't tell anyone about this."

"Agreed," she clasped his hand. "If you give me a few minutes to stay in this moment, I will give you the best blowjob of your life."

"I wasn't going to torture you because I saw how you handled the president. He did a number on you. If that didn't break you, nothing will," he whispered without looking away from the ceiling.

Stacy squeezed his hand, rolled, kissed him on the cheek, then rolled back and continued staring at the ceiling.

"That's not how you give a blowjob," Sam mumbled, the shock of the moment too great to divert his gaze.

"Fine," Stacy groaned as she stroked him with her free hand.

"Don't," Sam pushed her hand away. "You owe me nothing. You have earned your place. We are equals. If we fuck it will be from desire, not obligation. When you leave this room, you are free to make yourself at home, as my guest, until you are sent to your next assignment."

The pair lay motionless, holding hands, staring at the ceiling for hours as they drifted to sleep. Sam dreamt about his goddess, Sarah. They met in the bar, and Sarah's beauty was a spotlight in the midst of the ordinaries. She beckoned him as an aura of love radiated from her. They drank, flirted, laughed, and embraced before returning to her place. They couldn't keep their hands off each other as they yearned with unfettered happiness.

As they entered her room, she performed a slow, sensual strip tease before pushing him onto the bed and pulling him free of his clothes. Sarah climbed on top and kissed him as she guided him inside. Then something odd happened when she was lifting and lowering herself on his excitement.

Her body became liquid and formed itself into Valerie. They were no longer in Sarah's home or in bed. Valerie was straddling him in the rocky sand. He could feel his body baking in the hot sun. As Sam looked around, there was nothing. They were in the middle of a sand-dune desert.

When his eyes returned to Valerie, her arms were extended towards his face. Something blurry was in her hands. As his eyes focused, it molded itself into a gun. Her fingers squeezed the trigger. Fire from the barrel licked his face. Everything turned to black.

Sam remained in his nightmare for several minutes before realizing he was awake and his eyes were open. Panic-stricken, he clung to Stacy for a moment of reprieve, but she had disappeared. Sam had found himself abandoned in the darkness.

The pink room scared the hell out of him, and he realized why Muhammed enjoyed the Arboretum. With the Pink Room's isolation and the way the ceiling mesmerized him, it was too much. Spending time with the eights and nines was inappropriate, but he knew that at some point, he would need to find one or two to help keep his sanity and empty his juices.

Compared to the pink room, the garden was sweltering. The sun beat him in the face, the pollens clogged his nose and throat, and his eyes burned. He wondered if any of the guests enjoyed it or if it was another demonstration of power, beauty, and control. The society showed guests that even in this remote desert, they had the power to control nature itself and could create beauty among the most desolate of death bringers.

The conifer forest was the first to greet Sam. It was cool and reminded him of Christmas and a Bavarian road near a remote village. The cobblestones created a path that had been laid with slight arcs and valleys.

A sign greeted Sam at the intersection that read, "Asian, swamp, conifers, fruits & sweets."

Sam turned down the "fruits & Sweets" path. It was made from a dark soil and wood mulch mix. It was not long before white trees with peeling bark dotted the pines. Then, there were the occasional trees with leaves of bright oranges, reds, and yellows. Some had metal buckets hanging to the sides. As the final conifers dissipated from the forest, Sam found himself in the midst of apples, pears, plums, and an assortment of fruit bushes.

The light scent of peach pecked his nose, making him realize his allergies had cleared. He took a deep breath as he scanned for the peaches, they were his favorite. He crouched to see further but still saw none. He wondered if he had imagined the smell when he saw a shadow standing by a tree not too far from the path. It was a woman.

"Hey," he called as he walked toward her. She was turned away from him and did not respond. He could feel his heart start to pound as he slowed his pace.

"Hey you," he called to her, but nothing. He continued toeing towards her in the black dirt.

As he neared, her hair transformed from a dark shadow into luscious locks. She had one of the most feminine physiques he had ever seen.

"This can't be real. There's no way you are here. Do not make me kill you, Sarah. You are my love, but you know you can't be here," his thoughts continued as he froze.

He tip-toed closer. Her arms were raised in front of her, but he couldn't see why. When he was six feet away, he stopped.

"Tell me why you are here," he coaxed.

The woman turned, tears were streaking black lines from her eyes.

"Gross, what the fuck is that face? Who cries like that?" Sam asked himself as he looked at her wide, open-mouthed crying and heard the mucus-filled sniffles.

"You can't be here," Sam made his voice authoritative. "Return to the cages and cry with your nines, that is their job."

The woman wiped her eyes with a casted wrist as anger flashed in her face.

"You are injured," the woman hurled herself at the words with a lodge sword.

"Where the fuck did that come from?" Sam screamed to himself as he grabbed her wrists and rolled backward.

The soil cushioned the fall as they rolled through the landing. He mounted the woman as their bodies stopped rotating.

"That was a mistake," he growled as he twisted her broken wrist.

She winced in pain as he forced the blade toward her throat. The woman bucked hard. Sam released the blade, and his torso launched forward.

The woman rotated the blade toward him and sliced. Her wrist must have been in terrible pain because the blade kissed, creating a shallow gash.

Sam spun off the woman and stood. He kicked toward her head, but she rolled out of the way. She twisted to her feet and faced him. As she rose, her clothing moved enough for Sam to see her mark.

"You are safe. I am not your enemy," He held a hand up as he revealed his mark. "I am a twenty-two. You are my guest. You are safe."

The woman dropped the sword and collapsed on the ground. A streak of light that penetrated the forest's crown glinted against her golden mane. She held her thighs to her chest and lowered her face to her knees. She sobbed and sniffled while she rocked back and forth.

"Thank god she's one of us. That was close, but she's still an ugly crier," he thought as he examined his stomach.

The cut wasn't deep, and it would stop bleeding on its own. Her disgusting sniffling needed him more.

"Hey," he crouched, "I don't know what you are going through or what happened, but you might have come from Russia. I know you can't see it, but you are one of the strongest, bravest, most powerful among us. Everyone loves you and is here for you."

Sam didn't know if she had heard or if she even cared because she remained unchanged in her wide-mouthed sobbing.

"We are going to kill the bastards. We are going to kill them all. They started this, but they don't know how powerful we, you, are or the way we feel. I promise you, I will help you make them pay."

Sam thought he almost saw her look up from the corner of her eye.

"My loss is nothing compared to whatever you may be going through," he continued, "But it would help me if I could sit and hold you. I am going to sit behind you, let you rock in my arms, and hold you so you know you are loved and safe. Please do not kill me when I do it. If you don't want me to do it, give me a sign."

Sam stood and took a step back for a moment. She lowered her uninjured arm and lifted the handle of the sword.

"I can go if you need to be alone," he walked behind a tree.

The woman tossed the sword away and returned to the business of sobbing. Sam took a deep breath and thought about how Sarah might have reacted when she had learned of his murder. Or, worse, how Valerie might be doing considering the altercation he had orchestrated or the fact the police found his murdered body in her bathtub.

"That was a good choice," Sam whispered. "I need a good hug, too."

He rounded her and took his seat. He wrapped his legs around the side of her and situated his bits to ensure he would not get aroused before scooting forward. He wrapped his arms around her and held his hands together in front of her legs.

The woman turned and laid her head on his shoulder with her face pointed towards the trees. She lifted his arm so he was hugging her around the shoulders. Sam tightened the embrace and rocked.

"You are safe. We are your family, and we have your back. Whatever you need, we are here for you. Rest, you have been through a lot, and it is our turn to take your load. Welcome home, sister," every few sentences, he kissed the top of her head.

Sam continued to console his broken sister in the light, surrounded by the fruit of the Council of the Society of Ghost.

Returning Home

Stuck in the Past

There had been too much: too much silence, too much thinking, too much emotion. Alya had relived the extraction a hundred times in the past few days. She saw TaVi standing over her dying body. TaVi was surprising her at the train station. She saw the desperation on TaVi's face as she was pulled behind the building. She saw the fear and helplessness. It was all too much, and it was forever inked into her memory, like the tattoo that had been inked on the five-point. Inked into her memory like the site of the five-point being brutalized and tossed into the van.

She should have been the one to smash the man. She should have been the one to take him under control. She should be the one questioning him and exacting revenge for having the impudence to lay his eyes, much less his hands, on TaVi. There had been too much.

The car had been stopped for several minutes before Alya realized they had arrived. Lodge swordsmen were streaming from the Harem and amassing near the imperceptible helicopter pad. The landscaping hid the walls around it, and only those who knew of its existence could see it.

Alya looked at her casted wrist and took a deep breath. As she wiped her eyes with the casted hand, she pushed the car door open. As she stepped out of the vehicle, the swordsmen stopped moving and whispered.

"I would focus on your jobs and keep your eyes off of her," an unknown man yelled as he exited the Harem. The swordsmen diverted their focus but kept whispering as they continued moving into the island of green created by the driveway.

"The sisters have been moved. We offered the healer an apprenticeship, and she accepted. The older one has a normie job. It should not take long to find a new transporter," the man updated as he approached Alya.

"TaVi," The name had become difficult to say, but Alya managed to release it without tears.

"We are still trying to collect information. There are no reports, but there wouldn't be. An attack on a prominent Russian general is the kind of thing that gets covered up pretty quickly."

"I wish we could kill all the generals. It would make the world safer," a passing swordsman whispered.

Alya's brain swelled as her eyes became fuzzy. Without a conscious thought, she found herself ripping the sword from his sheath and thrusting it through his abdomen before pulling it out, spinning, and severing the head of his accomplice in one clean chop.

"There's two more to replace. I did warn them," the man's voice remained relaxed, but his mouth carried a slight frown as he took three steps away from Alya.

"Last warning," he yelled to the swordsmen who had witnessed the affair and were staring. "Ignore our esteemed guest and conduct your business in silence."

Once Alya realized what she had done, she shook uncontrollably. She was seething but also scared.

"What happened to me? I am the best in the world, how could I let myself lose control? I can fix this. This is something that happened once, and I can control it next time. When I make them pay,

everything will be back to normal," her brain was on overdrive.

"Breathe, sister," the man's tone was tender. "We are going to find out what happened, and they will suffer the full consequences."

"I want to be there," Alya snarled. "I want to give them their consequences.

"I have your back. I will support you when you are ready to request permission from the council," he replied as he took another step backward.

"No," Alya whispered. "Find him, bring him to me. There will be plenty of fives for the council. I want the one that took my TaVi."

"Sister, you know what you are demanding," he whispered.

"I don't care. I am owed this consequence. I have done everything they have asked," she clenched her teeth and burned her eyes into his.

"It will be done," he whispered. "Tell no one, if not for your safety, as a consequence for me being a good brother."

"I have had enough silence," Alya's chest still heaved with emotion, "but you have my word. Get all your men out, or I will."

"It seems we are no longer welcomed guests, so we will leave. I will ensure all the men stay on the island. I am assuming they will be safe until extracted."

"I will not order any consequences for any men who stay encircled by the driveway. If one foot steps into the driveway, there will be blood," Alya replied as she looked down at the two dead men. "Make sure you take your trash with you."

"You four," the man pointed at a group at the edge of the grass, "Come get these two after she has moved inside. Everyone else, if I see you looking or breathing on the driveway, I will end your life. Stay near the helicopter pad until you are extracted. This is your single warning."

"It looks like there is a lot happening inside," Alya turned toward the Harem entrance.

"Yes, the nines are moving the bodies to the garden and cleaning the blood," the man reported.

"The bodies are stored in the kiln house until burned," Alya raised an eyebrow, for the first time noticing her hands had unclenched, her breathing was normal, and her feet were getting sticky from drying blood pools.

"The body of the retired has been placed in there. It was thought best not to let anyone discover its condition," the man raised both eyebrows and lowered his chin.

Alya ascended two steps toward the harem entrance and removed her shoes. She tossed them on the bodies.

"Take the shoes too, they are ruined. I will ensure the retired is not discovered. He will be moved late this evening by myself and the other twenty-two who is running this place. I expect my train delay has made me the last to arrive, tell me where I can find him."

"I don't know why you're waiting," the man called to the men while pointing to the bodies. "Take the shoes, too. They have been ruined by your brothers' inability to listen." He turned to Alya.

"The new twenty-two is being interviewed by the sitting twenty-two. I didn't see them in the Office. They may be in the Pink Room or Blue Room."

"I will catch him when he is finished. Now is the time to tell me about any other surprises," she called over her shoulder as she ascended.

"He has been announced as the leader. We did not know how long it would take you to return. Once you meet with him, he will provide updates," the man yelled as he shooed the swordsmen toward their designated area.

"Then I have free time," Alya thought as she stepped inside.

It had been a long time since she had been home. So much had changed. She wasn't sure what to explore first and decided to turn right. After passing through a room she found boring, she entered the Office. Several women were carrying the corpses of men toward the back hallway.

"Stop," she directed. "Remove your head coverings."

The women looked at each other, dropping the bodies. They removed their head and face coverings. Their faces displayed fear and embarrassment. Some stood behind others to shield themselves from view.

"This is how you will be dressed in the Harem going forward," Alya stated. "You will not hide your faces. We serve a single goal but are not a single person. I want to see each of you line up."

As the women formed a line, a woman with short, black hair and pale skin stared into her eyes.

"TaVi?" The gasp trapped within Alya's brain.

"Go," Alya's voice shaky as she suppressed her emotion. "Hurry, remove these men from my site."

As the women lifted the bodies, Alya found herself desperate to feel TaVi's love one last time, even if it wasn't real.

"Wait," Alya's voice trembled. "You, with the black hair, I have a job for you. Help them get the bodies into the hall, then come back and close the door."

As the woman closed the door, Alya decided on the best way to feel TaVi's presence. Cuddling on the sofa seemed like the safest option. It wasn't difficult to find a comfortable position. Her hand patted a spot, and the woman obeyed. Her arms wrapped around the woman, and Alya realized something was wrong.

"TaVi was the big spoon, and she would never wear perfume that smelled so soapy. This is all wrong; this woman is nothing like TaVi. Okay, it's okay, she is an innocent following orders. Calm, calm, keep calm. She does have a nice body and kind of looks like TaVi. Maybe she can fuck like her too. I can find TaVi in the sex," Alya's brain refused to let silence return.

"Go and get something, you are going to fuck me," Alya pushed the woman to the floor.

The woman ran from the room and returned, holding a strap-on dildo. She stripped and donned the device.

"I am ready," the woman informed as she stood motionless by the door.

"Be rough, force me to be yours," Alya rose from the sofa. "Don't be afraid to make me feel your authority."

"Yes, ma'am," the woman replied as she approached. She took Alya's hand and led her to the desk. She stepped behind Alya and guided her upper body to the surface.

"That's too gentle," Alya complained.

The woman lifted Alya's skirt and yanked her panties hard. Alya could feel the material stretch and dig into her thighs. Grating her skin as they were pulled down.

The dildo's head pressed into her dry sex, and Alya thought for a moment TaVi was with her, then the woman said, "I hope that is not too painful."

The fantasy was broken, and Alya felt a wave of multiple emotions begin to drown her. She was embarrassed. Weakness had claimed her in front of a subordinate. She was fearful of the future. She was heartbroken she couldn't have Tavi. Devastated, she couldn't help Tavi. Angry at the five points for taking TaVi, the Council for extracting her, and the woman for ruining the fantasy. And she was sad, in total despair, that she was a failure.

"You're done, get out," she choked back the tears. "Now! Go before I get upset."

The dildo swung wildly as the woman dashed to her clothes, then from the room. Alya rolled on her side, pulled her thighs to her chest, and hugged them. She sobbed into her knees until her eyes had run out of tears. Not wanting to move, Alya wrestled her underwear up her thighs and over her ass and sex. They were digging into the side of her crotch, but she didn't care. Alya wanted to lay motionless, not free from the world, but not part of it either.

No Escape

It had been a while since Alya stopped crying. She watched the shadows walk across the floor behind the desk. They were longer. She knew she couldn't stay curled forever, and this weakness was not acceptable. Fortunately, a knock on the door gave her the prompt she needed. Alya struggled to her feet and fixed her panties as the door opened.

Several nines crept into the room carrying buckets of water. They froze when they spotted her. None of them were wearing their head coverings, and Alya knew her embarrassment must have spread to all ears.

"I have changed my mind," She kept her words unemotional despite the incredible embarrassment she felt. "Everyone will keep the same standards for dressing as before. Before you fix yourselves, tell me why you are here."

Alya knew if she kept running into the TaVi clone, she would continue to lose herself in regret and hostility. That was no way to lead the Harem.

"We have come to clean everything from the day's events," the ebony goddess in the front replied. Her voice was silky with a hint of something else. Alya couldn't decide what created the underlying uniqueness of the harmonious words but was enchanted. It was from someplace far from all her memories and pain.

"Clean first, I was about to tour the compound. Tell me where the other twenty-twos can be found."

The women turned to each other and whispered before a lean, tan-skinned woman stepped forward and spoke.

"No," Alya interrupted, "You, I want you to be the voice of the eights and nines. Nobody but you is allowed to speak to me. All others must send their messages through you unless I address someone else," she was pointing at the lanky, dark, goddess with the short hair. "I want my assistant to be from Africa, and you look like you might be from there. The woman restrained their laughter at the obviousness of the accusation.

"I am Maasai. None of us know where the others, the ones like you, can be found. They have vanished within these walls. There are good assistants who are not African, choosing based on continent might be considered prejudice," the designee answered.

"They haven't finished in the Pink room yet?" Alya questioned. *"Hopefully, he doesn't kill her. I might lose myself. I can't take another hit today."*

"It's not prejudice. You are my assistant because I will not kill you for triggering certain memories." Alya explained to the women. "Go, tell all the eights and nines your assignment. I will be touring soon and expect them to know their roles. The rest of you can begin cleaning."

Alya followed the goddess into the hallway. She stopped at a group of women who were carrying a headless body out of the Atrium. The group looked at Alya, dropped the body, and scattered in all directions.

"Finally," Alya thought, *"Something is going my way. Little wins, focus on the little wins."*

Alya stepped over the contorted corpse to enter the Atrium. It had already begun to smell like old beef, dried blood, and the death bile that brewed in the bowels of every departed. Alya had grown accustomed to the occasional smell of death, but it was still pungent and made her stomach churn.

"Found the head," Alya thought with an almost joyful tone as she used her bare foot to guide it to the owner in the hall. Upon reentering the Atrium, Alya found the spot where she would have sat if this had been the Atrium in her time. She walked to it and let her body flop. As her body smashed into the fabric, it hugged her. It provided a deep embrace that made her feel protected from all harm.

Alya rolled over and sat up, reminiscing about those days. The days when she was protected from all harm other than her stupidity and religiousness. She imagined her sisters being there with her, talking about how the Chinese team had messed up their visit with the Cambodian visitor, how the Russian team had attempted to escape, and even the time when the Ugandans had switched their eight and nine to protect the innocent virgin from the ravages of this life. Alya looked around the room at the high walls, the broken glass ceiling, and the raised circle in the middle.

"This is a beautiful room, despite the horrors," her eyes fixated on the couplings that surrounded the circle.

Alya knew she had some latitude to manipulate the ceremony, but, ultimately, it could never be less vile and haunting than the one she experienced. It was the thing that made her realize she had to become the best, become indispensable, and she wouldn't deprive any of the women the opportunity to one day have a chance of escape. A chance like the one nearing her and which, for a moment, she thought had arrived.

"This is taking a turn," she grimaced as she stood. *"No more reminiscing."* She looked at the door to the cages and then back at the door to the hallway. *"No fucking way am I interested in seeing more people. I will introduce myself tomorrow.*

Sound good brain? Yep, sounds good, Alya," she fake negotiated with herself. In the hallway, the women were lifting the body, inching it toward the garden.

"Make sure the bodies are neatly stacked. I will investigate the kiln house tomorrow, and they can be burned," Alya advised as she jogged past them to hold the door open.

None of the women spoke as they passed, which caused mixed emotions. Alya was relieved she didn't have to engage in conversation and that they were already obeying, but disappointed they were obeying without question and that nobody acknowledged her words. Ultimately, they were doing the right thing and making good choices, so she continued into the garden.

There were large embankments of flowers that gave the mirage of walls on three sides. The embankment towards the front of the compound was the lowest. It rose to the top step of the Harem entrance, and anyone riding in a vehicle could see most of the garden, including the fountains, low hedge rows, the Aviary, a gazebo, and some other structures.

Alya found a patch of grass surrounded by hedges and laid down to cook in the sun. A group of women passed and must not have seen her because they were chatty. Alya lay motionless, listening to their words, but they were foreign, incomprehensible. She took a deep breath as their voices became low in the distance. The flowers smelled amazing, and the sun was baking her in the best way.

Another group of voices was approaching. Alya strained to hear their words, but it didn't take long for her to regret the curiosity.

"I heard she told a Spanish nine to fuck her," the raspy first voice stated.

"And," a young, high-pitched voice full of excitement continued, "When the nine did it, she started crying and freaking out. I mean, she seems legit crazy."

"Stop," a mature voice whipped. "She is above our positions. I will not receive consequences because you want to gossip. If she is crazy, that is more of a reason to make yourselves invisible. No more talking outside the cage."

"Did you hear about the Russian general," the young one continued, "I would murder the entire world if I were—."

A loud slap startled Alya.

"Not outside the cage," the mature voice repeated.

"Okay, sorry," the young one sniffled.

Arboretum Delights

The dead swordsmen near the entrance let Alya know she wouldn't be alone long unless she explored deep into the forest. She took one of the swords to help pick fruit. The fruit forest always had something ripening.

Several yards off the path, she paralleled it all the way to the orchards. The fruit had always been the sweetest thing she had ever tasted. The plumbs were perfect for the picking.

The taste saturated her tongue, and the heavens rejoiced at the splendor of the divine flavor. Alya found herself devouring any fruit she could reach: plums, pears, red and green apples.

Alya soon turned her attention to berries on the bushes that lined the walls. The raspberries were too small, the blueberries were sour and needed to ripe, the boysenberries were perfect, but the blackberries were her favorite.

When her belly couldn't handle anymore, she walked back to the tree where the sword leaned. A man was approaching on the path. She looked at the sword and then back at the man. She decided to not reveal her edge until he was closer.

"Hey," he yelled and waived.

Alya turned away to wipe the fruit juices from her mouth.

"Hey, you," he called.

The memory of TaVi being pulled behind the building flashed in her brain. She felt the tears starting and couldn't stop them. She couldn't contain her weakness.

"You can't be here, return to the cages and cry with your nines, that is your job," said the man.

Alya's tears turned to rage at the ignorance. She wiped her eyes, this time to see her target. She seized the sword. It swung at the man and his arrogant display of misplaced authority. The soil was loose, causing her to tumble forward.

The man grabbed her and rolled through the fall. The next instant, Alya was staring up at him as he lowered the guillotine.

"*Fuck you, buddy, no man has ever overpowered me and you won't be the first.*" Alya cursed him as she provided a forceful blow, with her knee striking his crotch. She could tell she missed the gems, but he still bucked free.

Her wrist twitched with pain as she rotated the blade toward his belly. Her free hand pushed the blade. It kissed his skin, leaving a red slit. He spun away from the blade.

Alya rolled onto all fours and stood. She readied herself for another assault as the man yelled, but she could not hear through her rage and adrenaline. The man stripped and revealed a Mark of Ghost.

"I am the new twenty-two" formed from his incoherent screams. "You are safe. I am not your enemy," he continued. "You are my guest. You are safe."

Exhausted from life, the day, death, the world, Alya dropped the sword and collapsed in a beam of light that penetrated the canopy. She pulled her thighs to her chest, rocked, and stopped fighting the tears. It was all too much. She didn't know how to live anymore. The man, her brother, consoled her, but he was afraid of her. To show she was not going to harm him, she tossed the sword into the fruit bushes.

She felt the man slide against her back but didn't feel his manliness. He squeezed and whispered condolences, words of strength, and reassurances. Alya could feel herself warming and imagined it was TaVi holding her, consoling her, making her feel safe. She turned to lay her head on his shoulder and pretend, for one last time, TaVi was there, providing her the love and attention she needed, but her soul wanted more.

She knew it wasn't TaVi, but it was close enough to let her imagination warp reality. Alya turned away from the man and rolled forward. With her shins planted, she used her good arm to hold herself up as she reached back with the cast and lifted her skirt over her ass.

"No talking," Alya whispered as she crawled to the tree where the sword had been leaning. "I need this."

Alya laid her chest in the dirt, pressed her shoulder to the trunk, and hugged with both arms.

The man's hands froze her skin as they lowered her underwear. An unexpected heat covered her mound as he licked her lips. His tongue was muscular and exacting. It foraged her ravine, seeking sustenance. When it found her fragility, it devoured her inhibitions. Alya felt all the emotions of a Ghost overwhelm her, and she surrendered. She let the waves of pleasure pulsate and push away all the anguish.

The massaging was magical as it made her legs weaken. Alya could feel herself pushing towards the tongue, her sex begging for more. She was dripping with desire, and for the first time, she realized she wasn't thinking about TaVi. As she made the realization, her body tightened. She felt like a betrayer. She wondered how she could be enjoying what this *man* was doing when she had lost TaVi.

While she was deep in her thought, Alya had not noticed he had stopped massaging until her moisture cooled. She was about to look back to see if he had noticed her tense.

The top of his pleasure smashed against her cold, drying lips. They were too dry, and it felt like sandpaper had rubbed her while, at the same time, a spike of relief washed over her brain. He was going to be as brutal as TaVi. It was going to hurt, at first, before forcing her to experience a cathartic release.

His hammer struck its target, driving deeper. Alya covered her mouth to muffle her grunt, but he pushed the hand away, and she obeyed as he struck again. Alya let the grunt hum from her lips, accentuating it to please her penetrator.

As the next intrusion pushed further, Alya could feel herself getting wet as her sex grabbed the mast. He seemed to understand and pulled out the shaft, leaving the tip inside as he exploded forward. He slammed so hard it felt like Alya's cervix was going to be obliterated. Her shoulder pressed against the tree, and she let out a guttural yelp.

"Harder," she grunted.

His hands found her hips, and he carved his pleasure into her memory. With each strike, her shoulder became more bruised. The loud slapping was met by the jarring sounds of her painful pleasure. Alya could feel the emotions growing.

"Force me, don't stop," she croaked between grunts. Her mind danced with pictures of monumental moments. They filled her with the sorrow from losing TaVi and the joy of being promoted to a twenty-two.

The fear during the first ceremony and the triumph from her first mission. As the pictures danced, she teared and sobbed.

"Harder," she demanded as the tears turned to hilarity and laughter, then to calm.

The knowledge that TaVi was watching over her and did love her, even if it was a short relationship, soothed her. She could feel a psychological orgasm take hold and release all the pain, emotion, and hurt from her body, then there was nothing.

Just two people, strangers really, having rough sex in a strange place. The feeling was too disorientating. Alya faked an orgasm and reached back with a hand.

She pulled her ass cheek to the side. The man knew what to do. Her asshole unfurled pain as he punctured the gift. Alya screamed and reached back with both hands to slow his assault. His fingers hooked the sides of her mouth and pulled.

A pain ripped through Alya's face as she collapsed flat in the dirt. She worked to force his fingers from her mouth, but he was too strong. He pounded her ass harder, hurtling pain from her hips into her stomach. Alya knew he was too powerful and succumbed to her new master. He forced himself deeper into her ass than she had ever felt.

As the pain notified Alya that her face was going to rip in two, she forced her arms under her shoulders and pushed up. Her back made a deep arch.

"Stay like this," he instructed as he released her mouth. Alya felt her shirt lift over her breasts, then her bra. His hands found her hips and pulled her back to her knees.

His hands cupped her breasts and pulled. The pair rolled backward. Alya found herself sitting on his lap, her ass penetrated to the scrotum, which was not a short distance.

She was sitting, reclined, with her knees bent and her feet flat in the dirt. The man was popping his hips off the ground. Alya felt spikes of pain in her ass as she pogoed. Alya liked the way she was being handled, or rather, manhandled.

It wasn't long before he started moaning uncontrollably. Alya was starting to get a cramp in her leg and thought she better speed things along. She licked her fingers and massaged his balls as her ass stroked his mast.

He was saying words, but Alya couldn't make out what. She lowered her hand and massaged the skin behind his ball. It seemed like this made him lose more control, so Alya continued. She pressed a finger against his hole and tapped.

He pulled her hand away so she massaged the tops of his thighs around his manhood. His words were getting louder, but she still couldn't hear. Alya pressed her ass down hard, forcing him deep inside.

"Sarah," he groaned as his liquid filled her ass. Alya continued rocking on his rod until he was no longer solid. She had almost forgotten that they went soft, the ones TaVi used were never soft. As she slid him out, his joy juice dripped.

"Let's cuddle," he pulled Alya flat against his chest.

"It's sex, stop acting like a child. Do you want to date me, too?" Alya was disgusted.

"I wouldn't mind," the man replied, propping himself on his arm.

"*Is he serious? He hasn't earned cuddle privileges,*" she thought.

Alya used her panties to wipe herself, then tossed them at the man.

"Keep them as a souvenir. You are lucky I let you come near me after the way you ended your last assignment and how you treated Sarah."

"That was V..." the man shrugged. "You are lucky I didn't punish you more. You are my new fuck toy when I visit. It is your job to make sure none of the others try to play with me."

Alya smiled, she liked the idea of being the special one. The one who allowed to claim this man.

"The only one except for Sarah," her words made the man wince from some invisible wound. "Joking, you can fuck Sarah, too. We can be a thruple," she joked, but it was too late.

"You seem like fun even when you aren't on my cock," the man smiled.

"Right," Alya hated the word, and she would need to decide if it changed her feelings toward him. "Get dressed. We need to discuss business."

"Of course, you want a tour of the Harem and an update on the new twenty-two. She is weird but in a good way. It seems like she is going to make an exquisite addition."

"I wasn't talking about that," Alya was annoyed that he assumed he knew what she wanted.

"Oh," he lowered his voice. "You mean the retirement."

"No," Alya's voice was getting pitchy as her annoyance grew. "I am talking about Russia. I hope your listening is better than your guessing. If not, we will be destined for an eternity of ignorant servitude."

Taking the Reigns

"He has become paranoid, and I believe my extraction made it worse," Alya continued.

"That's unsettling. I assume there are other pitfalls that I should avoid," the man seemed interested.

He was attentive and probed the appropriate areas.

"There are two generals you should pay close attention to," Alya's mind constructed the potential emotional state of TaVi while also trying to distance the report from her vulnerability. "General Klopvor is a long-time loyalist to the president. He has been in his position for longer than either of us have been ghosts. His influence is formidable."

Alya's mind flashed to the general entering the dining hall and then to the Russian president's shocked face as she was dying, it forced a laugh.

"I don't understand why that is funny," Sam asserted.

"He was questioned by General Talia Vilonka. Klopvor was the only one who knew the president was in the hospital, and I led the president to believe Klopvor had been poisoning him. At the dinner, the one where I was murdered."

Alya became gleeful as she bragged about how she had faked her death.

"That night, he came with private security. He was weak and offered the president a bottle of the finest alcohol on earth. Naturally, I convinced the president I was the one who could be trusted."

"Naturally," Sam kicked her foot. "That's why you are the best, and everyone brags about you, even Guiying."

"You don't know Guiying," Alya retorted.

"We met at the lodge before she was sent out. She said she hoped she could garner as much pride, respect, and honor as you."

Alya's face burned with joy. Her personal hero admired her. It was more than her brain could handle. She became drunk with pride as she continued updating Sam.

"Anyway, there I was, scared, alone, and surrounded by the enemy on all sides. The Russian general had brought a gift for the Russian president, but little did he know, the Russian president had one remaining confidant: me! Hahaha, I still can't believe he was that easy to manipulate and so very, very stupid," Alya let out a deep laugh as she toppled into the dirt.

"So, there we were, with a bottle of the most expensive alcohol, and what does the president demand? He made me test the alcohol to see if it was poisoned. Naturally, I don't want the general to regain favor with the president."

"Naturally," Sam rotated his hand in the air to tell Alya to continue.

"So, of course, knowing I have to kill myself anyway, I poison the alcohol," Alya laughed. "You should have seen the president's face when I fell on the floor convulsing and foaming at the mouth, and it was the most hilarious thing you could ever imagine. Here was one of the most proud world leaders, almost shitting himself with fear as he ran from the room like a schoolboy being chased by a ruler-wielding nun." Alya had become manic as tears streamed down her face, and she laughed uncontrollably. She wiped her tears and calmed her breathing, but she could not stop laughing. Her brain knew it wasn't that funny, but her body did not agree.

"That is pretty funny," Sam chuckled. "I assume there are others besides Klopvor."

"Yes, whew, hold on," Alya stood. "Okay, calm, calm." Alya bent forward at the waist with her hands behind her head as she held her breath. "Okay, sorry about that. I don't know what that was," she explained while returning to her seat.

"Yes, as I faded into death, General Vilonka was standing over me shouting. She is going to be dangerous. I forced her to fall in love with me."

Alya kept her tone cold but felt the emotions well as she relived the moment, the expression on TaVi's face, and then there was the train station.

"General Vilonka," Sam repeated. "Is she—"

"She is a Russian general you need to stay away from," Alya interrupted. "You need to know she is influential and dangerous. If she discovers the slightest suggestion that you are untruthful about anything, she will seize and interrogate you until all your secrets are revealed or until she tires of keeping you alive."

"She sounds like a keeper," Sam teased. "I am sure I will be delighted to meet her."

"Seriously, stay away from her," Alya wasn't sure if she was trying to protect him or TaVi, but knew the idea of them meeting was bad. Then she realized what her brain wasn't ready to accept and what she had hidden from him. "Actually, you don't need to worry about her. She was murdered at a train station the day I egressed from Russia."

"I thought you withdrew from Russia by train," Sam tilted his head in confusion. "Did you—"

"No! I did leave by train, but I had nothing to do with her murder," Alya curled her thighs to her chest.

"Oh," Sam realized the implications. "Yeah, we don't need to discuss that. Tell me about the other threats," Sam continued to probe.

"The other threats are minor, and you are trained well enough to handle them. The generals and the president's paranoia are your main concerns and have created an intricate web of deceit, traps, and danger that will be impossible to navigate on a summer day, and let's face it, you are headed into a Siberian blizzard, so you better dress appropriately," Alya stood. "Introduce me to the new twenty-two. I want to congratulate her before I am alone with the underlings."

"She should be with the other Americans in the cage," Sam hoped as he brushed the dirt from his trousers and rose.

He didn't know where she had gone, and he gave her permission to do whatever she wanted.

"I didn't realize she was American," Alya was surprised. "We haven't had one of those promoted in quite a while."

"I checked. The last American to be promoted was 1989." Sam replied as they made their way to the path. The sun was low in the sky; pink lined the horizon as they strolled.

"I can't remember where you are from," Alya poked Sam in the ribs.

"I don't remember you saying where you were born either," Sam brushed the dirt off Alya's back and ass.

"The darkness, but I am glad I was relocated into the light," Alya shook her hips as she led Sam through the garden. "Don't stare too hard," she flirted as she flipped her skirt up to give him a final peek.

The Harem was ghostly as the patter of Alya's feet filled the air. The shadows were long, and the wind had begun to howl. The silence was eerie, and Alya wondered why nobody had remained to guard against any more attacks.

The hallway had no windows, and seeing the tip of her nose was impossible as they crept toward the cages. Alya had found it comforting to know Sam was by her side, even if he was useless. The hall was too dark. She needed to get to the Atrium where the stars could light her path.

A blanket of warmth greeted the twenty-twos as they opened the door to the cages. The fragrant smells of a million nations delighted their sniffers as Alya walked toward the North American hallway. She hadn't noticed the two women sitting cross-legged with plates beside the African hallway. They placed their plates on the floor and intercepted.

"Welcome back," the familiar voice of the tall ebony goddess delighted Alya's ears. "Tell us your message, and we will deliver it."

"You are too awe-inspiring," Alya's compliment was authentic as she stroked her fingers across the woman's cheek. "Go, finish your dinners, and return to your cages for the evening. You will be my assistant, not my slave. We will discuss boundaries and expectations in the morning."

"Thank you," the woman exclaimed with the most broad and sterling smile as she pulled her companion toward their meals.

"That was kind," Sam noted for no particular reason.

"This life is difficult and unfair, there is no reason to make it worse," Alya sighed as she continued to the North American hallway.

The American doorway was further than Alya would have expected, considering its prominence in the world, but it wasn't difficult to find. She used the knocker to announce her presence. After several minutes without a response, she looked at Sam with disdain.

"They must not have heard. They are some of the most respected in the building," Sam excused their delay, hoping the new girl hadn't taken liberties already.

Sam used the knocker, then banged on the door several times with the side of a closed fist. The doorway across the hall, the Canadian door, swung open, letting music spill out.

"I thought you were knocking on our door," the Canadian nine confessed. "They aren't there. Jane took them out. She said she is a twenty-two."

"Thank you for letting us know," Alya responded as she walked to the woman. "Tell us where they went."

"We don't know," a voice from inside yelled.

"Shh. It's the twenty-twos," the woman at the door yelled into the apartment, causing the music to silence. "They didn't tell us where they were going. We noticed them taking a car from the Arboretum lot when we finished stacking the dead."

"Go have fun with your sisters," Sam spoke over Alya's head. When the door shut, Sam walked toward the big room. "They aren't here. I did tell the new twenty-two to make herself at home. I am sure you remember when you were promoted."

"Yes, I do," Alya confessed. "I guess her night out with the girls without consequences will be her congratulations."

As they reached the big room, the Maasai nine ran to meet them.

"There is a man on the phone. He said he is waiting for you," she turned to Sam. "He said he has pulled the car to the front and has your papers."

"Thank you," Sam replied. "I believe she told you to enjoy the rest of your evening."

"It's okay, I can tell she is eager," Alya reminded Sam she was in charge. "No, he is correct. Go and spend time with your family. There will be plenty of time for you to answer phone calls and rise above your current expectations."

The woman spun and disappeared into her hallway. As Sam walked away, Alya grabbed his hand and pulled him back.

"We both know what is going to happen, but when it's over, you better come back and visit, or I will show you why everyone fears me," she warned as she kissed him on the cheek.

As the dull thud from the door rolled through the corridors. Alya turned in the dark room and almost jumped through the ceiling when she saw the woman standing in the hallway door. She was holding a thin white candle that made shadows dance on her face.

"Fuck, don't do that. You scared the shit out of me," Alya grabbed her chest.

"I am sorry," the woman apologized. "We drew straws, and I chose the short straw. I need to speak with you about your intentions towards my people."

"I can't see you, I don't know which people you mean," Alya waived the nine over before realizing it was too dark for the woman to see the gesture. "Come, sit on the sofa. Let's talk."

"Thank you," the woman said as her face floated in the dark behind the candle.

Alya walked to the woman and felt through the dark for the sofa. She sat, not sure she was going to hit cushion.

"Now, what is the problem? You are no different than anyone else. You know about consequences, good and bad."

"Yes, but we also know the numbers," the woman's voice was monotone. "We are Jewish."

"The numbers have nothing to do with the Jewish people," Alya was confused.

"A lot of our symbols have the evil number. Many have said that means the Society and the Council believe we are evil," she responded.

"I had not realized Mohammed treated your team any different than the other teams," Alya challenged.

"He didn't," she confirmed.

"That makes sense. Like it makes sense that I would not treat you any differently," Alya reached to pat the woman's leg. She missed and patted the cushion, then retracted her hand in embarrassment.

The woman must have felt or heard the gesture and confused the meaning because she scooted closer.

"I don't understand how our symbols can be determined to be evil if we are not determined to be the same," she was begging for more clarity.

"Let me share a secret with you. You have to promise it does not go beyond this conversation," Alya whispered.

"Of course, I don't want the consequences," the woman's answer reflected Alya's tone.

"No, not because of the consequences, because I am sharing something I do not want others to know. I keep my past private and want it to stay private," Alya corrected the misunderstanding.

"Ahh," the woman's eyes opened wide, and her voice no longer monotone. "I promise."

"I am Jewish, and the departed Iranian twenty-two was Jewish. The difference was that I follow the rules and am humble, and he lost his way. The society loves all humans no matter where they come from, or to which beliefs they ascribe."

"That can't be true." The woman's jaw slacked as she made an audible gasp.

"It is true, just because systems designed to control humans, like religions, government, and economies, harbor evil and evil symbology does not mean humans are evil. Sometimes humans get bastardized, distorted, abused, and so forth by those systems, but they are still humans, and all humans deserve love, kindness, respect, the chance at redemption, autonomy, and so many other words."

"Wait," the woman shook her head in disbelief, "So, what you are saying is that the Jewish people are not the Jewish nation, the Jewish religion, nor the Jewish faith?"

"You're quick. If more humans realized they are not their beliefs, government, or employment, this world would be a far safer, more loving, and human planet. Does that help assuage your concerns?"

"You asked a question," the woman noted.

"Yes, sometimes rules can be broken without consequences if it is merited," Alya embraced the woman. "Return to your place. It's getting late. I am keeping the candle; I prefer to walk in the light."

"I am glad we talked. We are all glad you are home, safe, surrounded by all the people who love you," the woman's words hung in the air long after she departed.

Alya sat, contemplating the sentiment. She was home. That night was her first in the Pink Room, and she let her do something she had not done since she was a child. Alya fell asleep smiling and without fear.

Full Circle

Embarrassing Ignorance

"Come on," Stacy glided into bed behind the line of cuddling women. "We are going to have a night on the town to celebrate."

"We can do that?" Prudence sparkled.

"Of course, Pru. I am a twenty-two. I can do pretty much anything," Stacy beamed. "Ginny, Bea, come on, get up."

"What is there to celebrate? Nancy is gone, the Harem got attacked, so many people died today," Bea snapped. "How can we celebrate? You abandoned us."

"Stop!" Prudence shouted. "Just stop it! You are always blaming Stacy, and it isn't fair."

"Thank you, Pru, but Bea has the freedom to be grumpy. Terrible things have happened, and I haven't been around. Let me make it up to you, Bea?" Stacy climbed over Ginny and Pru to curl against Beatrice.

"You can't cuddle your way out of this," Beatrice resisted as she scooted against Stacy. "You have to make it up to me."

"Then come with me. Let's have a night of freedom," Stacy pulled her arm as she got out of bed.

"Please, Bea," Prudence begged.

"All right, fine," Beatrice acted like getting out of bed was a struggle.

"I already have the dresses picked out," Ginny called from the closet. "They are the ones that will work."

"Let's see what ya got, Gin," Stacy called.

"Those are so pretty," Prudence fawned.

"I get the blue one," Beatrice declared.

"Purple for me," Stacy reached out a hand.

"Do you want red or nude, Ginny?" Prudence asked.

"I can't wear the nude. It washes me out. You can have it," Ginny handed the dress to Prudence.

"It's fine," prudence huffed. "I am sure someone was going to see me nude tonight anyway."

The women burst into laughter. They carried their heels as they snuck out, but the Canadian door swung open.

"It's too late to be wandering around dressed like that," a Canadian pointed at Prudence.

"It's late for a nine to be judging the orders of a twenty-two," Stacy growled.

"I didn't mean anything by it," the woman stammered. "I apologize. Should we tell anyone anything if they come looking for you?"

"Nobody is going to look for us, mind your business," Stacy replied. "You Canadians used to be so cool, what happened."

The woman stared, dumbfounded.

"Tell them you saw us leaving in a car when you were in the garden," Prudence offered peace.

The Canadian looked from Prudence to Stacy for confirmation.

"Close your door and go back to your friends," Stacy demanded.

When the door closed, Ginny said, "That was mean. They have always had our backs."

"I am sorry, Gin. Let's go have some fun and forget this place for a while."

The pungent stench of death soaked their clothing as they crossed the garden. Ginny swore she heard someone having sex when they passed the Arboretum, but the others didn't believe her.

In the parking lot, the keys were in the sedan. After some debate, Stacy drove with Prudence in the front seat. Beatrice and Ginny were not happy about being in the back, but the fact they were going out made nothing else matter.

Prudence flicked on the radio and searched through the stations until she found the perfect music. A rhythmic thumping shook the windows.

"Nope," Stacy said as she changed the station. "Find something with words."

"Like what?" Prudence squinted her nose.

"Something to get us pumped. We are badass bitches that are going to wreck the city. Let's find something like that."

"Deal," Prudence flipped through the stations until they found their song.

"These be red bottoms," rapped the radio.

All the women sang the words as their excitement grew.

When they reached the edge of the city, Beatrice was performing a solo, *"Now we have problems, and I really don't think we can solve them."*

Stacy wasn't sure where to go or how to find the man, so she drove around exploring.

"Are we lost?" Ginny asked.

"No," Stacy replied, "We are exploring. We don't get out often, so let's find the best party."

"Have you been here before?" Beatrice asked.

"Stacy said we are exploring until we find the best party," Prudence echoed. "Tell us if you see a place that looks interesting."

The red light offered no clues as she stopped. There were lights everywhere, and it seemed like the choices were endless. She took a right, deciding to keep taking right turns, driving further between each turn, to spiral through the city until she found the target.

As she took the next right, she smiled. At the entrance of the hotel was her pot of gold.

"I see what I am looking for," she informed the others.

"The hotel?" Prudence gave her a funny look. "We have beds at home."

"Nope, not the hotel," Stacy replied as she pulled up to the valet.

A young man circled the front of the car and opened her door. "Welcome to the, nope. You need to leave. We can't park you." He closed the door.

"What do you mean you can't park me, this is a valet stand," Stacy argued as she stepped out.

"No," he replied. "Not for you. You are bad news. Last time I met you, someone shot at me, and the car was damaged. My boss had to pay a large bill for the damage. No service, you have to leave."

"I made you a promise, remember?" Stacy used her sultry voice.

"I remember, but I do not want to die tonight," Nasir ushered her back toward the seat.

"My friends want to thank you, too," Stacy giggled as she stroked his arm.

"Are they as much trouble as you?" He asked as he looked into the car.

"We want to thank you and have fun," Stacy smiled.

"No, I can't, I am working. They look like trouble. They are much too attractive to be interested in me."

"True, they are too attractive for you, but you saved me, and they owe me a favor. They are my gift, and I am keeping my promise," Stacy winked at the women.

Prudence spread her legs to let the man see she was not wearing underwear.

"Wow," he was flabbergasted. "Let me see if I can go on break, but I will not go to your place. That is too dangerous."

"This is a hotel," Stacy smiled. "Hop in, we'll park together."

"I have to drive," Nasir replied. "All women must go in the back."

"Even me?" Stacy made her flirtiest face.

"Especially you. But maybe not her. I am going to see the rest of her tonight." He looked at Prudence.

"Told you so," Prudence whispered to Ginny and Beatrice.

The women in the car let out a deep laugh as Stacy sat in the back seat. The ladies kept Nasir entertained while Stacy rented a room. When she returned, it was clear Nasir was nervous despite his obvious excitement.

"We are on the third floor," Stacy opened the door. "Be sure to hide our hero on the way up so he doesn't get in trouble for taking his break with guests."

"Is this our night out?" Beatrice asked as she looked at Ginny.

"Look, he saved my life and is the one who drove me back to the house. I promised him I would repay his kindness. After this, we can go dancing."

"That sounds fair," Ginny hedged. "What's the catch?"

"No catch," Stacy replied as they walked inside, Prudence was making out with Nasir. "We take turns riding his dick until he is finished, then we dance."

"Can I go first?" Beatrice requested. "I can't remember the last time a real one was in me."

Prudence laughed in the man's mouth, causing the others to cackle. The closer they were to the room, the more sweat appeared on his brow. By the time they reached the door, his knees appeared to be getting shaky.

"You're nervous," Beatrice hissed in his ear. Hold these for support. She placed his hands over her breasts as Stacy opened the door.

"I can't do this," Nasir freaked out.

"Pull him in, ladies," Stacy ordered as she held the door.

"He's a lot weaker than he looks," Ginny giggled as the women worked him through the door. "Where do you want him?"

"Put him on the bed!" Beatrice trumpeted.

"Calm, ladies," Stacy's voice soothed the mood. "Sit him on the bed and go into the bathroom. I need a minute to speak with our guest."

When the bathroom door shut, Stacy straddled Nasir's lap and held his cheeks in her hands.

"Hey, how are you doing?" She ground her crotch into his lap. "Remember how brave and strong you were when we met?"

"I have fantasized about this so many times," he confided in hushed tones. "But I have never been with a woman. It's embarrassing, and I am too nervous. What if I don't do it right or hurt one of you?"

Stacy gave him a tender, sensual kiss, "You are a true prince. You can do no wrong tonight, and you aren't strong enough to hurt us. Be brave. We will do the work, lay back and enjoy yourself."

"I can't. I am too nervous. I am really, really sorry," he was about to cry.

"Hey, it's okay. You don't need to do anything. Lay and relax. I'll make sure the women don't touch you. If you want to play in a bit, don't ask permission; you already have it. Does that sound fair?"

"Nobody will touch me?"

"Yeah, nobody will touch you unless you ask us," Stacy stepped off his lap. "Is that better?"

"Yes, I can do that," Nasir wiped his face and moved to the armchair.

"Ladies, you can come out," Stacy announced. "You are going to have to arouse yourselves. Nasir is feeling shy. He might join in a bit."

The women exited the bathroom without a noise and disrobed. Prudence and Beatrice were the first to climb onto the bed. Standing on their knees, they made out and rubbed each others' arms and sides.

Ginny gave Stacy a look, requesting guidance on what she should do. Stacy flapped her hands toward the bed. Ginny climbed on the bed behind the kissing couple and spread her legs. She moistened two fingers in her mouth. Using her middle finger and her thumb, she spread her lips and massaged her clitoris.

Beatrice paused from kissing Prudence, glancing down at Ginny. She turned and lowered her front half to the bedspread, rotating her body so her sex was pointed at Nasir. She clasped Ginny's hands and pushed them over her head as she lapped at Ginny's opening. A moan caught Nasir's attention.

As Stacy watched him, it was clear his nervousness was vanishing. She walked to Prudence, who was sitting on her knees watching Ginny and Beatrice. Prudence pulled Stacy's dress down as Stacy shimmied. When she felt the dress on her feet, Stacy lifted each foot and removed her heels.

Stacy laid Prudence backward beside Beatrice and climbed on top. She slipped the index and middle fingers of each hand into her mouth, then found Prudence's and Beatrice's openings. She worked her fingers inside. Beatrice had not been dishonest. She was extremely tight.

As Stacy fingered, she ensured to stimulate the clitorises as much as possible while also finding the G-spots. She was so focused that she didn't feel Prudence start to stroke her love button with a thumb. Stacy looked over her shoulder at Nasir. He had begun stroking his member.

"Join us," she mouthed.

"In a minute," he mouthed back as he undressed.

Stacy had felt his staff but never saw it. When she did, she was delighted. Stacy had become so delighted that Prudence noticed.

"You got super wet," Prudence announced as her hips gyrated to the rhythm of Stacy's fingers.

"He has a pretty dick," Stacy mouthed.

Prudence cocked her head to sneak a peak. "It's average size," she whispered.

"Yeah," Stacy smiled, "But look at the shape and the head. It's pretty."

"I don't see it," Prudence shrugged.

Nasir took a half step toward the bed when Ginny let out a deep moan. He was staring at Beatrice's backside as Stacy continued probing. He stepped closer and readied his spear. He placed a foot on the bed and thrust towards her lips.

The tip of his pleasure poked her ass cheek as he lost his balance. He had to use his hand to stop himself from falling. Stacy pulled her fingers out of Prudence and covered her mouth. The site was so awkward and hilarious. Having seen the event, Prudence snatched a pillow and covered her face to seal her laughter with both hands.

"What's going on," Beatrice lifted her mouth from Ginny's sex.

"He is getting ready to enter you," Stacy struggled to keep serious. "I am going to guide him in."

"I am so fucking ready," Beatrice moaned.

Prudence's muffled laughter erupted. Stacy twisted her body, trying to get a better view. The position stretched her side too much, so she climbed off Prudence. Taking him with her hand, she guided his passion into her mouth for lubrication.

"Ready?" She asked, looking into his wide eyes.

He nodded. Stacy wrapped an arm around his waist and moved him into position as she lined up his staff.

"Bea, open up," she said as she pulled him toward the bed. Beatrice reached back with a hand to spread her lips.

"Gently," Stacy smiled as she rocked the tip of his member up and down between Beatrice's lips as he pressed forward. "Good, grab her hips and show her who's boss."

"Fuck!" Beatrice moaned as he thrust. "I deserve this," she moaned as she clutched the bedspread. "Nasir, yes."

Ginny smiled at Stacy, who shrugged her shoulders. They both watched as Nasir did his best to be an expert. He slipped out a couple of times, but Beatrice's hand was there to guide him.

"What do we do?" Ginny whispered.

"I don't know," Stacy replied as Prudence peaked from beneath the pillow.

Ginny swung her leg over Beatrice's head, and Prudence caught it. She removed the pillow and guided Ginny's mound to her lips. Ginny looked at Stacy and shrugged.

"Fuck her face," Stacy said as she stuck out her tongue.

Feeling left out, Stacy laid her head between Prudence's legs. She knew this night was for them and wanted to make sure her favorite, Prudence, was satisfied.

Prudence always smelled sweet, and the reason was a mystery. Stacy looked at Beatrice, whose eyes had rolled back as her breasts slapped with every thrust by the mediocre man. She turned back to Prudence, used her thumbs to spread the lips, and worked.

It never took Prudence long to get aroused or to get her hips to figure eight as she neared completion. Stacy knew the key to Prudence was three flat tongues, one sharp tongue swipe, one sharp tongue circle, wiggle the tongue inside, and repeat. After a few iterations of Prudence's combination, Stacy felt hands burrow their fingers into her hair. As Prudence spasmed, an unexpected feeling appeared hands on her hips.

She turned to look over her shoulder. Nasir was standing behind her, holding his dick. She looked at Beatrice, who was lying beside her heaving for air.

"It's the best I have had in a long time, don't judge," Beatrice panted. "Let me catch my breath, and I will go again."

"I thought you said I would have anyone tonight?" Nasir asked as Stacy looked at him.

"I'm waiting, big boy," Stacy flirted as she used one hand to open herself and the other to help him find the entrance.

Stacy pretended it was good sex but made her pretending obvious. This night was not about her; it was about the others. They deserved a real man that wasn't there to beat the shit out of them.

"I am lame," Stacy confessed. "Prudence, the one I have been pleasuring, or Ginny, the one standing on her knees with her pussy in Prudence's mouth, are much better at sex. Which do you want first?"

"I don't want to offend anyone," Nasir's cheeks pinked.

"Beatrice, go recover in the chair," Stacy pushed Beatrice toward the edge of the bed. Stacy slapped Ginny's thigh. "Lay over there. Prudence will lay here. Let Nasir choose what he wants."

Both women lay on their backs with their hands behind their heads. Their knees were bent, and their legs spread.

"I'd fuck them both, but the choice is yours. Go get them, tiger," Stacy slapped Nasir on the ass as she felt herself taking on the role of his sex coach. "Fuck them hard and deep. Make them beg for more," she laughed until Nasir gave her an uncomfortable look. Even the ladies seemed puzzled.

"Sorry," Stacy whispered. "Do your thing. Beatrice and I will be over here."

Nasir pulled Prudence to the end of the bed and placed her feet against his shoulders. He wiggled his way inside and thumped.

"Wait," Prudence was shocked, "How are you going this deep?"

Nasir smiled as he squeezed each of her breasts and pounded faster.

"Holy shit! Stacy, he does have a beautiful penis," Prudence's voice was vibrating like she was talking through a fan.

Nasir worked his hammer for several minutes as Prudence squealed all manners of compliments and pleasurable sounds.

"I want this. Cum in me. I want to feel your cum," she whispered as his body stiffened. As she rubbed his chest affectionately, she moaned, "Good boy."

When he pulled out and let her feet find the floor, Prudence grabbed his neck and pulled him down. She kissed him an authentic kiss of passion, then pushed him away.

"Who's next?" Prudence stepped off the bed. "Saving the best for last. Ginny is the fucking best."

"Yeah, I am so good that everyone forgets about me," Ginny looked disappointed.

Nasir didn't seem to notice. He walked to the bedside where Ginny's head was resting. With his flaccid mass dangling in front of her, Ginny opened her mouth and swallowed it. Nasir grunted as he stacked the pillows on the edge.

"Is he building a fort?" Beatrice whispered.

"Shh..." Stacy hushed.

Ginny was magic with her mouth, and it was not long before Nasir was ready for another round. He took her hand and assisted her from the bed. Nasir led her to the stack of pillows and rotated her toward them.

"Ohhh," Beatrice blurted.

Nasir guided Ginny's hips onto the stack of pillows and knelt. He spread her lips with his fingers and licked.

"mmmm," Ginny moaned.

Nasir took that as a sign and stood. He entered Ginny and penetrated her pleasure. He bent forward and kissed her back as he pushed.

"Why's he trying to be romantic?" Prudence asked.

"Who knows, but hush," Stacy held a finger to her mouth.

After a few minutes of delicate probing, Nasir rolled Ginny off the stack of pillows and onto her side. He stepped over her lower leg and wrapped the top around his waist. Holding her nape in one hand and a breast in the other, he crossed the threshold into Ginny's enjoyment.

"This is so cheesy, but it feels so good. Why does this feel so good?" Ginny was smiling as she placed a hand over her mouth.

Nasir smiled as he bent forward and kissed her with intense sexual love. As their lips parted, a single strand of the kiss kept their mouths momentarily connected.

"I'm ready," Ginny smiled, looking into Nasir's eyes. "Fill me with your love. She stretched her arms and pulled his hips. He smiled as he rocked back and collided their delights.

"Please," Ginny begged, "I want your love. Release into me."

Nasir bent his knees and pushed against her, "For you, anything,"

He held their bodies together as he finished filling Ginny. When he extracted himself, the three onlookers smiled and shook their heads in approval. Nasir's face became red as he walked to his clothes.

"I'm sorry," he said as he put on his underwear.

"Hey, no. Stacy lifted his chin so their eyes met. "Look around the room. Four of the most beautiful women in the world were pleasured by you. And Ginny, she may be in love with you. You have nothing to apologize for. You were great. I wish, hell, we all wish more men were like you."

"But you all only had sex with me because you had a debt to pay. You didn't really want me," he slipped his legs into his pants.

"Beatrice," Stacy called over her shoulder. "Did anyone force you to have sex with Nasir? Did you fake your pleasure?"

"Fuck no," Beatrice snapped back. "It really has been a long time since I got some dick, and that was some good dick."

The women looked at each other and cackled.

"Sorry for laughing," Stacy struggled to stop. "We have never heard her talk like that."

"That's how you know it was some good dick," Beatrice's voice was serious, and the others laughed.

"Enough about Beatrice," Stacy said as Nasir put his shirt on. "Ginny and Prudence, what are your thoughts."

"I thought you had a small dick," Prudence shrugged, "but I don't know what that thing was where you put my feet against your chest, or shoulders, or whatever, that was amazing. I liked it. If you have enough in you, we can go again."

"Back off, love you bitch, but if he has another run, he's mine," Ginny demanded from the bed.

"Ginny doesn't talk that way either or demand things. She might be trying to top Beatrice, but she liked your performance. Have more self-confidence. You will get further," Stacy recommended.

"What about you?" He asked. "Why didn't you want me?"

"I am kind of a party girl. They never get to leave the house. I wanted them to have fun on their night out. Plus, I was being honest, I am pretty bad and boring at sex. I end up falling on the floor and breaking my nose or something," Stacy kissed Nasir on the chin. "If I am ever back in town, it will be you and me."

"I believe you," he smiled as he slipped his shoes on. "I am way late returning to work, but it was so worth it. The others will never believe my story."

As the door closed behind Nasir, Stacy turned to the group, "Who wants to go dancing?"

The Dance Continues

"I like your hat, my dad likes the Redwings, too. What can I get you?" A perky voice inquired.

It had been a long time since he was free to choose how to answer. He lowered the paper to let his eyes find the face. She was attractive and ignorant.

"They may have a chance this year. May I have an iced mocha?" He had always wondered how they tasted.

"Ooo, those are my favorite. We must be kindred spirits," the woman smiled. "Anything else?"

The man contemplated the question, getting lost in thought, not noticing he was lowering the paper and revealing his face.

"Oh my god," the woman gasped. "I'm sorry. I didn't mean it," she rambled as her face became a rose garden. "I have never—. Are you a firefighter? I am talking too much. I am aware I am talking too much. I'm sorry. I am going to get that mocha. Wait, did you want anything else?" The way she fidgeted screamed she was antsy and needed the permission to leave.

"It's fine. You are doing perfect. The mocha is all I would like at the moment," the man replied, trying to calm any anxiety and embarrassment.

He watched the woman from the corner of his eye as she scurried behind the counter, staying behind the large bakery case to hide from the world.

The man wondered what her life had been like and what it would hold. He closed his eyes and imagined how his life would be different if he had a daughter. He wondered what she would be like and if he would have been able to spare her from the pain of his reality.

"Are you sleeping?" the voice whispered. "I forgot to ask your name when I took your order."

"My name?" He questioned without opening his eyes. "You don't bring the orders to the table?"

"Yes, I am going to bring your drink to you, but it's policy. We are supposed to ask your name and write it on the cup so we know the correct person gets the correct drink."

The absurdity of the explanation made him chuckle. He had somehow entered a comedy bit that even the likes of Abbott and Costello could appreciate.

"Nestor," he offered.

"Thank you. I will be back with your drink in a minute. And sorry for before, I..." the woman walked away without finishing.

He let his mind muse on the idea of having lived a different life. One which included a family. The sound of the drink being placed on the table interrupted his imagination. He opened his eyes as the woman was trying to sneak away.

"Wait," he called as he removed a money clip from his pocket. "Take this. You deserve more than what you get." He handed her a twenty dollar bill, "I don't want the change, it's yours."

The woman accepted the gratuities, which seemed to fix her posture. She stood up and walked behind the counter.

As he sipped the chocolatey caffeine, he watched the door across the walkway. The aircraft was maneuvered into position, and the ramp attached in the windows beside the door. He had been waiting six hours for it to reveal his target, and the time was drawing near.

His heart started to race. The room became hot, and he had to pee. He became aware that he was being obvious. The newspaper was lifted, and he pretended to read. Needing to relieve the discomfort of his dry mouth, he lifted the drink without releasing the paper. The paper poked him in the eye as he took a sip. Putting the drink down, it landed on the corner of the paper.

The door was opening. He stood and failed to move the drink to free the paper without spilling. People were starting to exit the door. He pushed the drink across the table, and it stopped, teetering on the edge. Was that her, could she see him?

He plunged back into the chair and raised the paper in front of his face. His heart was racing. His hands trembled. He sat motionless as the paper rattled in his hands.

"You might have had too much caffeine," the woman whispered from behind the counter. "Would you like some water or a muffin?"

The man bumped the table as he shook his head. The drink tumbled to the floor. Cold, brown embarrassment splattered the floor and his leg.

He looked at the woman behind the counter, "I am sorry."

"It's okay, you are a good tipper," she smiled.

He removed a five-dollar bill and placed it on the table as she pulled a mop from the swinging door behind her. The man lowered the paper. All of the people had exited the aircraft, and the door had been shut.

As the woman approached with the mop, he said, "I didn't mean to. Please take this extra five as my apology."

"Who am I to turn down free money?" She smiled as she mopped.

The man stalked his prey. She was hiding in the crowd of travelers. He knew she must be headed for the luggage carousel but wasn't sure which head was hers. He knew she was shorter than that woman and taller than the one over there. She wasn't that fat or as lanky as that one. He made his way through the crowd, trying to spot his mark without being seen.

He needed to be discrete around the cameras. After all, he was supposed to be dead. He hovered from wall to wall as he advanced, stopping when he might be approaching the intended, but he made it all the way to the carousel without finding her. As he watched people collect their luggage, he was miffed. How had he missed her?

Then, from the corner of his eye, he spotted a woman walking towards the taxis outside. He turned and sprinted toward the door as a man jogging with a luggage cart passed in front of him.

The collision was ugly. He fell headlong over the cart as a carry-on dropped on his belly. It almost knocked the wind out of him, but he was transfixed. The cart pusher helped him to his feet while apologizing and trying to escape blame. He had no time for that. He ran with a sore leg.

As he made it to the curb, he reached into his pocket and removed a phone. He held it up and snapped photos of the woman while the taxi driver placed her luggage in the trunk. As the driver slammed the trunk, she turned and looked in his direction. He ducked behind a black SUV that had stopped to let people out.

As the SUV pulled away, the man stepped back onto the curb. The woman and the taxi were gone. He dialed the phone.

"Are you ready?" A young woman asked.

"Yes, I have confirmed it's her. Were you able to secure the apartment?"

"Yeppers, I've been waiting in the cell phone lot. I will be there in a minute. I can't wait to see the photos. Does she know we are tracking her?"

"No, but I hope that she accepts the intent and extent. If not, we may be fucked."

"She would never betray the society," the young woman replied.

"People change, she is advancing in her career and may not know the limits or protocols that have been provided."

"She is the one that will save us all. I just hope she is as we believe," she brushed off the doubt.

"This isn't a fairytale. You know that you were one of the best. You have been on missions with me. She can't do it alone, and there will be death, lots of death. You should be prepared to watch me be murdered, or her, or even you. We are all in a new world where there are no rules, no society, and no safety."

"I know," her voice was faint. "But, we are going to do as much damage as we can. When we lay down, too exhausted to continue, then we will be defeated."

"Do you have the documents? We need to go back to the apartment and rehearse," a white sedan stopped in front of him. As he sat, he continued, "We need to rehearse our identities and roles. What is your name?"

"I'm sorry, Nestor, or do I call you step-daddy?" She was snarky, "I will ensure everyone knows I am Olivia."

"Thank you, Olivia. You should call me 'dad' or 'papa.' The word 'daddy' is too sexual," he explained.

"What if I want to be sexual?" She gave him a perverted smile. "Step-daughters have needs, too."

"Watch yourself," he smirked. "I like the meat."

"I know what you like, Daddy. I have toys," she continued.

"The future is far less predictable than any of us could have ever anticipated," he replied. "Now, let's get back to the apartment before the dark swallows us."

"That was a super weird way to say that," she laughed. "You are so weird, but I kind of like it. We could have been friends in our other life if we weren't so afraid of the rules."

"The rules have a use, but yes, when the rules prevent humans from being human, it may be time to redesign the rulebook to ensure humans come first and can develop the kinds of relationships which allow societies to flourish."

"I have no idea what that means, but you just offered to be my daddy," she looked at him with crossed eyes.

"It means we should be friends without expectation. No matter what, I am here for you," he intertwined her fingers with his.

Unsettling Arrivals

"On behalf of North Star Airlines, I would like to thank the flight attendants and all of our passengers for choosing to fly with us. I would also like to be the first to welcome home everyone who lives in the D.M.V. If you are visiting or have a connecting flight, I welcome you to Washington, D.C., where taxes are harvested, and legislation is stalled. The temperature outside is a perfect fifty-four degrees, so sweatshirts are advised, especially if you are traveling with little ones. We will be arriving at gate twenty-two in eight minutes. Please remain seated until we have reached the gate and the crew has opened the door," the captain announced.

To say the flight had been turbulent was an understatement. Not more than twenty minutes before, the plane dropped one hundred feet and slammed against the sky beneath. Several luggage bins had flown open, and one woman was upset that her underwear had flung onto a man's head. He didn't seem to mind as much.

"I don't know why she is so upset," Stacy thought, *"She isn't even attractive. She should be glad someone is willing to enjoy her granny panties."*

Focusing on the short, greasy woman helped keep Stacy's mind off her nerves and belly. This was her first true mission, and she experienced stomach-churning nausea since she departed the Harem.

Her last mission wasn't a success, and this one was far more consequential. The destiny of the entire world was dependent on her. Stacy grabbed her belly and moaned as it bubbled into her throat.

"Do you need to get up?" the man in the tank top beside her asked. "I'm sure they'll make an exception if you still feel ill."

He raised his arm to summon a flight attendant, causing his stink to clobber her remaining self-control.

Stacy gagged as the man jumped to his feet in the aisle. She held up an arm, shaking her hand in descent as she covered her mouth. Vomit spewed through her fingers and covered his seat.

"I am going to be ill," he gagged into a closed fist. The man walked several steps toward the rear of the plane as more puke punched through her fingers and puddled on the seat.

The inside of Stacy's throat burned from the acids, and the smell hung heavy in the air. It burned her eyes, and the outcry of complaints and admonishments from fellow passengers was not helping. A flight attendant walked to the vacant seat and threw her hands up.

"Hell no," she said as she turned around. "Linda, you are going to have to deal with this shit. I do not get paid enough. There's a woman throwing up everywhere. Bring paper towels."

Another flight attendant approached from the rear, holding a stack of paper towels and a bag. As she squeezed around the hairy man, he pressed his crotch against her and said something. Disgust filled her face as she slid away.

"If I sat next to him, I would be vomiting, too," the woman said as she spread the paper towels across the puddle. She raised her voice slightly, "He smells like shit, has a tiny dick, and says the nastiest things."

"Thank you," Stacy managed.

"Don't thank me," the woman replied. "Just be glad the rest of the passengers are so calm. This could have gotten a lot worse. I recommend we let them off first."

"Okay," Stacy disagreed but wasn't going to argue.

"Plus," the flight attendant whispered. "It's not like the airline is going to stop someone from sitting here in twenty minutes when the next crew boards the next flight. You would be surprised how many people sit in others' fluids and never realize."

"That's super gross," Stacy laughed.

"There we go, you are feeling better. Take this bag. If you feel ill, get it in the bag. We will leave these paper towels on the seat for the cleaning crew."

The flight attendant returned to the plane's tail, glaring at the hairy man as she approached. He sucked in his gut and stared at the ceiling as she passed. During the commotion, the plane had docked, and the crew was scrambling to open the door and get the passengers off.

"This is the fastest I have ever seen a plane cleared," the flight attendant said. "You are the last one. Do you feel well enough to walk, or should we ask for a medic?"

"Sorry," Stacy apologized. "I am going. Her legs were weak, but she managed. As she walked up the ramp, the airline attendant was waiting to close the door.

"Last one," the attendant jeered. "I hope you enjoy your visit."

"Thank you," the airport seemed more relaxing. Stacy could breathe easier, and her stomach settled. An uneasy feeling like someone was watching tingled her senses. She looked around, but nothing seemed odd. There was a café, a tiny convenience store, and a newsstand.

The luggage carousel was crowded when she arrived. She pulled her bag free and headed for the door. A ride had been scheduled, but she didn't know who to expect. A taxi stopped in front of her when she raised an arm in the air.

"Where ya headed?" A short-haired woman asked.

"I am waiting for my ride," Stacy responded.

"I can be your ride. I'll even give you a discount."

"No, sorry. I didn't mean to signal you," Stacy requested forgiveness.

"That's why I hate you fucking tourists," the woman replied. "You are all a bunch of fucking teases."

"I'm sorry," Stacy called as tires squealed.

bew-woop! Bew-woop!

A police vehicle appeared from nowhere and pulled behind the taxi. Stacy observed the driver punching the steering wheel as the taxi navigated to the side.

"Choices and consequences," Stacy giggled internally.

Another taxi stopped in front of Stacy. The driver didn't move, say anything, or seem to be breathing as the passenger window rolled down.

"Kimberly?" He asked without moving his head.

"Are you my ride?" Stacy asked.

"Alexandria sent me for Kimberly. I am supposed to wait five minutes and am permitted to circle five times. If Kimberly misses me, she will have to find herself a ride. It's five miles to her new apartment. That may make it difficult for her to arrive at work by five in the morning."

"I have a bag," Stacy replied.

"Ahh, Kimberly, I am honored to be your driver," he vaulted from the taxi. As he lifted her bag into the trunk, he continued, "Are you aware of your admirer? He is to my right, by the black SUV. Take a peak, then get in the cab. He may be someone unfriendly."

Stacy appeared as though she was looking at her surroundings. She saw the man, and they locked eyes as he darted behind the SUV.

"*What the fuck?*" Her brain was not able to accept what she had seen. "*Why are you playing games on me, stupid eyes? This is my first mission, you better stop acting up, or we are going to have issues.*"

"Anyone you know?" The driver inquired while navigating through the airport traffic.

"No, and I don't believe he was looking at me. He looked too young and attractive to be interested in me," Stacy worked to change how the driver remembered the man. "He looked Italian or maybe Greek. What are your thoughts?"

"If you don't mind me saying, you are a beauty. Any man would be lucky to have you, Greek, Italian, or otherwise," the driver smiled in the mirror.

"I appreciate the feedback. How long until we reach my apartment?"

"The GPS says thirty-eight minutes. It will be longer. Rush hour is terrible."

"I am going to shut my eyes and relax. I won't fall asleep, so please do not try to wake me," Stacy closed her eyes.

"Sounds good," he replied. "The further we travel from where we started, the longer it takes to return to our proper state of being. We need to make one stop in Alexandria before heading to the apartment."

"Tonight?' Stacy whined.

"Afraid so, I was told to wait, so it should be quick."

"Lovely," Stacy grumbled.

The Beltway was miserable. Stacy understood large cities and traffic, but the driver was terrible. As the traffic flowed, he stomped the pedal, throwing Stacy backward. One hundred feet later, he stomped on the brakes.

"Hey," she could feel her stomach begin to churn. "Is it much further?"

"We are the next exit. First time in the D.M.V.?"

"What's that?" She returned.

"D.C., Maryland, Virginia; it's this area. Nova is Northern Virginia, and I take that as a yes, you are a first-timer. The traffic is never this bad," he bemoaned.

"It seems like people enjoy slamming on the brakes." she hinted.

"Folks move here a lot. You would hope they would learn to drive," he agreed as the tires screeched and Stacy flung forward.

The driver laid across the front seat to look out the passenger window.

"Close enough," he muttered as he careened into the brake down lane and raced.

Just as the lines on the highway were about to create an exit lane, a car darted in front of the taxi and stopped.

"Every time?" the driver mumbled. "Once we arrive, I will drop you near the bus stop. Someone should be waiting. When you're finished, I will take you to the apartment."

"Sounds good," she looked at the ocean of cars. "Do this many people work here?"

"Even more, these are people who park close. More park further, and most take the metro," he educated. "This is where I let you out. Do you know him?"

"I don't know anyone, I am super new," she was delighted to escape the roller coaster.

"We have arrived," he announced with his most regal impression, holding out a hand.

"Thank you, my good sir," Stacy played along.

"Kimberly?" The man standing in a dark blue suit inquired. She nodded, and he continued, "Welcome to the Pentagon. Let's get you inside. Top is waiting to read you in."

"Lead the way," she gestured with her hand. "I didn't catch your name."

"I didn't drop it," he replied.

Stacy wasn't sure if he was an asshole or trying to be funny, but either way, she did not like him.

"That took a while," the driver commented when she returned.

"It sure did, and it could have waited until the morning. I have no idea why they wanted me to perform meet-and-greets this evening," she complained.

"Welp, I am the driver, so I can't make those decisions. Let's get you home so you can rest. Is the address they gave me correct?" He pointed to the GPS screen.

"Those are correct," Stacy assumed. The driver worked his way onto the freeway as she found her new driver's license and checked the address.

"*Kimberly Wainscot, who comes up with these names? I wonder if I look like Kimberly or Kim. Kimberly or Kim, which is better, sounds better? I should be Kimberly, it's more formal and suits the last name, like I am from old money,*" Stacy obsessed about the fine details and nuances of her identity as the taxi made its way to the apartment.

"Wow, these are nice," the driver fawned. "I was going to move here, but it felt overly secure, like a prison. It's all too much for me, but it's wonderful for you. A pretty lady like you deserves to feel safe and protected. A man like me, I like the freedom."

"Haha, that's funny," Stacy felt the words burst forth before she realized he was being serious. "Thank you for the ride."

"It was my pleasure, let me grab your bag," he requested as the car stopped in front of the door.

As the car pulled away, Stacy stood in front of the keypad door, wondering what to do. She had not been told the combination. She searched the purse and wallet she had been given and found nothing. Out of a growing sense of frustration, she pressed *1234*. The lock clicked. Stacy opened the door and stepped into her future.

Final Twists

Bathroom Issues

"Welcome home. It's not often I transport a hero," the driver opened the sedan door. "They called to ask if you had landed. I let them know I was waiting for the crew to let you out."

"Thank you," Sam replied. "Do I have time for a nap, or are we headed to the Kremlin?"

"We must drive straight to the meeting site. Taking an hour for the crew to release the passengers put us behind schedule. I am sure you understand," the driver closed the door.

It had not been a long flight, but Sam needed to take a shit and wasn't sure how long he could hold it.

"We need to hurry. I need a few minutes to freshen up before I enter the meeting," he advised.

"Let me pull to the hangar. The toilet is there," the driver pointed at a door.

"I will be a few," Sam carefully waddled to the door. It was locked. He looked at the driver for advice and was prompted to knock. Sam banged on the door. The deadbolt slid. A tall, thin, blond man in an old flight suit pushed past in a hurry. Sam rushed inside.

As Sam washed his hands and prepared to leave, he noticed something etched on the door.

Do not resist the inevitable.
Use it against your enemies
so you can survive to continue
the fight. Your loved ones are
counting on you.

"*How can someone resist the inevitable? It is inevitable.*" Sam pondered the words as he walked to the car.

301

"Is everything okay?" The driver pried. "We should report the incident so it can be investigated and the pilot punished."

"I just destroyed that toilet. I hope the airport has a plumber. As for the pilot, I will handle him," Sam replied. "Get me to the meeting and be quiet."

"Will do," the driver consented.

Sam was not familiar with Russia, so he didn't realize the driver was taking him away from Moscow. The buildings became smaller and spread further apart. Trees were starting to become part of the roadside scenery.

"What is the meaning of this?" Sam demanded.

"I have been ordered to reroute you to a new meeting location. It is secured where there is less likelihood of the meeting being interrupted," the driver informed.

"Is the president paranoid? I am bringing good reports from the front lines in Ukraine, and they are hardly secret," Sam probed.

The doors locked, and a glass partition rose between the men. Sam's stomach grew heavy as his palms became icy. There was nothing he could do as he watched the residential homes transform into forest. Not long after, the pavement became dirt.

The trees squeezed the sides of the car as Sam spotted a field ahead. He considered running but wasn't sure where to run or who to trust. With a bounce over a rut, the car was in the clearing.

Outside, a door in a cement wall was pressed into a hillside. Sam pulled the door handle. It was still locked. He laid on the seat and kicked the window with both feet. As it was about to burst, the door above his head opened, and two men yanked him by the armpits. He was thrown to the ground.

The barrel of an AK-47 was inches from Sam's face. A petite woman stepped out of the hillside door as the car drove away. She had short black hair and wore the same Russian uniform. Even with the jagged scar over her eye, she was highly attractive.

"We have been waiting for you, Christian. Your people have been naughty." She stepped forward and knocked the wind out of Sam with her boot.

"Get him inside," she commanded.

Sam's lungs heaved with pain as the men dragged his body down a cement corridor. He resisted, but without oxygen, his rebellion was quelled. They strapped him to an odd-looking chair. It had hinges at every joint.

"We are going to be good friends, Christian," the woman's voice was foreboding. "I have plans for you. You cannot keep your secrets. Telling me everything is inevitable."

"Please," Sam panted, still trying to catch his breath. "My troops have served with honor and pride."

The woman crouched before Sam. She forced his head back using a handful of his hair.

"You do not understand the seriousness of this situation. You are not here because of the war in Ukraine. You are here because Alya did her best to kill me. You are a dirty fucking American, and your associate told us everything. After he failed to kill me at the train station, he became my good friend, too."

"You have it all wrong," Sam protested.

The woman turned to one of the men who had removed a paper from his pocket. Taking it, she held it up to Sam's face, "Is this you with the United States president?"

"*Fuck!*" Sam panicked. "*Fuck, fuck fuck. Okay, Sam, think. It could be a deepfake. Yes, tell her it is a deepfake.*"

"That is a deepfake from another ambitious general," he offered.

His offer was rejected with a fist to the eye, "This photo came from an American newspaper."

Sam knew he was in serious trouble and wracked his brain for more ideas.

"It's a secret," he whispered. "Get the guards out, and I can update you. Our president had me on a limited operation, but I can't reveal it in front of them. Let me free, and I will not report your insubordination and treason."

Another punch greeted his face.

"Who do you believe ordered your interrogation? After Alya 'died' and failed to murder me, we interrogated your operative. He was willing to tell us everything. He told us about your plot to murder the president. How Alya used me. How she worked to gain my favor and love, then betrayed me. What kind of subhuman tricks someone into falling in love with them and then forces them to watch as they die? I still see the way she convulsed, foaming at the mouth, dying. Then, she didn't even respect me enough to hide the fact she faked her murder? What kind of despicable subhuman causes such pain?"

"I don't know who you interrogated, but he is lying," Sam pleaded, knowing the Russian president wouldn't have betrayed the Society; No world leader would risk those consequences. "There is no plan to kill the Russian president. Alya killed herself to protect you, not hurt you. Consider it: if she wanted to kill the president, she could have. She was the one he trusted. TaVi, I am telling the truth."

As Sam uttered that name, he thought the woman's expression seemed to soften, but she pulled his head forward as she jumped with a bent knee. It squished his teeth into his cheek. As he worked it away with his tongue, he tasted blood. His head spun as his eyes pulsated.

"Get out. He needs some special attention, and I don't want you to get in trouble," she began shoving the guards toward the door.

"But our orders—" one protested.

"Unless you want to trade places with Christian, you will listen to my orders. I am in charge," she growled.

"We will be listening through the door to make sure you are safe," one stated as they stepped into the hallway and closed the door.

"Why did you use that name?" She asked as she pressed their cheeks together.

"Alya only knows you by that name. She thinks you are dead. She couldn't stop crying after we pulled her out. Your death is a loss she may not be able to recover from," he spoke in her ear.

"Tell me what I want to know," she screamed as she stepped back and slapped Sam's face with a clap. "You will talk, fucking American pig!" Another slap. "I need my tools."

The woman opened the door, "Get my tools."

"Where are they?" A guard asked.

"In closet 7H. Bring them at once. He needs to be incentivized to tell us what he knows."

"Where is 7H?" The same guard asked.

"You know where 7H is located. Go with him and make sure he gets the specified tools. You know which ones I prefer. Send Peska to take your place while you are getting my things," she pushed the men, and they walked.

Moments later, a tall blond took their spots.

"Get in here," TaVi heaved the new guard into the room.

"What the fuck?" Sam was flabbergasted. "What are you doing?"

"She is saving your ass. Tell Alya I survived. I will find her and explain everything," TaVi responded.

"I told you, I play for keeps, Sam," the blond replied as she helped TaVi undo the restraints. "We need to hurry. Those guards may be stupid, but they work quickly."

"Make it look good," TaVi said as Sam found his footing and prepared to strike.

"Not you, darling, I have this. Nobody touches my man," Sarah kissed Sam's cheek.

She grabbed TaVi's head and interlocked her fingers. TaVi's head lowered as Sarah's knee exploded into her face. When the knee connected, Tavi's eyes rolled. Sarah helped the body to the ground, ensuring the head did not receive another blow.

"If we are going to have our happily-ever-after, we need to go," Sarah tugged Sam from the room.

As they burst through the doors and found themselves in the middle of the Russian wilderness, screams nipped at their heels.

"What now?" Sam asked.

"Now we run," Sarah scrambled into the tree line as she pulled a GPS and satellite phone from a bag.

"Where did the bag come from?"

"They store them by the door so they can chase anyone who escapes without worrying about getting lost," Sarah smirked. "I have been on more than one mission and know how to prepare and improvise. Weren't you taught the same stuff?"

"Speaking of being chased..." Sam pointed at the growing group trickling out of the door.

"Let's move," the GPS says the nearest town is that way, so let's head this way. There is a field about four miles away."

"You can get an extraction that quickly? That is prepared, but how are you going to explain me to your superiors?" He huffed as they jogged.

"I'm not. I have a local contact who owns a helicopter and owes me a favor."

Sarah motioned for Sam to stop speaking. He was happy to oblige. His lungs burned from TaVi and the jogging. They stopped at the edge of the clearing. Sarah dialed the satellite phone.

"Get your chopper. I have a guest, and we need to get out." She disconnected the call, "Let's circle the field. We want to know they are coming."

"God, you are fucking amazing," Sam worshiped.

"Come here," Sarah pulled their lips together. "We aren't Romeo and Juliet. We are going to survive this shit. But, if you die, I am sorry, but I won't be going with you. So, get your head in the game."

"Yes, ma'am," Sam exaggerated a salute, then pulled Sarah in for another kiss. "Lead the way."

The next forty-five minutes was the longest of Sam's life. He loved the fact he could spend some time in nature with Sarah in his lap, but the whole Russians chasing them for the purposes of torture was a real mood dampener.

"Do you hear that?" Sam sat erect.

"Yes, they brought out the dogs. It won't be long before they arrive, but do you hear that?"

"What?" Sam strained to hear something, anything other than those fucking dogs.

"Listen closer," Sarah put a hand over his eyes.

There was a low rumble that was growing louder. The rumble became thumping. It was the helicopter.

"God, you're amazing, " Sam clung to Sarah as they watched the helicopter hover over the field.

The pair hopped to their feet and sprinted into the field, vaulting themselves into the back.

One Happy Ending

"I have bread. Do you want breakfast?" Sarah called as Sam rolled over in bed. He was getting accustomed to life outside the society, and waking up later was one of his favorite perks.

"Good morning, sleepy head," Sarah entered the room. "I went to the bakery. Which jam do you want? I'm sampling the blueberry."

"Just coffee, I need coffee," Sam yawned.

"I am making some," She shook his leg, "but you can't have any unless you join me."

"On my way," Sam swung his legs off the bed and sat up as Sarah departed.

He examined the snow caps through the compact Swiss windows. He could barely believe it had been a week since they made it to Switzerland and purchased the cottage.

"You know what we should do today?" He called as he walked to the dining room. "I have always wanted to go to a Christmas market. I hear they are a thing."

"We might have to wait until Christmas, or at least the winter," Sarah snickered. "But speaking of Christmas, I do have to reveal a secret and am scared of how you will react."

"How are secrets related to Christmas?" Sam asked as he sat at the table.

"Hmm," Sarah paused while looking at the low ceiling. "I guess they are not related. But that's not the point. Can I tell you something without you getting upset?"

Sam half-stood, leaned over the table, and pecked Sarah on the lips.

"What is it, my love? You know you are perfection, there is nothing you could tell me that would change that."

"Hopefully, you hang on to that feeling," Sarah frowned as she spread jam across her bread roll. "I used to be a man."

"What?" Sam's face contorted in confusion. "That's super weird, but I still love you." He swallowed and coughed on his spit.

"See, it's a problem," Sarah shrieked.

"No, No, it is so unexpected. Really? You used to be a man?"

"No, that wasn't the secret. I thought it would be funny to see your reaction. Funnier than it actually was," she took the bread.

"I need coffee, where is the coffee," Sam looked around.

"This one is yours," Sarah handed Sam the drink.

"So there is no secret?" Sam asked as he finished guzzling.

"No, there is," Sarah took another bite.

"This isn't a fun game, Sarah," Sam sliced his roll and spread orange jam.

"All right," Sarah huffed. "I have a sister. This is the last photo I have of her. She was attending college." Sarah held up a wallet-sized photo.

"That's not a very big secret," Sam shrugged.

"She disappeared four years ago. I have concluded the Society of Ghost took her," Sarah winced as the words finished leaving the station.

Sam sat wide-eyed, staring at Sarah after that punch to the face.

"That's not possible," he managed as a gloop of jam dripped into his lap.

"Why is that not possible?" Sara proceeded.

"It's not possible. There are methods and protocols. Backgrounds and consents. The society doesn't kidnap girls off the streets," Sam rambled.

"Calm, I didn't mean to upset you. I didn't mean 'the Society' itself. Maybe the transporters. Is it possible the transporters broke the rules?"

"This is such a ridiculous conversation. That would not, no, that could not happen. How do you even know this much about this kind of stuff?"

"I am trying to find my sister. I didn't mean to upset you. She was twenty-two when she was taken from her college. We know the man she was talking to online tricked her. We found messages; she seemed to love him, but he doesn't exist," her words remained calm as her face began to sadden.

"I am sorry about your sister, but there is no way she was taken by the society. I can't," Sam stood and headed for the door.

"Her name is Ginny. Please, Sam, I need your help," Sarah pleaded as Sam put on his coat and stepped outside.

This was their first argument, and it felt like a substantial one. Sam needed to check to see if this 'Ginny' had ever been at the Harem. He made his way into town and found the train station.

At the ticket counter, he inquired about round-trip tickets to Lubbock. The person behind the counter stated that no such place existed and slipped him a folded map while recommending he find a new destination. Sam shoved it in his pocket.

He found a cozy alley and pulled the map from his pocket. He unfolded it to find a black phone. There were four numbers in the phone. Sam dialed the third.

"Alya, it's me. We may have a problem. A source told me one of the transporters may not be following protocol. Check the records for the past couple of years to see if there has been an American named 'Ginny.'"

"You are supposed to be dead. Calling could jeopardize everything, but still, it's good to hear your voice," Alya replied.

"I can't wait to find you in the Arboretum again, but I need info on the girl."

"She is the senior American nine. She is scheduled to graduate next month," Alya replied.

Sam was shocked by the answer and looked around to see if anyone heard. He thought he saw someone run from view at the end of the alley but there was no way they heard.

"Are you sure?" He confirmed.

"I am sure. There was a fight earlier; she is savage. I am considering giving her a test for possible promotion."

"I need her with me. I will meet her at the Munich train station in two days," Sam waited for a response.

"I can't just export a nine. Have you found the five-point for me yet?"

"Say you retired her early; do what you have to do. I claimed you, remember? Get her to me." Sam's voice was on the edge between demanding and pleading.

"Will it help you with your orders? I want the five-point that took TaVi from me," Alya was adamant.

"I am still working on finding that five-point. Don't freak out or be mad, but I have to tell you something. I was trying to get more information first, so please don't be mad."

"You've been in me. If I get upset you know how to fix me," she giggled.

"TaVi is not dead, and she is still in love with you. She helped me escape from Russia, but she is pissed at you. She may be dangerous."

Sam looked up and down the alley. He thought he heard footsteps, but nobody was around. Alya was silent, and Sam wasn't sure if the call had been disconnected.

"Don't be mad. I will get more details when I find the five that attacked her. I know he is still somewhere. I am working to get access to their resources." After the proper sendoffs the call was disconnected.

Sam returned to the train station and slid the map back across the counter with the phone inside. The man behind the counter used a pencil to slide the map into a black metal trashcan before dumping a bottle of liquid on top.

"Sarah!" Sam called as he entered the cottage. "Where are you? I have some great news."

The sound of a toilette whooshing was followed by the washing of hands. When the water closet door opened, Sarah was rubbing her stomach.

"I don't know if that bread had something weird in it, but it's best that I stay close to the bathroom. It cleaned me out."

"That's pretty gross," Sam responded. "I was going to say Munich is supposed to have a year-round Christmas market. It's not far by train, but it is an overnight trip. Maybe I should plan it for another day."

"No!" Sarah almost yelled. "I mean, no, it's okay," she calmed her tone. "I can visit a Christmas market closer to Christmas. I will be more in the mood."

"Are you sure? It would be a fun trip. I can pick out a nice present for you," Sam didn't want her to miss the arrival, even if it needed to be delayed a day or two.

"Seriously, love. I can see you are excited. I will go next time," Sarah smiled.

"God, you are so perfect," Sam strode to Sarah and hugged her as they kissed.

"You are going to squeeze the shit out of me," Sarah ran into the bathroom and slammed the door. "You may want to leave. I am going to be in here a while, and it is going to smell."

Sam thought he heard whispering so he crept toward the bathroom and placed an ear against the door.

"I can see your shadow, you know I can't go unless I am alone. I get nervous," Sarah called.

"Love you, I am leaving now. I will stay an extra day if it is busy." Sam shouted as he departed.

"Love you," Sarah screamed.

Traveling to Munich took longer than Sam expected because he hadn't checked to see how long it would take. When he arrived, he booked a hotel for two nights and then explored the city.

The first thing on his agenda was finding a Christmas ornament for Sarah. He scoured dozens of small shops until he found the perfect item. It was a porcelain carousel that played three different classic Christmas songs. As the shiny horses danced around the center, he knew she deserved far more, but this was a start. Later, he found an amazing Turkish restaurant that had the best falafel.

On the second day, he explored the markets further and found the most delectable fire-side chicken. He loved the cobble streets and old architecture.

The morning of Ginny's arrival, he surveilled the train depot from every reasonable angle he could locate. A group of girls in school uniforms giggled at one end of the platform. One pulled a pack of cigarettes from a backpack and offered them to the others. One girl took a cigarette as they smoked in the huddle.

"Bad ass kids," Sam grinned as he decided it was time to head to the platform. It was a cool grey day, and the ground was wet from the night before. The cobbles had changed from gray to black. The parking lot was small and empty. Sam didn't see anything unusual as he approached.

The commuter pulled away from the station as a mob surrounded and passed Sam. Three people, other than the group of bad ass children, remained on the train platform: a short balding woman, a young woman that was a striking match to the photo, and an old man who used his phone to asked his wife why she wasn't waiting.

"Ginny," Sam called as he waved to the woman. "How are you? Did you have any trouble during your trip?"

"I do not understand why I am here. I am a nine, not a twenty-two," she said as she approached.

"I will explain everything. It is a terrible story, and the Society owes you more than it can ever repay."

"I have no idea what you are talking about," She looked startled.

As they walked toward the road, a horn started honking from the parking lot. Sam talked over it, but the car zoomed beside them. The window rolled down.

"Hurry, get in!" Sarah shouted in a panic.

"Wait, why are you here?" Sam looked at Sarah with disbelief.

"Hurry before the other five-points arrive. They tracked Ginny and are on their way," She pleaded.

Sam turned to Ginny, "Get in the back, I'm up front."

Ginny looked super confused but complied. As the doors were closed, Ginny seemed to recognize Sarah.

"You look so familiar. Trisha, is that you?"

Sarah turned to face Sam with a knife in her hand.

"I am sorry, my love. If there was any other way..." her voice trailed as she pressed the knife into his side.

Everything happened so fast Sam couldn't comprehend what was transpiring. He reached down and felt his burning side. He lifted his fingers to his eyes. They were covered in bright red liquid.

"I am sorry. I really do love you," Sarah pressed a second hole then leaned across him and opened the door.

"*Who the fuck is Trisha? Why are you doing this, Sara?*" Sam's mind questioned.

Everything was in slow motion as Sam watched his body get pushed from the vehicle. The car sped from the parking lot, but it happened so slowly.

Sam felt blood warming his hands as it seeped through his fingers. He looked to where the school girls had been, but they were gone. Sam realized he was hurt, alone, and in the dark as he accepted his fate.

Epilogue

Stacy found her floor as a buzzing sounded from her purse. It was her phone, and she had an email.

Congratulations, you have won a free sunset cruise on the "Sailing Victory." To claim your cruise, please call the number below. We look forward to Servicing your every need, and creating memories that will last a lifetime.

"Free cruise? The last time I did that, I ended up in the Harem. And, what kind of name is 'Sailing Victory' anyway? Wait, the 'Sailing Victory' that name sounds familiar. I wonder..."

Stacy dialed the number, and a man answered, "Hi, this is the captain of the 'Sailing Victory.' how can I help you?"

Stacy's breathing stopped. That voice, that horrible, wretched voice. It was the same voice. It was the same boat. She had no idea if she was marked for death, but she knew one thing: she was going to give the captain the consequences he earned.

"Hello? If you are speaking, I can't hear you. I am going to hang up. Please call back," the voice pierced her eardrum.

"Wait," she gasped. "I got an email. A free sunset cruise. I would like to book my trip."

"That is exciting," he replied. "There should be a number under the signature box in the email. Can you please read that to me?"

"Yes, of course. Let me see," Stacy fumbled with the phone as her excitement at the opportunity grew. "X843SDF73."

"It looks like this is a group sunset cruise. The other couple has confirmed their reservation. I look forward to meeting you in an hour, Ms. Wainscot. Please be on time. You may want to bring a coat. Do you have any questions?"

"Will there be an opportunity to get to know you better? It has been a long time since I was alone with a captain, and I want to have fun."

There was a long silence before the voice said, "I cannot make promises, but there are private rooms. If you find you need a moment of privacy, I might be able to escort you to ensure your comfort."

"Excellent," Stacy replied. "I'm horny and hairless. I hope you like frisky women and have a big cock."

"That is the exact kind of information I should know, and I do. Is there anything else I should know before you arrive? Are there any special considerations or requests? For instance, will a rain jacket be required?"

"You can cum inside of me if you fuck me like you mean it," Stacy tantalized.

She was getting ecstatic, but not by the sex. The idea of toying with her killer, making him squirm with excitement, letting him believe he was about to get gratification, only to reveal on the boat the thing he would be getting was gutted. It was all too much. Stacy squealed with delight.

"You are going to be a handful," the captain replied.

"You have no idea," she giggled. "I will see you in an hour."

"Don't be late," his warning was firm.

"I am too excited, you would have to kill me first," Stacy laughed into the phone as she disconnected the call and entered her new home.

It was exquisite. It wasn't much larger than the cages at the Harem, but it was everything she wanted. The marble countertops, the felt sofa, a giant television, even the fine details were correct. She had the correct pans, soaps, and even the fruits in the fridge. Someone had done their homework.

In Stacy's mind, there was no way this assignment could start any better. She changed into a see-through dress with no bra or panties. On the way out, she grabbed a banana and ordered a ride share.

The sun was low in the sky when she arrived at the dock. She scarfed down the banana and tossed the peel in a public trashcan. She recognized the boat and walked toward it. The muscular captain leered as she approached.

"Are you my troublemaker?" He was drooling.

"If you can handle me," Stacy smiled and held out a hand.

He hopped over the side of the boat and landed by her. He grabbed her by the waist, lifted her over the boat's railing, and placed her on the deck.

"You need to take off the heels," he stated as he climbed aboard.

"Already trying to get me naked?" Stacy gave him a flirty smile as she bent over to display her vagina while removing her shoes.

"There is plenty of time for that," the captain said as he stepped behind her, pressed his crotch against her, and let his hands slide to her breasts.

"I thought you said there were others," Stacy became alarmed that they may be alone and she was the target.

"They are freshening up below deck. They asked me to get them when the sun is starting to set," he replied as he thumped his crotch against her.

Stacy reached behind her and grabbed his dick.

"I want this, but not on the docks in front of everyone."

"Let's be on our way," the captain pulled away as he became firm. "Do you want to learn how to drive this boat?"

"No," Stacy replied, wondering if that was his only pick-up line. "I would much rather have a drink. I will explore while you take us out."

"Drinks are inside, make yourself at home," the captain proposed as he untied the ropes. "I will get us going shortly."

Stacy took her time walking around. She envisioned where she had been sunbathing the first time. She remembered how the captain seemed so protective and charming when he stopped the old man from molesting her. So much had changed.

She walked to where it had happened. The doors to the rooms were shut. Holding her ear to each door, one at a time, she heard nobody. Her fear grew.

"Was there another couple?" She wondered.

She tried the handle on the guest door, it was locked. As she jiggled the handle, a loud moan perforated the wood. Worrying she was going to get caught snooping, Stacy hurried back to the deck where the captain was dropping the anchor.

"We have an hour and a half before the sun sets. Do you want the 'Captain's Tour'?"

"I would love that," Stacy replied as she shivered.

"You look cold," the captain said as he pulled their bodies together. "I can heat you up."

Stacy felt his icy hands take hold of her ass as he bent down and bit her nipples through her dress.

"Fuck that feels good," Stacy lied. "But people can see. Let's go somewhere private."

The captain led her by the hand to the master room. It was not as nice as she imagined. It was a mattress beside a deep oval.

"How about this?" The captain asked as he patted the bed beside him.

"This will work," Stacy was nervous as she removed her dress. She wasn't sure if the other couple would try to enter.

"Give me a taste," the captain tugged her hand.

"I'm embarrassed," Stacy looked at her feet.

"Look at you. You are the sexiest chick that has ever been on this boat. What is there to be embarrassed about?"

"There's only one way I get really excited," Stacy closed the door and locked it.

"I like getting excited. What gets your motor running?"

The captain wasn't paying attention as he pulled his shirt over his head. He unbuckled his pants and let them slide to the floor.

"I like to be on top while I am getting choked," She gave him a mischievous grin.

"I love that for you," he exclaimed, flopping backward on the bed naked.

"Such a charmer," Stacy bent down and picked up his belt. She inserted the end into the buckle to make a loop. "To choke me," she held it up."

"Whatever you need," he was like a gleeful child on Christmas morning.

Stacy climbed on the bed and crawled with one of his legs centered below her body. She stared into his eyes as she crawled closer. When she felt her knee bump his scrotum, she stopped and looked down.

"Don't want to hurt these," she patted them as she lifted her knee. With as forceful a maneuver as she could manage, Stacy stomped her kneecap into his scrotum.

His body crunched into a sitting position as his hands covered his damaged danglers. Stacy slipped the belt over his head and centered the buckle on the back of his neck. She yanked. He struggled to get his hands under the belt.

Stacy pounced forward. Her knees landed on his shoulders, and slammed him back to the mattress. She turned and kneed him in the side of the face. When his head turned, she placed one knee on his cheek and the other on his sternum. She pressed her toes into the mattress, arched her back, and wrenched the leather.

The captain's body bucked, and his arms flailed. He punched her in the abdomen, knocking the wind out of her. She struggled to keep a grip on the belt as she gasped for air.

He swung again, but she was ready. She wrapped the tail of the belt around his wrist. She slid one leg across his face and the other into the loop created by his wrist, neck, and belt. He was spitting and sputtering as he bucked. The veins in the side of his neck and his forehead were bulging as his face turned crimson. She laid backward and yanked with all her might.

When Stacy was sure he could no longer resist the inevitable, she let the belt slack. She climbed on him and lowered her face to his.

"Use your legs to pull me deeper, and I will give you a fighting chance," she whispered.

"What?" The captain sputtered as he continued fighting for air.

"Use your legs to pull me deeper, and I will give you a fighting chance," she screamed as she began punching his face.

The captain's eyes grew large as his pupils dilated. Stacy knew he remembered her. She lay sideways and jerked the belt. She bent her knees and pushed his shoulder and head with her feet. It took longer than she expected. As he lay motionless, she ensured there was no pulse.

"Fucking asshole," Stacy screamed as she stood beside the bed.

There was a knocking at the door.

"*Shit! The other couple. What the fuck am I going to do?*" Stacy wondered as she looked around for a way to hide the body.

"Is everything okay in there, Stacy?" The voice asked.

"*Wait, wait, no, no, no. This is all wrong. How do they know my name?*" She became frantic as the door exploded open.

"It's us, are you okay? Did he hurt you?" A man asked.

"You are dead," Stacy was in complete shock.

"I am dead, too," A woman stepped around the man. "We are ghosts. We are your ghost family."

"Want to help us burn this bitch to the ground?" The man asked.

www.ingramcontent.com/pod-product-compliance
Ingram Content Group UK Ltd.
Pitfield, Milton Keynes, MK11 3LW, UK
UKHW031504181224
452569UK00005B/521